KU-487-777

BLACK BEAUTY

BLACKIE & SON LIMITED
16/18 William IV Street, Charing Cross, LONDON, W.C.2
17 Stanhope Street, GLASGOW

BLACKIE & SON (INDIA) LIMITED
103/5 Fort Street, BOMBAY

BLACKIE & SON (CANADA) LIMITED
TORONTO

G 843

IN THE ORCHARD

BLACK BEAUTY

Anna Sewell

BLACKIE & SON LIMITED
LONDON AND GLASGOW

Printed in Great Britain by Blackie & Son, Ltd., Glasgow

CONTENTS

CHAP.   Page

Part I

I.	MY EARLY HOME	11
II.	THE HUNT	14
III.	MY BREAKING IN	17
IV.	BIRTWICK PARK	22
V.	A FAIR START	25
VI.	LIBERTY	30
VII.	GINGER	32
VIII.	GINGER'S STORY CONTINUED	37
IX.	MERRYLEGS	41
X.	A TALK IN THE ORCHARD	44
XI.	PLAIN SPEAKING	51
XII.	A STORMY DAY	55
XIII.	THE DEVIL'S TRADE-MARK	59
XIV.	JAMES HOWARD	62
XV.	THE OLD OSTLER	66
XVI.	THE FIRE	69
XVII.	JOHN MANLY'S TALK	74
XVIII.	GOING FOR THE DOCTOR	78
XIX.	ONLY IGNORANCE	82
XX.	JOE GREEN	85
XXI.	THE PARTING	88

Part II

XXII.	EARLSHALL	95
XXIII.	A STRIKE FOR LIBERTY	99
XXIV.	THE LADY ANNE	103

CHAP.   Page

XXV.   REUBEN SMITH   110

XXVI.   HOW IT ENDED   114

XXVII. RUINED, AND GOING DOWNHILL   118

XXVIII. A JOB HORSE AND HIS DRIVERS   121

XXIX.   COCKNEYS   125

XXX.   A THIEF   132

XXXI.   A HUMBUG   135

Part III

XXXII.   A HORSE FAIR   141

XXXIII.   A LONDON CAB HORSE   145

XXXIV.   AN OLD WAR HORSE   149

XXXV.   JERRY BARKER   155

XXXVI.   THE SUNDAY CAB   162

XXXVII.   THE GOLDEN RULE   167

XXXVIII. DOLLY AND A REAL GENTLEMAN   171

XXXIX.   SEEDY SAM   176

XL.   POOR GINGER   180

XLI.   THE BUTCHER   182

XLII.   THE ELECTION   185

XLIII.   A FRIEND IN NEED   188

XLIV.   OLD CAPTAIN AND HIS SUCCESSOR   193

XLV.   JERRY'S NEW YEAR   198

Part IV

XLVI.   JAKES AND THE LADY   207

XLVII.   HARD TIMES   211

XLVIII.   FARMER THOROUGHGOOD AND HIS GRANDSON WILLIE   216

XLIX.   MY LAST HOME   220

PART I

BLACK BEAUTY

CHAPTER I

MY EARLY HOME

THE first place that I can well remember was a large pleasant meadow with a pond of clear water in it. Some shady trees leaned over it, and rushes and water-lilies grew at the deep end. Over the hedge on one side we looked into a ploughed field, and on the other we looked over a gate at our master's house, which stood by the roadside; at the top of the meadow was a plantation of fir trees, and at the bottom a running brook overhung by a steep bank.

Whilst I was young I lived upon my mother's milk, as I could not eat grass. In the daytime I ran by her side, and at night I lay down close by her. When it was hot, we used to stand by the pond in the shade of the trees, and when it was cold, we had a nice warm shed near the plantation.

As soon as I was old enough to eat grass, my mother used to go out to work in the daytime, and come back in the evening.

There were six young colts in the meadow besides me; they were older than I was; some were nearly as large as grown-up horses. I used to run with them, and had great fun; we used to gallop all together round and round the field as hard as we could go. Sometimes we had rather rough play, for they would frequently bite and kick as well as gallop.

One day, when there was a good deal of kicking, my mother whinnied to me to come to her, and then she said:

" I wish you to pay attention to what I am going to say to you. The colts who live here are very good colts, but they are cart-horse colts, and, of course, they have not learned manners. You have been well bred and well born; your father has a great name in these parts, and your grandfather won the cup two years at the Newmarket races; your grandmother had the sweetest temper of any horse I ever knew, and I think you have never seen me kick or bite. I hope you will grow up gentle and good, and never learn bad ways. Do your work with a good will, lift your feet up well when you trot, and never bite or kick, even in play."

I have never forgotten my mother's advice; I knew she was a wise old horse, and our master thought a great deal of her. Her name was Duchess, but he often called her Pet.

Our master was a good, kind man. He gave us good food, good lodging, and kind words; he spoke as kindly to us as he did to his little children. We were all fond of him, and my mother loved him very much. When she saw him at the gate, she would neigh with joy and trot up to him. He would pat and stroke her and say, " Well, old Pet, and how is your little Darkie?" I was a dull black, so he called me Darkie; then he would give me a piece of bread, which was very good, and sometimes he brought a carrot for my mother. All the horses would come to him, but I think we were his favourites. My mother always took him to the town on a market day in a light gig.

There was a ploughboy, Dick, who sometimes came into our field to pluck blackberries from the hedge. When he had eaten all he wanted, he would have what he called fun with the colts, throwing stones and sticks at them to make them gallop. We did not much mind him, for we could gallop off; but sometimes a stone would hit and hurt us.

One day he was at this game and did not know that the master was in the next field, but he was there, watching what was going on. Over the hedge he jumped in a snap, and, catching Dick by the arm, he gave him such a box on the ear as made him roar with the pain and surprise. As soon as we saw the master, we trotted up nearer to see what went on.

" Bad boy !" he said. " Bad boy to chase the colts ! This is not the first time, nor the second, but it shall be the last. There—take your money and go home. I shall not want you on my farm again." So we never saw Dick any more. Old Daniel, the man who looked after the horses, was just as gentle as our master, so we were well off.

CHAPTER II

THE HUNT

BEFORE I was two years old, a circumstance happened which I have never forgotten. It was early in the spring; there had been a little frost in the night, and a light mist still hung over the plantations and meadows. I and the other colts were feeding at the lower part of the field when we heard, quite in the distance, what sounded like the cry of dogs. The oldest of the colts raised his head, pricked his ears, and said, " There are the hounds!" and immediately cantered off, followed by the rest of us, to the upper part of the field where we could look over the hedge and see several fields beyond. My mother and an old riding horse of our master's were also standing near, and seemed to know all about it.

" They have found a hare," said my mother, " and if they come this way we shall see the hunt."

And soon the dogs were all tearing down the field of young wheat next to ours. I never heard such a noise as they made. They did not bark, nor howl, nor whine, but kept on a " Yo! Yo, o, o! Yo! Yo, o, o!" at the top of their voices. After them came a number of men on horseback, some of them in green coats, all galloping as fast as they could. The old horse snorted and looked eagerly after them, and we young colts wanted to be galloping with them, but they were soon away into the fields lower down. Here it seemed as if they had come to a stand; the dogs left off barking and ran about every way with their noses to the ground.

"They have lost the scent," said the old horse. "Perhaps the hare will get off."

"What hare?" I said.

"Oh! I don't know *what* hare. Likely enough it may be one of our own hares out of the plantation; any hare they can find will do for the dogs and men to run after." And before long the dogs began their "Yo! Yo, o, o!" again, and back they came all together at full speed, making straight for our meadow at the part where the high bank and hedge overhang the brook.

"Now we shall see the hare," said my mother; and just then a hare, wild with fright, rushed by and made for the plantation. On came the dogs; they burst over the bank, leapt the stream, and came dashing across the field, followed by the huntsmen. Six or eight men leaped their horses clean over, close upon the dogs. The hare tried to get through the fence; it was too thick, and she turned sharp round to make for the road, but it was too late; the dogs were upon her with their wild cries; we heard one shriek, and that was the end of her. One of the huntsmen rode up and whipped off the dogs, who would soon have torn her to pieces. He held her up by the leg, torn and bleeding, and all the gentlemen seemed well pleased.

As for me, I was so astonished that I did not at first see what was going on by the brook, but when I did look, there was a sad sight; two fine horses were down, one was struggling in the stream, and the other was groaning on the grass. One of the riders was getting out of the water covered with mud, the other lay quite still.

" His neck is broken," said my mother.

" And serve him right too," said one of the colts.

I thought the same, but my mother did not join with us.

" Well, no," she said, " you must not say that; but though I am an old horse, and have seen and heard a great deal, I never yet could make out why men are so fond of this sport; they often hurt themselves, often spoil good horses and tear up the fields, and all for a hare or a fox or a stag, that they could get more easily some other way; but we are only horses, and don't know."

Whilst my mother was saying this, we stood and looked on. Many of the riders had gone to the young man; but my master, who had been watching what was going on, was the first to raise him. His head fell back and his arms hung down, and every one looked very serious. There was no noise now; even the dogs were quiet, and seemed to know that something was wrong. They carried him to our master's house. I heard afterwards that it was young George Gordon, the Squire's only son, a fine, tall young man, and the pride of his family.

There was now riding off in all directions to the doctor's, to the farrier's, and, no doubt, to Squire Gordon's, to let him know about his son. When Mr. Bond, the farrier, came to look at the black horse that lay groaning on the grass, he felt him all over, and

(G 845)

shook his head; one of his legs was broken. Then someone ran to our master's house and came back with a
gun; presently there was a loud bang and a dreadful
shriek, and then all was still; the black horse moved
no more.

My mother seemed much troubled; she said she had
known that horse for years, and that his name was
" Rob Roy "; he was a good bold horse, and there was
no vice in him. She never would go to that part of the
field afterwards.

Not many days after we heard the church bell tolling
for a long time, and, looking over the gate, we saw a
long strange black coach that was covered with black
cloth and was drawn by black horses; after that came
another and another and another, and all were black,
while the bell kept tolling, tolling. They were carrying
young Gordon to the churchyard to bury him. He
would never ride again. What they did with Rob Roy
I never knew; but 'twas all for one little hare.

CHAPTER III

MY BREAKING IN

I was now beginning to grow handsome; my coat had
grown fine and soft, and was bright black. I had one
white foot, and a pretty white star on my forehead. I
was thought very handsome; my master would not
sell me till I was four years old; he said lads ought not

to work like men, and colts ought not to work like horses till they were quite grown up.

When I was four years old, Squire Gordon came to look at me. He examined by eyes, my mouth, and my legs; he felt them all down; and then I had to walk and trot and gallop before him. He seemed to like me, and said, " When he has been well broken in, he will do very well." My master said he would break me in himself, as he should not like me to be frightened or hurt, and he lost no time about it, for the next day he began.

Every one may not know what breaking in is, therefore I will describe it. It means to teach a horse to wear a saddle and bridle and to carry on his back a man, woman, or child; to go just the way they wish, and to go quietly. Besides this, he has to learn to wear a collar, a crupper, and a breeching, and to stand still whilst they are put on; then to have a cart or a chaise fixed behind him, so that he cannot walk or trot without dragging it after him; and he must go fast or slow, just as the driver wishes. He must never start at what he sees, nor speak to other horses, not bite, nor kick, nor have any will of his own, but always do his master's will, even though he may be very tired or hungry; but the worst of all is, when his harness is once on, he may neither jump for joy nor lie down for weariness. So you see this breaking in is a great thing.

I had, of course, long been used to a halter and a headstall, and to be led about in the field and lanes quietly, but now I was to have a bit and a bridle. My master gave me some oats as usual, and after a good deal of coaxing, he got the bit into my mouth and the bridle fixed, but it was a nasty thing! Those who have never had a bit in their mouths cannot think how bad it feels; a great piece of cold, hard steel as thick as a man's finger to be pushed into one's mouth, between one's teeth and over one's tongue, with the ends coming out at the corner of your mouth, and held fast there by straps over your head, under your throat, round your nose, and under your chin, so that no way in the world can you get rid of the nasty, hard thing. It is very bad— yes, very bad! At least I thought so; but I knew my mother always wore one when she went out, and all horses did when they were grown up; and so, what with the nice oats, and what with my master's pats, kind words, and gentle ways, I got to wear my bit and bridle.

Next came the saddle, but that was not half so bad; my master put it on my back very gently, whilst old Daniel held my head; he then made the girths fast under my body, patting and talking to me all the time; then I had a few oats, then a little leading about, and this he did every day till I began to look for the oats and the saddle. At length, one morning my master got on my back and rode me round the meadow on the soft grass. It certainly did feel queer, but I must say I felt rather proud to carry my master, and as he contin- ued to ride me a little every day, I soon became accus- tomed to it.

The next unpleasant business was putting on the iron shoes; that, too, was very hard at first. My master went with me to the smith's forge, to see that I was not hurt or got any fright. The blacksmith took my feet in his hand one after the other and cut away some of the hoof. It did not pain me, so I stood still on three legs till he had done them all. Then he took a piece of iron the shape of my foot and clapped it on, and drove some nails through the shoe quite into my hoof so that the shoe was firmly on. My feet felt very stiff and heavy, but in time I got used to it.

And now having got so far, my master went on to break me to harness. There were more new things to wear; first, a stiff heavy collar just on my neck, and a bridle with great sidepieces against my eyes, called blinkers, and blinkers indeed they were, for I could not see on either side, but only straight in front of me; next there was a small saddle with a nasty stiff strap that went right under my tail; that was the crupper. I hated the crupper—to have my long tail doubled up and poked through that strap was almost as bad as the bit. I never felt more like kicking, but of course I could not kick such a good master, and so in time I got used to everything and could do my work as well as my mother.

I must not forget to mention one part of my training, which I have always considered a very great advantage. My master sent me for a fortnight to a neighbouring farmer's, who had a meadow which was skirted on one side by the railway. Here were some sheep and cows, and I was turned in amongst them.

I shall never forget the first train that ran by. I was feeding quietly near the pales which separated the meadow from the railway when I heard a strange sound at a distance, and before I knew whence it came—with a rush and a clatter, and a puffing out of smoke—a long

black train of something flew by, and was gone almost
before I could draw my breath. I turned and galloped
to the farther side of the meadow as fast as I could go,
and there I stood snorting with astonishment and fear.
In the course of the day many other trains went by,
some more slowly; these drew up at the station close
by, and sometimes made an awful shriek and groan
before they stopped. I thought it very dreadful, but the
cows went on eating very quietly, and hardly raised
their heads as the black frightful thing came puffing
and grinding past.

For the first few days I could not feed in peace,
but as I found that this terrible creature never came
into the field or did me any harm, I began to dis-
regard it, and very soon I cared as little about the
passing of a train as the cows and sheep did.

Since then I have seen many horses much alarmed
and restive at the sight or sound of a steam engine, but,
thanks to my good master's care, I am as fearless at
railway stations as in my own stable.

Now if any one wants to break in a young horse well,
that is the way.

My master often drove me in double harness with
my mother, because she was steady and could teach
me how to go better than a strange horse. She told me
the better I behaved the better I should be treated,
and it was wisest always to do my best to please my
master. " But," said she, " there are a great many kinds
of men; there are good, thoughtful men like our master
that any horse may be proud to serve; but there are
bad, cruel men who never ought to have a horse or dog

to call their own. Beside, there are a great many foolish
men, vain, ignorant, and careless, who never trouble
themselves to think; these spoil more horses than all,
just for want of sense; they don't mean it, but they do
it for all that. I hope you will fall into good hands;
but a horse never knows who may buy him, or who may
drive him; it is all a chance for us, but still I say, do
your best, wherever it is, and keep up your good name."

CHAPTER IV

BIRTWICK PARK

At this time I used to stand in the stable, and my coat
was brushed every day till it shone like a rook's wing.
It was early in May when there came a man from
Squire Gordon's, who took me away to the Hall. My
master said, " Good-bye, Darkie. Be a good horse,
and always do your best." I could not say " good-bye,"
so I put my nose into his hand; he patted me kindly,
and I left my first home. As I lived some years with
Squire Gordon, I may as well tell something about the
place.

Squire Gordon's Park skirted the village of Birtwick.
It was entered by a large iron gate, at which stood the
first lodge, and then you trotted along on a smooth
road between clumps of large old trees; then another
lodge and another gate which brought you to the house
and the gardens. Beyond this lay the home paddock,

the old orchard, and the stables. There was accommodation for many horses and carriages, but I need only describe the stable into which I was taken; this was very roomy, with four good stalls; a large swinging window opened into the yard, which made it pleasant and airy.

The first stall was a large square one, shut behind with a wooden gate; the others were common stalls, good stalls, but not nearly so large; it had a low rack for hay and a low manger for corn; it was called a loose box, because the horse that was put into it was not tied up, but left loose to do as he liked. It is a great thing to have a loose box.

Into this fine box the groom put me; it was clean, sweet, and airy. I never was in a better box than that, and the sides were not so high but that I could see all that went on through the iron rails that were at the top.

He gave me some very nice oats, he patted me, spoke kindly, and then went away.

When I had eaten my corn I looked round. In the stall next to mine stood a little fat grey pony, with a thick mane and tail, a very pretty head, and a pert little nose.

I put my head up to the iron-rails at the top of my box and said, " How do you do? What is your name?"

He turned round as far as his halter would allow, held up his head, and said, " My name is Merrylegs. I am very handsome, I carry the young ladies on my back, and sometimes I take our mistress out in the low chair. They think a great deal of me, and so does James. Are you going to live next door to me in the box?"

I said, " Yes."

" Well, then," he said, " I hope you are good-tempered; I do not like anyone next door who bites."

Just then a horse's head looked over from the stall beyond; the ears were laid back and the eye looked rather ill-tempered. This was a tall chestnut mare, with a long handsome neck. She looked across to me and said:

" So it is you who have turned me out of my box; it is a very strange thing for a colt like you to come and turn a lady out of her own home."

" I beg your pardon," I said. " I have turned no one out; the man who brought me put me here, and I had nothing to do with it; and as to my being a colt, I am turned four years old, and am a grown-up horse. I never had words yet with horse or mare, and it is my wish to live at peace."

" Well," she said, " we shall see. Of course I do not want to have words with a young thing like you." I said no more.

In the afternoon, when she went out, Merrylegs told me all about it.

" The thing is this," said Merrylegs, " Ginger has a bad habit of biting and snapping; that is why they call her Ginger, and when she was in the loose box she used to snap very much. One day she bit James in the arm and made it bleed, and so Miss Flora and Miss Jessie, who are very fond of me, were afraid to come into the stable. They used to bring me nice things to eat—an apple or a carrot, or a piece of bread, but after Ginger stood in that box they dare not come, and I missed them very much. I hope they will now come again, if you do not bite or snap."

I told him I never bit anything but grass, hay, and corn, and could not think what pleasure Ginger found in it.

" Well, I don't think she does find pleasure," says Merrylegs; " it is just a bad habit. She says no one was ever kind to her, and why should she not bite? Of course it is a very bad habit; but I am sure, if all she says be true, she must have been very ill-used before she came here. John does all he can to please her, and James does all he can, and our master never uses a whip if a horse acts right, so I think she might be good-tempered here. You see," he said, with a wise look, " I am twelve years old; I know a great deal, and I can tell you there is not a better place for a horse all round the country than this. John is the best groom that ever was—he has been here fourteen years; and you never saw such a kind boy as James is, so that it is all Ginger's own fault that she did not stay in that box."

CHAPTER V

A FAIR START

THE name of the coachman was John Manly; he had a wife and one little child, and they lived in the coachman's cottage, very near the stables.

The next morning he took me into the yard and gave

me a good grooming, and just as I was going into my box with my coat soft and bright, the Squire came in to look at me and seemed pleased. "John," he said, " I meant to have tried the new horse this morning, but I have other business. You may as well take him a round after breakfast. Go by the common and the Highwood, and back by the watermill and the river; that will show his paces."

" I will, sir," said John. After breakfast he came and fitted me with a bridle. He was very particular in letting out and taking in the straps, to fit my head comfortably; then he brought a saddle, but it was not broad enough for my back; he saw it in a minute and went for another, which fitted nicely. He rode me first slowly, then a trot, then a canter, and when we were on the common he gave me a light touch with his whip, and we had a splendid gallop.

" Ho, ho, my boy!" he said as he pulled me up. " You would like to follow the hounds, I think."

As we came back through the Park we met the Squire and Mrs. Gordon walking; they stopped and John jumped off.

" Well, John, how does he go?"

" First-rate, sir," answered John. " He is as fleet as a deer, and has a fine spirit too; but the lightest touch of the rein will guide him. Down at the end of the common we met one of those travelling carts hung all over with baskets, rugs, and such like. You know, sir, many horses will not pass those carts quietly; he just took a good look at it, and then went on as quiet and pleasant as could be. They were shooting rabbits near

the Highwood, and a gun went off close by; he pulled
up a little and looked, but did not stir a step to right or
left. I just held the rein steady and did not hurry him,
and it's my opinion he has not been frightened or ill-
used while he was young."

"That's well," said the Squire. "I will try him myself to-morrow."

The next day I was brought up for my master. I
remembered my mother's counsel and my good old
master's, and I tried to do exactly what he wanted me
to do. I found he was a very good rider, and thoughtful
for his horse too. When we came home, the lady was
at the hall door as he rode up.

"Well, my dear," she said, "how do you like him?"

"He is exactly what John said," he replied. "A
pleasanter creature I never wished to mount. What
shall we call him?"

"Would you like Ebony?" said she. "He is as
black as ebony."

"No, not Ebony."

"Will you call him Blackbird, like your uncle's old
horse?"

"No; he is far handsomer than old Blackbird ever
was."

"Yes," she said, "he is really quite a beauty, and
he has such a sweet good-tempered face and such a
fine intelligent eye—what do you say to calling him
Black Beauty?"

"Black Beauty—why, yes, I think that is a very good
name. If you like, it shall be his name," and so it was.

When John went into the stable, he told James that

master and mistress had chosen a good sensible English name for me that meant something, not like Marengo or Pegasus or Abdullah. They both laughed, and James said, " If it was not for bringing back the past, I should have named him Rob Roy, for I never saw two horses more alike."

" That's no wonder," said John. " Didn't you know that Farmer Grey's old Duchess was the mother of them both?"

I had never heard that before. And so poor Rob Roy who was killed at that hunt was my brother! I did not wonder that my mother was so troubled. It seems that horses have no relations; at least, they never know each other after they are sold.

John seemed very proud of me; he used to make my mane and tail almost as smooth as a lady's hair, and he would talk to me a great deal. Of course I did not understand all he said, but I learned more and more to know what he *meant*, and what he wanted me to do. I grew very fond of him, he was so gentle and kind; he seemed to know just how a horse feels, and when he cleaned me he knew the tender places and the ticklish places; when he brushed my head he went as carefully over my eyes as if they were his own, and never stirred up any ill-temper.

James Howard, the stable boy, was just as gentle and pleasant in his way, so I thought myself well off. There was another man who helped in the yard, but he had very little to do with Ginger and me.

A few days after this I had to go out with Ginger in the carriage. I wondered how we should get on together, but, except for laying her ears back when I was led up to her, she behaved very well. She did her work honestly and did her full share, and I never wish to have a better partner in double harness. When we came to a hill, instead of slackening her pace, she would throw her weight right into the collar and pull away straight up. We had both the same sort of courage at our work, and John had oftener to hold us in than to urge us forward; he never had to use the whip with either of us. Then our paces were much the same, and I found it very easy to keep step with her when trotting, which made it pleasant; and master always liked it when we kept step well, and so did John. After we had been out two or three times together we grew quite friendly and sociable, which made me feel very much at home.

As for Merrylegs, he and I soon became great friends; he was such a cheerful, plucky, good-tempered little fellow that he was a favourite with everyone, and especially with Miss Jessie and Flora, who used to ride him about in the orchard, and have fine games with him and their little dog Frisky.

Our master had two other horses that stood in another stable. One was Justice, a roan cob, used for riding or for the luggage cart; the other was an old brown hunter, named Sir Oliver. He was past work now, but was a great favourite with the master, who gave him the run of the Park; he sometimes did a little light carting on the estate, or carried one of the young ladies when they rode out with their father, for he was very gentle, and could be trusted with a child as well as Merrylegs. The cob was a strong, well-made, good-tempered horse, and we sometimes had a little chat in the paddock, but of course I could not be so intimate with him as with Ginger, who stood in the same stable.

CHAPTER VI

LIBERTY

I WAS quite happy in my new place, and if there was one thing that I missed it must not be thought I was discontented; all who had to do with me were good, and I had a light airy stable and the best of food. What more could I want? Why, liberty! For three years and a half of my life I had had all the liberty I could wish for; but now, week after week, month after month, and no doubt year after year, I must stand up in a stable night and day except when I am wanted, and then I must be just as steady and quiet as any old horse who has worked twenty years; straps here and straps there, a bit in my mouth, and blinkers over my eyes. Now I am not complaining, for I know it must be so. I only mean to say that for a young horse full of strength and spirits who has been used to some large field or plain, where he can fling up his head and toss up his tail and gallop away at full speed, then round and back again with a snort to his companions—I say it is hard never to have a bit more liberty to do as you like. Sometimes, when I have had less exercise than usual, I have felt so full of life and spring that when

John has taken me out to exercise I really could not keep quiet; do what I would, it seemed as if I must jump or dance or prance, and many a good shake I know I must have given him, specially at the first; but he was always good and patient.

" Steady, steady, my boy," he would say. " Wait a bit, and we'll have a good swing, and soon get the tickle out of your feet." Then, as soon as we were out of the village, he would give me a few miles at a spanking trot, and then bring me back as fresh as before, only clear of the fidgets, as he called them. Spirited horses, when not enough exercised, are often called skittish when it is only play; and some grooms will punish them, but our John did not; he knew it was only high spirits. Still, he had his own ways of making me understand by the tone of his voice or the touch of the rein. If he was very serious and quite determined, I always knew it by his voice, and that had more power with me than anything else, for I was very fond of him.

I ought to say that sometimes we had our liberty for a few hours; this used to be on fine Sundays in the summer-time. The carriage never went out on Sundays, because the church was not far off.

It was a great treat for us to be turned out into the home paddock or the old orchard. The grass was so cool and soft to our feet; the air so sweet, and the freedom to do as we liked was so pleasant—to gallop, to lie down and roll over on our backs, or to nibble the sweet grass. Then it was a very good time for talking as we stood together under the shade of the large chestnut tree.

CHAPTER VII

GINGER

One day when Ginger and I were standing alone in the shade, we had a great deal of talk; she wanted to know all about my bringing up and breaking in, and I told her.

" Well," she said, " if I had had your bringing up I might have had as good a temper as you, but now I don't believe I ever shall."

" Why not?" I said.

" Because it has been all so different with me," she replied. " I never had any one, horse or man, that was kind to me, or that I cared to please; for, in the first place, I was taken from my mother as soon as I was weaned, and put with a lot of other young colts; none of them cared for me, and I cared for none of them. There was no kind master like yours to look after me and talk to me and bring me nice things to eat. The man that had the care of us never gave me a kind word in my life. I do not mean that he ill-used me, but that he did not care for us one bit further than to see that we had plenty to eat and shelter in the winter.

" A footpath ran through our field, and very often the great boys passing through would fling stones to make us gallop. I was never hit, but one fine young colt was badly cut in the face, and I should think it would be a scar for life. We did not care for them, but, of course, it made us more wild, and we settled it in our minds that boys were our enemies.

" We had very good fun in the free meadows, galloping up and down and chasing each other round and round the field, then standing still under the shade of the trees. But when it came to breaking in, that was a bad time for me; several men came to catch me, and when at last they closed me in at one corner of the field, one caught me by the forelock, another caught me by the nose, and held it so tight I could hardly draw my breath; then another took my under jaw in his hard hand and wrenched my mouth open, and so by force they got on the halter and the bar into my mouth; then one dragged me along by the halter, another flogging behind, and this was the first experience I had of men's kindness. It was all force; they did not give me a chance to know what they wanted. I was high bred and had a great deal of spirit, and was very wild, no doubt, and gave them, I dare say, plenty of trouble, but then it was dreadful to be shut up in a stall day after day instead of having my liberty, and I fretted and pined and wanted to get loose. You know yourself it's bad enough when you have a kind master and plenty of coaxing, but there was nothing of that sort for me.

" There was one—the old master, Mr. Ryder, who, I think, could soon have brought me round, and could have done anything with me, but he had given up all the hard part of the trade to his son and to another experienced man, and he only came at times to oversee. His son was a strong, tall, bold man; they called him Samson, and he used to boast that he had never found a horse that could throw him. There was no gentleness in him as there was in his father, but only hardness— a hard voice, a hard eye, a hard hand; and I felt from the first that what he wanted was to wear all the spirit out of me, and just make me into a quiet, humble, obedient piece of horse-flesh. ' Horse-flesh!' Yes, that is all that he thought about." And Ginger stamped her foot as if the very thought of him made her angry.

She went on: " If I did not do exactly what he wanted, he would get put out and make me run round with that long rein in the training field till he had tired me out. I think he drank a good deal, and I am quite sure that the oftener he drank the worse it was for me. One day he had worked me hard in every way he could, and when I laid down I was tired and miserable and angry; it all seemed so hard. The next morning he came for me early and ran me round again for a long time. I had scarcely had an hours' rest when he came again for me with a saddle and bridle and a new kind of bit. I could never quite tell how it came about; he had only just mounted me on the training ground when something I did put him out of temper and he chucked me hard with the rein. The new bit was very painful and I reared up suddenly, which angered him still more, and he began to flog me. I felt my whole spirit set against him, and I began to kick and plunge and rear as I had never done before, and we had a regular fight. For a long time he stuck to the saddle and punished me cruelly with his whip and spurs, but my blood was thoroughly up and I cared for nothing he could do if only I could get him off. At last, after a terrible

struggle, I threw him off backwards. I heard him fall
heavily on the turf, and without looking behind me I
galloped off to the other end of the field; there I turned
round and saw my persecutor slowly rising from the
ground and going into the stable. I stood under an
oak tree and watched, but no one came to catch me.
The time went on, the sun was very hot, the flies
swarmed round me, and settled on my bleeding flanks
where the spurs had dug in. I felt hungry, for I had not
eaten since the early morning, but there was not enough
grass in that meadow for a goose to live on. I wanted
to lie down and rest, but with the saddle strapped tightly
on there was no comfort, and there was not a drop of
water to drink. The afternoon wore on and the sun
got low. I saw the other colts led in and I knew they
were having a good feed.

" At last, just as the sun went down, I saw the old
master come out with a sieve in his hand. He was a
very fine old gentleman with quite white hair, but his
voice was what I should know him by amongst a thousand. It was not high, nor yet low, but full and clear
and kind, and when he gave orders it was so steady and
decided that every one knew, both horses and men,
that he expected to be obeyed. He came quietly along,
now and then shaking the oats about that he had in the
sieve, and speaking cheerfully and gently to me:
' Come along, lassie; come along, lassie; come along,
come along.' I stood still and let him come up; he held
the oats to me and I began to eat without fear; his
voice took all my fear away. He stood by, patting and
stroking me whilst I was eating, and seeing the clots of

blood on my side, he seemed very vexed. ' Poor lassie! It was a bad business, a bad business!' Then he quietly took the rein and led me to the stable. Just at the door stood Samson. I laid my ears back and snapped at him. ' Stand back,' said the master, ' and keep out of her way; you've done a bad day's work for this filly.' He growled out something about a vicious brute. ' Hark ye,' said the father, ' a bad-tempered man will never make a good-tempered horse. You've not learned your trade yet, Samson.' Then he led me into my box, took off the saddle and bridle with his own hands, and tied me up; then he called for a pail of warm water and a sponge, took off his coat, and while the stableman held the pail, he sponged my sides a good while so tenderly that I was sure he knew how sore and bruised they were. ' Whoa, my pretty one!' he said. ' Stand still, stand still.' His very voice did me good, and the bathing was very comfortable. The skin was so broken at the corners of my mouth that I could not eat the hay—the stalks hurt me. He looked closely at it, shook his head, and told the man to fetch a good bran mash and put some meal into it. How good that mash was, and so soft and healing to my mouth! He stood by all the time I was eating, stroking me and talking to the man. ' If a high-mettled creature like this,' said he, ' can't be broken in by fair means, she will never be good for anything.'

" After that he often came to see me, and when my mouth was healed, the other breaker, Job they called him, went on training me. He was steady and thoughtful, and I soon learned what he wanted."

CHAPTER VIII

GINGER'S STORY CONTINUED

THE next time that Ginger and I were together in the paddock she told me about her first place. " After my breaking in," she said, " I was bought by a dealer to match another chestnut horse. For some weeks he drove us together, and then we were sold to a fashionable gentleman and were sent up to London. I had been driven with a bearing rein by the dealer, and I hated it worse than anything else; but in this place we were reined far tighter, the coachman and his master thinking we looked more stylish so. We were often driven about in the Park and other fashionable places. You who never had a bearing rein on don't know what it is, but I can tell you it is dreadful.

" I like to toss my head about and hold it as high as any horse; but fancy now yourself, if you tossed your head up high and were obliged to hold it there and that for hours together, not able to move it at all, except with a jerk still higher, your neck aching till you did not know how to bear it. Beside that, to have two bits instead of one; and mine was a sharp one; it hurt my tongue and my jaw, and the blood from my tongue coloured the froth that kept flying from my lips, as I chafed and fretted at the bits and rein. It was worse when we had to stand by the hour waiting for our mistress at some grand party or entertainment; and if I fretted or stamped with impatience the whip was laid on. It was enough to drive one mad."

"Did not your master take any thought for you?" I said.

"No," said she, "he only cared to have a stylish turn-out, as they call it. I think he knew very little about horses; he left that to his coachman, who told him I had an irritable temper; that I had not been well broken to the bearing rein, but I should soon get used to it; but *he* was not the man to do it, for when I was in the stable, miserable and angry, instead of being soothed and quieted by kindness, I got only a surly word or a blow. If he had been civil, I would have tried to bear it. I was willing to work and ready to work hard too; but to be tormented for nothing but their fancies angered me. What right had they to make me suffer like that? Besides the soreness in my mouth and the pain in my neck, it always made my windpipe feel bad, and if I had stopped there long I know it would have spoiled my breathing; but I grew more and more restless and irritable—I could not help it—and I began to snap and kick when any one came to harness me. For this the groom beat me, and one day as they had just buckled us into the carriage and were straining my head up with that rein, I began to plunge and kick with all my might. I soon broke a lot of harness and kicked myself clear; so that was an end of that place.

"After this I was sent to Tattersalls to be sold. Of course I could not be warranted free from vice, so nothing was said about that. My handsome appearance and good paces soon brought a gentleman to bid for me, and I was bought by another dealer; he tried me in all kinds of ways and with different bits, and soon found out what I could bear. At last he drove me quite without a bearing rein, and then sold me as a perfectly quiet horse to a gentleman in the country; he was a good master, and I was getting on very well, but his old groom left him and a new one came. This man was as hard-tempered and hard-handed as Samson; he always spoke in a rough, impatient voice, and if I did not move in the stall the moment he wanted me, he would hit me above the hocks with his stable broom or the fork, whichever he might have in his hand. Everything he did was rough, and I began to hate him; he wanted to make me afraid of him, but I was too high-mettled for that; and one day when he had aggravated me more than usual I bit him, which of course put him in a great rage, and he began to hit me about the head with a riding whip. After that he never dared to come into my stall again; either my teeth or my heels were ready for him, and he knew it. I was quite quiet with my master, but, of course, he listened to what the man said, and so I was sold again.

" The same dealer heard of me and said he thought he knew one place where I should do well. ' 'Twas a pity,' he said, ' that such a fine horse should go to the bad for want of a real good chance,' and the end of it was that I came here not long before you did; but I had then made up my mind that men were my natural enemies and that I must defend myself. Of course it is very different here, but who knows how long it will last? I wish I could think about things as you do, but I can't after all I have gone through."

"Well," I said, "I think it would be a real shame if you were to bite or kick John or James."

"I don't mean to," she said, "while they are good to me. I did bite James once, pretty sharp, but John said, 'Try her with kindness,' and instead of punishing me as I expected, James came to me with his arm bound up and brought me a bran mash and stroked me; and I have never snapped at him since, and I won't either."

I was sorry for Ginger, but, of course, I knew very little then and I thought most likely she made the worst of it; however, I found that as the weeks went on, she grew much more gentle and cheerful, and had lost the watchful, defiant look that she used to turn on any strange person who came near her; and one day James said, "I do believe that mare is getting fond of me; she quite whinnied after me this morning when I had been rubbing her forehead."

"Aye, aye, Jim, 'tis the Birtwick balls," said John. "She'll be as good as Black Beauty by and by; kindness is all the physic she wants, poor thing!" Master noticed the change too, and one day when he got out of the carriage and came to speak to us as he often did, he stroked her beautiful neck. "Well, my pretty one, well, how do things go with you now? You are a good bit happier than when you came to us, I think."

She put her nose up to him in a friendly, trustful way while he rubbed it gently.

"We shall make a cure of her, John," he said.

"Yes, sir; she's wonderfully improved; she's not

the same creature that she was. It's the Birtwick balls, sir," said John, laughing.

This was a little joke of John's. He used to say that a regular course of the Birtwick horse-balls would cure almost any vicious horse. These balls, he said, were made up of patience and gentleness, firmness and petting, one pound of each to be mixed up with half a pint of common sense and given to the horse every day.

CHAPTER IX

MERRYLEGS

MR. BLOMEFIELD, the Vicar, had a large family of boys and girls; sometimes they used to come and play with Miss Jessie and Flora. One of the girls was as old as Miss Jessie; two of the boys were older, and there were several little ones. When they came there was plenty of work for Merrylegs, for nothing pleased them so much as getting on him by turns and riding him all about the orchard and the home paddock, and this they would do by the hour together.

One afternoon he had been out with them a long time, and when James brought him in and put on his halter, he said:

" There, you rogue, mind how you behave yourself, or we shall get into trouble."

" What have you been doing, Merrylegs?" I asked.

" Oh !" said he, tossing his little head, " I have only been giving those young people a lesson; they did not know when they had had enough, nor when I had had enough, so I just pitched them off backwards. That was the only thing they could understand."

" What?" I said. " You threw the children off? I thought you did know better than that! Did you throw Miss Jessie or Miss Flora?"

He looked very much offended, and said:

" Of course not; I would not do such a thing for the best oats that ever came into the stable. Why, I am as careful of our young ladies as the master could be, and as for the little ones, it is I who teach them to ride. When they seem frightened or a little unsteady on my back, I go as smooth and as quiet as old pussy when she is after a bird; and when they are all right, I go on again faster, you see, just to use them to it, so don't you trouble yourself preaching to me; I am the best friend and the best riding master those children have. It is not them; it is the boys. Boys," said he, shaking his mane, " are quite different; they must be broken in, as we were broken in when we were colts, and just be taught what's what. The other children had ridden me about for nearly two hours, and then the boys thought it was their turn; and so it was, and I was quite agreeable. They rode me by turns, and I galloped them about up and down the fields and all about the orchard for a good hour. They had each cut a great hazel stick for a riding whip and laid it on a little too hard; but I took it in good part, till at last I thought we had had enough, so I stopped two or three times by way

of a hint. Boys, you see, think a horse or a pony is like
a steam-engine or a thrashing machine, and can go on
as long and as fast as they please; they never think
that a pony can get tired, or have any feelings; so as
the one who was whipping me could not understand,
I just rose up on my hind legs and let him slip off
behind—that was all; he mounted me again, and I
did the same. Then the other boy got up, and as soon
as he began to use his stick I laid him on the grass,
and so on, till they were able to understand, that was all.
They are not bad boys; they don't wish to be cruel.
I like them very well, but, you see, I had to give them
a lesson. When they brought me to James and told
him, I think he was very angry to see such big sticks.
He said they were only fit for drovers or gipsies, and
not for young gentlemen."

"If I had been you," said Ginger, " I would have
given those boys a good kick, and that would have
given them a lesson."

"No doubt you would," said Merrylegs, " but then
I am not quite such a fool (begging your pardon) as to
anger our master or make James ashamed of me;
besides, those children are under my charge when they
are riding; I tell you they are entrusted to me. Why,
only the other day I heard our master say to Mrs.
Blomefield, ' My dear madam, you need not be anxious
about the children; my old Merrylegs will take as
much care of them as you or I could. I assure you I
would not sell that pony for any money, he is so perfectly
good-tempered and trustworthy.' And do you think I
am such an ungrateful brute as to forget all the kind

treatment I have had here for five years, and all the trust they place in me, and turn vicious because a couple of ignorant boys used me badly? No, no! You never had a good place where they were kind to you, and so you don't know and I'm sorry for you, but I can tell you good places make good horses. I wouldn't vex our people for anything; I love them, I do," said Merrylegs, and he gave a low " ho, ho, ho " through his nose, as he used to do in the morning when he heard James's footstep at the door.

" Besides," he went on, " if I took to kicking, where should I be? Why, sold off in a jiffy, and no character, and I might find myself slaved about under a butcher's boy, or worked to death at some seaside place where no one cared for me except to find out how fast I could go, or be flogged along in some cart with three or four great men in it going out for a Sunday spree, as I have often seen in the place I lived in before I came here. No," said he, shaking his head, " I hope I shall never come to that."

CHAPTER X

A TALK IN THE ORCHARD

GINGER and I were not of the regular tall carriage-horse breed; we had more of the racing blood in us. We stood about fifteen and a half hands high; we were therefore just as good for riding as we were for driving, and our master used to say that he disliked either horse or man that could do but one thing; and as he did not want to show off in London parks, he preferred a more active and useful kind of horse. As for us, our greatest pleasure was when we were saddled for a riding party— the master on Ginger, the mistress on me, and the young ladies on Sir Oliver and Merrylegs. It was so cheerful to be trotting and cantering all together that it always put us in high spirits. I had the best of it, for I always carried the mistress; her weight was little, her voice was sweet, and her hand was so light on the rein that I was guided almost without feeling it.

Oh, if people knew what a comfort to horses a light hand is, and how it keeps a good mouth and a good temper, they surely would not chuck and drag and pull at the rein as they often do. Our mouths are so tender that where they have not been spoiled or hardened with bad or ignorant treatment, they feel the slightest move- ment of the driver's hand, and we know in an instant what is required of us. My mouth had never been spoiled, and I believe that was why the mistress pre- ferred me to Ginger, although her paces were cer- tainly quite as good. She used often to envy me, and said it was all the fault of breaking in and the gag bit in London, that her mouth was not so perfect as mine; and then old Sir Oliver would say, "There, there! Don't vex yourself; you have the greatest honour; a mare that can carry a tall man of our master's weight, with all your spring and sprightly action, does not need to hold her head down because she does not carry the lady. We horses must take things as they come, and always be contented and willing so long as we are kindly used."

I had often wondered how it was that Sir Oliver had such a very short tail; it was only six or seven inches long, with a tassel of hair hanging from it; and on one of our holidays in the orchard I ventured to ask him by what accident it was that he had lost his tail. " Accident!" he snorted, with a fierce look. " It was no accident! It was a cruel, shameful, cold-blooded act! When I was young, I was taken to a place where these cruel things were done; I was tied up and made fast so that I could not stir, and they then came and cut off my long beautiful tail, through the flesh and through the bone, and took it away."

" How dreadful!" I exclaimed.

" Dreadful! Ah! It was dreadful. But it was not only the pain, though that was terrible and lasted a long time; it was not only the indignity of having my best ornament taken from me, though that was bad; but it was this—how could I ever brush the flies off my sides and my hind legs any more? You who have tails just whisk the flies off without thinking about it, and you can't tell what a torment it is to have them settle upon you and sting and sting, and have nothing in the world to lash them off with. I tell you it is a lifelong wrong and a lifelong loss; but, thank Heaven they don't do it now."

" What did they do it for, then?" said Ginger.

" For fashion!" said the old horse with a stamp of his foot. " For fashion—if you know what that means. There was not a well-bred horse in my time that had not his tail docked in that shameful way, just as if the good God that made us did not know what we wanted and what looked best."

" I suppose it is fashion that makes them strap our heads up with those horrid bits that I was tortured with in London," said Ginger.

" Of course it is," said he. " To my mind, fashion is one of the wickedest things in the world. Now look, for instance, at the way they serve dogs, cutting off their tails to make them look plucky, and shearing up their pretty little ears to a point to make them look sharp, forsooth! I had a dear friend once, a brown terrier—' Skye,' they called her. She was so fond of me that she never would sleep out of my stall; she made her bed under the manger, and there she had a litter of five as pretty little puppies as need be; none were drowned, for they were a valuable kind, and how pleased she was with them! And when they got their eyes open and crawled about, it was a real pretty sight; but one day the man came and took them all away; I thought he might be afraid I should tread upon them, but it was not so. In the evening poor Skye brought them back again, one by one in her mouth; not the happy little things that they were, but bleeding and crying pitifully; they had all had a piece of their tails cut off, and the soft flap of their pretty little ears was cut quite off. How their mother licked them, and how troubled she was, poor thing! I never forgot it. They healed in time, and they forgot the pain, but the nice soft flap that of course was intended to protect the delicate part of their ears from dust and injury was gone for ever.

Why don't they cut their own children's ears into points
to make them look sharp? Why don't they cut the end
off their noses to make them look plucky? One would
be just as sensible as the other. What right have they to
torment and disfigure God's creatures?"

Sir Oliver, though he was so gentle, was a fiery old
fellow, and what he said was all so new to me and so
dreadful that I found a bitter feeling toward men rise
up in my mind that I had never had before. Of course
Ginger was much excited; she flung up her head with
flashing eyes and distended nostrils, declaring that
men were both brutes and blockheads.

"Who talks about blockheads?" said Merrylegs,
who just came up from the old apple tree where he
had been rubbing himself against the low branch.
"Who talks about blockheads? I believe that is a bad
word."

"Bad words were made for bad things," said Ginger,
and she told him what Sir Oliver had said. "It is all
true," said Merrylegs sadly, "and I've seen that about
the dogs over and over again where I lived first; but
we won't talk about it here. You know that master and
John and James are always good to us, and talking
against men in such a place as this doesn't seem fair or
grateful, and you know there are good masters and good
grooms besides ours, though, of course, ours are the
best." This wise speech of good little Merrylegs, which
we knew was quite true, cooled us all down, especially
Sir Oliver, who was dearly fond of his master; and to
turn the subject I said, "Can any one tell me the use
of blinkers?"

" No," said Sir Oliver shortly, " because they are no use."

" They are supposed," said Justice in his calm way, " to prevent horses from shying and starting and getting so frightened as to cause accidents."

" Then what is the reason they do not put them on riding horses—especially on ladies' horses?" said I.

" There is no reason at all," said he quietly, " except the fashion. They say that a horse would be so frightened to see the wheels of his own cart or carriage coming behind him that he would be sure to run away, although, of course, when he is ridden, he sees them all about him if the streets are crowded. I admit they do sometimes come too close to be pleasant, but we don't run away; we are used to it and understand it, and if we never had blinkers put on we should never want them; we should see what was there and know what was what, and be much less frightened than by only seeing bits of things that we can't understand."

Of course there may be some nervous horses who have been hurt or frightened when they were young, and may be the better for them, but as I never was nervous, I can't judge.

" I consider," said Sir Oliver, " that blinkers are dangerous things in the night; we horses can see much better in the dark than man can, and many an accident would never have happened if horses might have had the full use of their eyes. Some years ago, I remember, there was a hearse with two horses returning one dark night, and just by Farmer Sparrow's house, where the pond is close to the road, the wheels went too near the edge, and the hearse was overturned into the water; both the horses were drowned, and the driver hardly escaped. Of course, after this accident a stout white rail was put up that might be easily seen, but if those horses had not been partly blinded, they would of themselves have kept farther from the edge, and no accident would have happened. When our master's carriage was overturned, before you came here, it was said that if the lamp on the left side had not gone out John would have seen the great hole that the roadmakers had left; and so he might, but if old Colin had not had blinkers on, he would have seen it, lamp or no lamp, for he was far too knowing an old horse to run into danger. As it was, he was very much hurt, the carriage was broken, and how John escaped nobody knew."

"I should say," said Ginger, curling her nostril, "that these men, who are so wise, had better give orders that in future all foals should be born with their eyes set in the middle of their foreheads instead of on the side; they always think they can improve upon Nature and mend what God has made."

Things were getting rather sore again, when Merry-legs held up his knowing little face, and said, " I'll tell you a secret; I believe John does not approve of blinkers; I heard him talking with master about it one day. The master said that ' if horses had been used to them, it might be dangerous in some cases to leave them off ', and John said he thought it would be a good thing if all colts were broken in without blinkers, as was the case in some foreign countries. So let us cheer up, and have a run to the other end of the orchard; I believe the wind has blown down some apples, and we might just as well eat them as the slugs."

Merrylegs could not be resisted, so we broke off our long conversation and got up our spirits by munching some very sweet apples which lay scattered on the grass.

CHAPTER XI

PLAIN SPEAKING

THE longer I lived at Birtwick, the more proud and happy I felt at having such a place. Our master and mistress were respected and beloved by all who knew them; they were good and kind to everybody and everything—not only men and women, but horses and donkeys, dogs and cats, cattle and birds. There was no oppressed or ill-used creature that had not a friend in them, and their servants took the same tone. If any of the village children were known to treat any creature cruelly, they soon heard about it from the Hall.

The Squire and Farmer Grey had worked together, as they said, for more than twenty years, to get bearing reins on the cart horses done away with, and in our parts you seldom saw them; but sometimes, if mistress met a heavily-laden horse with his head strained up, she would stop the carriage and get out and reason with the driver in her sweet serious voice, and try to show him how foolish and cruel it was.

I don't think any man could withstand our mistress;

I wish all ladies were like her. Our master, too, used to come down very heavy sometimes. I remember he was riding me towards home one morning when we saw a powerful man driving towards us in a light pony chaise, with a beautiful little bay pony with slender legs and a high-bred sensitive head and face. Just as we came to the Park gates, the little thing turned towards them; the man, without word or warning, wrenched the creature's head round with such a force and suddenness that he nearly threw it on its haunches; recovering itself, it was going on when he began to lash it furiously; the pony plunged forward, but the strong, heavy hand held the pretty creature back with force almost enough to break its jaw, whilst the whip still cut into him. It was a dreadful sight to me, for I knew what fearful pain it gave that delicate little mouth; but master gave me the word, and we were up with him in a second.

"Sawyer," he cried in a stern voice, "is that pony made of flesh and blood?"

"Flesh and blood and temper," he said. "He's too fond of his own will, and that won't suit me." He spoke as if he was in a strong passion; he was a builder who had often been to the Park on business.

"And do you think," said master sternly, "that treatment like this will make him fond of your will?"

"He had no business to make that turn; his road was straight on!" said the man roughly.

"You have often driven that pony up to my place," said master. "It only shows the creature's memory and intelligence. How did he know that you were not going there again? But that has little to do with it. I must say,

Mr. Sawyer, that more unmanly, brutal treatment of a little pony it was never my painful lot to witness; and by giving way to such passions you injure your own character as much, nay more, than you injure your horse, and remember, we shall all have to be judged according to our works, whether they be towards man or towards beast."

Master rode me home slowly, and I could tell by his voice how the thing had grieved him. He was just as free to speak to gentlemen of his own rank as to those below him, for another day, when we were out, we met a Captain Langley, a friend of our master's; he was driving a splendid pair of greys in a kind of brake. After a little conversation the Captain said:

" What do you think of my new team, Mr. Douglas? You know you are the judge of horses in these parts, and I should like your opinion."

The master backed me a little, so as to get a good view of them. " They are an uncommonly handsome pair," he said, " and if they are as good as they look, I am sure you need not wish for anything better; but I see you get hold of that pet scheme of yours for worrying your horses and lessening their power."

" What do you mean?" said the other. " The bearing reins? Oh, ah! I know that's a hobby of yours. Well, the fact is I like to see my horses hold their heads up."

" So do I," said master, " as well as any man, but I don't like to see them *held up*; that takes all the shine out of it. Now you are a military man, Langley, and no doubt like to see your regiment look well on parade.

'Heads up,' and all that; but you would not take much credit for your drill if all your men had their heads tied to a backboard! It might not be much harm on parade, except to worry and fatigue them, but how would it be in a bayonet charge against the enemy, when they want the free use of every muscle, and all their strength thrown forward? I would not give much for their chance of victory, and it is just the same with horses; you fret and worry their tempers and decrease their power; you will not let them throw their weight against their work, and so they have to do too much with their joints and muscles, and, of course, it wears them up faster. You may depend upon it, horses were intended to have their heads free, as free as men's are; and if we could act a little more according to common sense and a good deal less according to fashion, we should find many things work easier. Besides, you know as well as I, that if a horse makes a false step, he has much less chance of recovering himself if his head and neck are fastened back. And now," said the master, laughing, "I have given my hobby a good trot out, can't you make up your mind to mount him too, Captain? Your example would go a long way."

"I believe you are right in theory," said the other, "and that's rather a hard hit about the soldiers, but— well—I'll think about it." And so they parted.

CHAPTER XII

A STORMY DAY

ONE day late in the autumn my master had a long journey to go on business. I was put into the dogcart and John went with his master. I always liked to go in the dogcart, it was so light and the high wheels ran along so pleasantly. There had been a great deal of rain, and now the wind was very high and blew the dry leaves across the road in a shower. We went along merrily till we came to the toll-bar and the low wooden bridge. The river banks were rather high, and the bridge, instead of rising, went across just level, so that in the middle, if the river was full, the water would be nearly up to the wood-work and planks; but as there were good substantial rails on each side, people did not mind it.

The man at the gate said the river was rising fast and he feared it would be a bad night. Many of the meadows were under water, and in one low part of the road the water was halfway up to my knees; the bottom was good and master drove gently, so it was no matter.

When we got to the town, of course, I had a good wait, but as the master's business engaged him a long time, we did not start for home till rather late in the afternoon. The wind was then much higher, and I heard the master say to John he had never been out in such a storm; and so I thought, as we went along the skirts of a wood, where the great branches were swaying about like twigs and the rushing sound was terrible.

"I wish we were well out of this wood," said my master.

"Yes, sir," said John. "It would be rather awkward if one of these branches came down upon us."

The words were scarcely out of his mouth when there was a groan and a crack and a splitting sound, and tearing, crashing down amongst the other trees came an oak, torn up by the roots, and it fell right across the road just before us. I will never say I was not frightened, for I was; I stopped still and I believe I trembled; of course I did not turn round or run away; I was not brought up to that. John jumped out and was in a moment at my head.

"That was a very near touch," said my master. "What's to be done now?"

"Well, sir, we can't drive over that tree nor get round it; there will be nothing for it but to go back to the four crossways, and that will be a good six miles before we get round to the wooden bridge again; it will make us late, but the horse is fresh."

So back we went and round by the crossroads; but by the time we got to the bridge it was very nearly dark; we could just see that the water was over the middle of it, but as that happened sometimes when the floods were out, master did not stop. We were going along at a good pace, but the moment my feet touched the first part of the bridge, I felt sure there was something wrong; I dare not go forward and I made a dead stop.

" Go on, Beauty," said my master, and he gave me a touch with the whip. But I dare not stir; he gave me a sharp cut; I jumped, but I dare not go forward.

" There's something wrong, sir," said John, and he sprang out of the dogcart and came to my head and looked all about. He tried to lead me forward. " Come on, Beauty. What's the matter?" Of course I could not tell him, but I knew very well that the bridge was not safe.

Just then the man at the toll-gate on the other side ran out of the house, tossing a torch about like one mad.

" Hoy, hoy, hoy, halloo, stop !" he cried.

" What's the matter?" shouted my master.

" The bridge is broken in the middle and part of it is carried away; if you come on, you'll be into the river."

" Thank God !" said my master.

" You Beauty !" said John, and took the bridle and gently turned me round to the right-hand road by the river-side.

The sun had set some time; the wind seemed to have lulled off after that furious blast which tore up the tree; it grew darker and darker, stiller and stiller. I trotted quietly along, the wheels hardly making a sound on the soft road. For a good while neither master nor John spoke, and then master began in a serious voice. I could not understand much of what they said, but I found they thought if I had gone on, as the master wanted me, most likely the bridge would have given way under us, and horse, chaise, master, and man would have fallen into the river; and as the current was flowing very strongly, and there was no light and no help at hand, it was more than likely we should all have been drowned. Master said God had given men reason by which they could find out things for themselves, but He had given animals knowledge which did not depend on reason, and which was much more prompt and perfect in its way, and by which they had often saved the lives of men. John had many stories to tell of dogs and horses and the wonderful things they had done; he thought people did not value their animals half enough, nor make friends of them as they ought to do. I am sure he makes friends of them if ever a man did.

At last we came to the Park gates and found the gardener looking out for us. He said that mistress had been in a dreadful way ever since dark, fearing some accident had happened, and that she had sent James off on Justice, the roan cob, towards the wooden bridge to make inquiry after us.

We saw a light at the hall door and at the upper windows, and as we came up, mistress ran out, saying, "Are you really safe, my dear? Oh! I have been so anxious, fancying all sorts of things. Have you had an accident?"

"No, my dear; but if your Black Beauty had not been wiser than we were, we should all have been carried down the river at the wooden bridge." I heard no more, as they went into the house, and John took me to the stable. Oh! What a good supper he gave me that night—a good bran mash and some crushed beans with my oats, and such a thick bed of straw, and I was glad of it, for I was tired.

CHAPTER XIII

THE DEVIL'S TRADE-MARK

ONE day when John and I had been out on some business of our master's and were returning gently on a long straight road, at some distance we saw a boy trying to leap a pony over a gate. The pony would not take the leap, and the boy cut him with the whip, but he only turned off on one side; he whipped him again, but the pony turned off on the other side. Then the boy got off and gave him a hard thrashing, and knocked him about the head; then he got up again and tried to make him leap the gate, kicking him all the time shamefully, but still the pony refused. When we were nearly at the spot, the pony put down his head and threw up his heels and sent the boy neatly over into a broad quickset hedge, and with the rein dangling from his head he set off home at a full gallop. John laughed out quite loud. " Served him right," he said.

" Oh! Oh! Oh!" cried the boy as he struggled about amongst the thorns. " I say, come and help me out."

" Thank ye," said John, " I think you are quite in the right place, and maybe a little scratching will teach you not to leap a pony over a gate that is too high for him!" And so with that John rode off. " It may be," said he to himself, " that young fellow is a liar as well as a cruel one. We'll just go home by Farmer Bushby's, Beauty, and then if anybody wants to know, you and I can tell 'em, ye see." So we turned off to the right, and soon came up to the stackyard and within sight of the house. The farmer was hurrying out into the road, and his wife was standing at the gate looking very frightened.

"Have you seen my boy?" said Mr. Bushby as we came up. "He went out an hour ago on my black pony, and the creature is just come back without a rider."

"I should think, sir," said John, "he had better be without a rider, unless he can be ridden properly."

"What do you mean?" said the farmer.

"Well, sir, I saw your son whipping and kicking and knocking that good little pony about shamefully because he would not leap a gate that was too high for him. The pony behaved well, sir, and showed no vice; but at last he just threw up his heels and tipped the young gentlemen into the thorn hedge. He wanted me to help him out. But I hope you will excuse me, sir, I did not feel inclined to do so. There's no bones broken, sir; he'll only get a few scratches. I love horses, and it roiles me to see them badly used. It is a bad plan to aggravate an animal till he uses his heels; the first time is not always the last."

During this time the mother began to cry, "Oh, my poor Bill! I must go and meet him; he must be hurt."

"You had better go into the house, wife," said the farmer. "Bill wants a lesson about this, and I must see that he gets it. This is not the first time nor the second that he has ill-treated that pony, and I shall stop it. I am much obliged to you, Manly. Good-evening."

So we went on, John chuckling all the way home; then he told James about it, who laughed and said, " Serve him right. I knew that boy at school; he took great airs on himself because he was a farmer's son; he used to swagger about and bully the little boys. Of course, we elder ones would not have any of that nonsense, and let him know that in the school and the playground farmers' sons and labourers' sons were all alike. I well remember one day, just before afternoon school, I found him at the large window catching flies and pulling off their wings. He did not see me, and I gave him a box on the ears that laid him sprawling on the floor. Well, angry as I was, I was almost frightened, he roared and bellowed in such a style. The boys rushed in from the playground, and the master ran in from the road to see who was being murdered. Of course I said fair and square at once what I had done, and why; then I showed the master the poor flies, some crushed and some crawling about helpless, and I showed him the wings on the window-sill. I never saw him so angry before; but as Bill was still howling and whining, like the coward that he was, he did not give him any more punishment of that kind, but set him up on a stool for the rest of the afternoon, and said that he should not go out to play for that week. Then he talked to all the boys very seriously about cruelty, and said how hard-hearted and cowardly it was to hurt the weak and the helpless. But what stuck in my mind was this; he said that cruelty was the devil's own trade-mark, and if we

saw any one who took pleasure in cruelty, we might
know who he belonged to, for the devil was a murderer
from the beginning and a tormentor to the end; on
the other hand, where we saw people who loved their
neighbours and were kind to man and beast, we might
know that was God's mark, for ' God is Love '."

"Your master never taught you a truer thing,"
said John. "There is no religion without love, and
people may talk as much as they like about their religion, but if it does not teach them to be good and kind
to man and beast, it is all a sham—all a sham, James,
and it won't stand when things come to be turned inside out and put down for what they are."

CHAPTER XIV

JAMES HOWARD

ONE morning early in December John had just led me
into my box after my daily exercise and was strapping
my cloth on, and James was coming in from the corn
chamber with some oats, when the master came into
the stable; he looked rather serious, and held an open
letter in his hand. John fastened the door of my box,
touched his cap, and waited for orders.

"Good-morning, John," said the master. "I want
to know if you have any complaint to make of James?"

"Complaint, sir? No, sir."

"Is he industrious at his work and respectful to you?"

" Yes, sir; always."

" You never find he slights his work when your back is turned?"

" Never, sir."

" That's well; but I must put another question. Have you any reason to suspect that when he goes out with the horses to exercise them or to take a message, he stops about talking to his acquaintances, or goes into houses where he has no business, leaving the horses outside?"

" No, sir, certainly not, and if anybody has been saying that about James, I don't believe it, and I don't mean to believe it unless I have it fairly proved before witnesses. It's not for me to say who has been trying to take away James's character, but I will say this, sir, that a steadier, pleasanter, honester, smarter young fellow I never had in this stable. I can trust his word and I can trust his work; he is gentle and clever with the horses, and I would rather have them in his charge than in that of half the young fellows I know in laced hats and liveries; and whoever wants a character of James Howard," said John, with a decided jerk of his head, " let them come to John Manly."

The Master stood all this time grave and attentive, but as John finished his speech a broad smile spread over his face, and looking kindly across at James, who all this time had stood still at the door, he said: " James, my lad, set down the oats and come here: I am very glad to find that John's opinion of your character agrees so exactly with my own. John is a cautious man," he said, with a droll smile, " and it is not always easy to get his opinion about people, so I thought if I beat the bush on this side, the birds would fly out and I should learn what I wanted to know quickly; so now we will come to business. I have a letter from my brother-in-law, Sir Clifford Williams, of Clifford Hall; he wants me to find him a trustworthy young groom, about twenty or twenty-one, who knows his business. His old coachman, who has lived with him twenty years, is getting feeble, and he wants a man to work with him and get into his ways, who would be able, when the old man was pensioned off, to step into his place. He would have eighteen shillings a week at first, a stable suit, a driving suit, a bedroom over the coachhouse, and a boy under him. Sir Clifford is a good master, and if you could get the place, it would be a good start for you. I don't want to part with you, and if you left us, I know John would lose his right hand."

"That I should, sir," said John, "but I would not stand in his light for the world."

"How old are you, James?" said master.

"Nineteen next May, sir."

"That's young. What do you think, John?"

"Well, sir, it is young; but he is as steady as a man, and is strong and well grown, and though he has not had much experience in driving, he has a light, firm hand, and a quick eye, and he is very careful, and I am quite sure no horse of his will be ruined for want of having his feet and shoes looked after."

"Your word will go the furthest, John," said the master, "for Sir Clifford adds in a postcript, 'If I could find a man trained by your John, I should like

im better than any other.' So James, lad, think it
over, talk to your mother at dinner-time, and then let
me know what you wish."

In a few days after this conversation it was fully
settled that James should go to Clifford Hall in a month
or six weeks, as it suited his master, and in the meantime he was to get all the practice in driving that could
be given to him. I never knew the carriage go out so
often before. When the mistress did not go out, the
master drove himself in the two-wheeled chaise; but
now, whether it was master or the young ladies, or
only an errand, Ginger and I were put into the carriage
and James drove us. At the first, John rode with him
on the box, telling him this and that, and after that
James drove alone.

Then it was wonderful what a number of places the
master would go to in the city on Saturday, and what
queer streets we were driven through. He was sure to
go to the railway station just as the train was coming
in, and cabs and carriages, carts and omnibuses were
all trying to get over the bridge together; that bridge
wanted good horses and good drivers when the railway
bell was ringing, for it was narrow and there was a very
sharp turn up to the station, where it would not have
been at all difficult for people to run into each other
if they did not look sharp and keep their wits about
them.

CHAPTER XV

THE OLD OSTLER

AFTER this it was decided by my master and mistress to pay a visit to some friends who lived about forty-six miles from our home, and James was to drive them. The first day we travelled thirty-two miles; there were some long, heavy hills, but James drove so carefully and thoughtfully that we were not at all harassed. He never forgot to put on the drag as we went downhill, nor to take it off at the right place. He kept our feet on the smoothest part of the road, and if the uphill was very long, he set the carriage wheels a little across the road, so as not to run back, and gave us a breathing. All these little things help a horse very much, particularly if he gets kind words into the bargain.

We stopped once or twice on the road, and just as the sun was going down, we reached the town where we were to spend the night. We stopped at the principal hotel, which was in the market place; it was a very large one. We drove under an archway into a long yard, at the farther end of which were the stables and coach-houses. Two ostlers came to take us out. The head ostler was a pleasant, active little man, with a crooked leg and a yellow-striped waistcoat. I never saw a man unbuckle harness so quickly as he did, and with a pat and a good word he led me to a long stable, with six or eight stalls in it, and two or three horses.

The other man brought Ginger; James stood by whilst we were rubbed down and cleaned.

I was never cleaned so lightly and quickly as by that little old man. When he had done, James stepped up and felt me over, as if he thought I could not be thoroughly done, but he found my coat as clean and smooth as silk.

" Well," he said, " I thought I was pretty quick, and our John quicker still, but you do beat all I ever saw for being quick and thorough at the same time."

" Practice makes perfect," said the crooked little ostler, " and 'twould be a pity if it didn't; forty years' practice, and not perfect! Ha, ha! That would be a pity. And as to being quick, why bless you! that is only a matter of habit; if you get into the habit of being quick, it is just as easy as being slow—easier I should say; in fact, it don't agree with my health to be hulking about over a job twice as long as it need take. Bless you! I couldn't whistle if I crawled over my work as some folks do! You see, I have been about horses ever since I was twelve years old, in hunting stables and racing stables; and being small, ye see, I was jockey for several years; but at the Goodwood, ye see, the turf was very slippery and my poor Larkspur got a fall, and I broke my knee, and so, of course, I was of no more use there; but I could not live without horses, of course, I couldn't, so I took to the hotels, and I can tell ye it is a downright pleasure to handle an animal like this, well-bred, well-mannered, well-cared for. Bless ye! I can tell how a horse is treated. Give me the handling of a horse for twenty minutes, and I'll tell you what sort of groom he has had. Look at this one, pleasant, quiet, turns about just as you want him, holds up his feet to be cleaned out, or anything else you please to wish; then you'll find another, fidgety, fretty, won't move the right way, or starts across the stall, tosses up his head as soon as you come near him, lays his ears, and seems afraid of you; or else squares about at you with his heels. Poor things! I know what sort of treatment they have had. If they are timid, it makes them start or shy; if they are high-mettled, it makes them vicious or dangerous; their tempers are mostly made when they are young. Bless you! they are like children: train 'em up in the way they should go, as the good Book says, and when they are old they will not depart from it—if they have a chance, that is."

" I like to hear you talk," said James. " That's the way we lay it down at home, at our master's."

" Who is your master, young man, if it be a proper question? I should judge he is a good one from what I see."

" He is Squire Gordon, of Birtwick Park, the other side the Beacon hills," said James.

" Ah, so, so! I have heard tell of him. Fine judge of horses, ain't he? The best rider in the county?"

" I believe he is," said James, " but he rides very little now since the poor young master was killed."

" Ah, poor gentleman. I read all about it in the paper at the time. A fine horse killed too, wasn't there?"

" Yes," said James, " he was a splendid creature, brother to this one, and just like him."

" Pity! Pity!" said the old man. " 'Twas a bad place

to leap, if I remember; a thin fence at top, a steep bank down to the stream, wasn't it? No chance for a horse to see where he is going. Now, I am for bold riding as much as any man, but still there are some leaps that only a very knowing old huntsman has any right to take. A man's life and a horse's life are worth more than a fox's tail; at least I should say they ought to be."

During this time the other man had finished Ginger and had brought our corn, and James and the old man left the stable together.

CHAPTER XVI

THE FIRE

LATER on in the evening a traveller's horse was brought in by the second ostler, and whilst he was cleaning him a young man with a pipe in his mouth lounged into the stable to gossip.

" I say, Towler," said the ostler, " just run up the ladder into the loft and put some hay down into this horse's rack, will you? Only lay down your pipe."

" All right," said the other, and went up through the trapdoor; and I heard him step across the floor over-head and put down the hay. James came in to look at us the last thing, and then the door was locked.

I cannot say how long I had slept, nor what time in the night it was, but I woke up very uncomfortable, though I hardly knew why. I got up; the air seemed all thick and choking. I heard Ginger coughing, and one of the other horses moved about restlessly. It was quite dark and I could see nothing, but the stable was very full of smoke, and I hardly knew how to breathe.

The trapdoor had been left open, and I thought that was the place it came through. I listened and heard a soft rushing sort of noise and a low crackling and snapping. I did not know what it was, but there was something in the sound so strange that it made me tremble all over. The other horses were now all awake; some were pulling at their halters, others were stamping.

At last I heard steps outside, and the ostler who had put up the traveller's horse burst into the stable with a lantern, and began to untie the horses and try to lead them out; but he seemed in such a hurry and so frightened himself that he frightened me still more. The first horse would not go with him; he tried the second and third—they too would not stir. He came to me next and tried to drag me out of the stall by force; of course that was no use. He tried us all by turns and then left the stable.

No doubt we were very foolish, but danger seemed to be all round, and there was nobody we knew to trust in, and all was strange and uncertain. The fresh air that had come in through the open door made it easier to breathe, but the rushing sound overhead grew louder, and as I looked upward through the bars of my empty rack, I saw a red light flickering on the wall. Then I heard a cry of " Fire!" outside, and the old ostler quietly and quickly came in; he got one horse out and went to another, but the flames were playing round the trapdoor and the roaring overhead was dreadful.

The next thing I heard was James's voice, quiet and cheery, as it always was.

"Come, my beauties, it is time for us to be off, so wake up and come along." I stood nearest the door, so he came to me first, patting me as he came in.

"Come, Beauty, on with your bridle, my boy; we'll soon be out of this smother." It was on in no time; then he took the scarf off his neck and tied it lightly over my eyes, and patting and coaxing he led me out of the stable. Safe in the yard, he slipped the scarf off my eyes, and shouted, "Here, somebody! Take this horse while I go back for the other."

A tall broad man stepped forward and took me, and James darted back into the stable. I set up a shrill whinny as I saw him go. Ginger told me afterwards that whinny was the best thing I could have done for her, for had she not heard me outside, she would never have had the courage to come out.

There was much confusion in the yard, the horses being got out of other stables, and the carriages and gigs being pulled out of houses and sheds, lest the flames should spread farther. On the other side the yard, windows were thrown up and people were shouting all sorts of things; but I kept my eye fixed on the stable door, where the smoke poured out thicker than ever, and I could see flashes of red light. Presently I heard above all the stir and din a loud clear voice, which I knew was master's:

"James Howard! James Howard! Are you there?"

There was no answer, but I heard a crash of something falling in the stable and the next moment I gave a loud joyful neigh, for I saw James coming through the smoke leading Ginger with him; she was coughing violently and he was not able to speak.

" My brave lad!" said master, laying his hand on his shoulder. " Are you hurt?"

James shook his head, for he could not yet speak.

" Aye," said the big man who held me, " he is a brave lad and no mistake."

" And now," said master, " when you have got your breath, James, we'll get out of this place as quickly as we can," and we were moving towards the entry, when from the market-place there came a sound of galloping feet and loud rumbling wheels.

" 'Tis the fire engine! The fire engine!" shouted two or three voices. " Stand back! Make way!" and clattering and thundering over the stones two horses dashed into the yard with the heavy engine behind them. The firemen leaped to the ground; there was no need to ask where the fire was—it was torching up in a great blaze from the roof.

We got out as fast as we could into the broad, quiet market-place; the stars were shining, and except the noise behind us, all was still. Master led the way to a large hotel on the other side, and as soon as the ostler came, he said, " James, I must now hasten to your mistress. I trust the horses entirely to you; order whatever you think is needed," and with that he was gone. The master did not run, but I never saw mortal man walk so fast as he did that night.

There was a dreadful sound before we got into our stalls—the shrieks of those poor horses that were left burning to death in the stable; it was very terrible, and made both Ginger and me feel very bad! We, however, were taken in and well done by.

The next morning the master came to see how we were and to speak to James. I did not hear much, for the ostler was rubbing me down, but I could see that James looked very happy and I thought the master was proud of him. Our mistress had been so much alarmed in the night that the journey was put off till the afternoon, so James had the morning on hand, and went first to the inn to see about our harness and the carriage, and then to hear more about the fire. When he came back, we heard him tell the ostler about it. At first no one could guess how the fire had been caused, but at last a man said he saw Dick Towler go into the stable with a pipe in his mouth, and when he came out he had not one and went to the tap for another. Then the under ostler said he had asked Dick to go up the ladder to put down some hay, but told him to lay down his pipe first. Dick denied taking the pipe with him, but no one believed him. I remember our John Manly's rule, never to allow a pipe in the stable, and thought it ought to be the rule everywhere.

James said the roof and floor had all fallen in, and that only the black walls were standing; the two poor horses that could not be brought out were buried under the burnt rafters and tiles.

CHAPTER XVII

JOHN MANLY'S TALK

THE rest of our journey was very easy, and a little after sunset we reached the house of my master's friend. We were taken into a clean, snug stable; there was a kind coachman, who made us very comfortable and who seemed to think a good deal of James when he heard about the fire.

"There is one thing quite clear, young man," he said; "your horses know who they can trust. It is one of the hardest things in the world to get horses out of a stable when there is either fire or flood. I don't know why they won't come out, but they won't—not one in twenty."

We stopped two or three days at this place and then returned home. All went well on the journey; we were glad to be in our own stable again, and John was equally glad to see us.

Before he and James left us for the night, James said, " I wonder who is coming in my place."

" Little Joe Green at the lodge," said John.

" Little Joe Green! Why, he's a child!"

" He is fourteen and a half," said John.

" But he is such a little chap."

" Yes, he is small, but he is quick and willing and kind-hearted too, and then he wishes to come and his father would like it; and I know the master would like to give him the chance. He said, if I thought he would

not do, he would look out for a bigger boy; but I said
I was quite agreeable to try him for six weeks."

"Six weeks!" said James. "Why, it will be six
months before he can be of much use! It will make you
a deal of work, John."

"Well," said John with a laugh, "work and I are
very good friends; I never was afraid of work yet."

"You are a very good man," said James. "I wish
I may ever be like you."

"I don't often speak of myself," said John, "but as
you are going away from us out into the world to shift
for yourself, I'll just tell you how I look on these things.
I was just as old as Joseph when my father and mother
died of the fever, within ten days of each other, and left
me and my crippled sister, Nelly, alone in the world,
without a relation that we could look to for help. I was
a farmer's boy, not earning enough to keep myself,
much less both of us, and she must have gone to the
workhouse, but for our mistress (Nelly calls her her
angel, and she has good right to do so). She went and
hired a room for her with old widow Mallet, and she
gave her knitting and needlework when she was able to
do it; and when she was ill she sent her dinners and
many nice comfortable things, and was like a mother
to her. Then the master, he took me into the stable
under old Norman, the coachman that was then. I had
my food at the house, and my bed in the loft, and a
suit of clothes, and three shillings a week, so that I
could help Nelly. Then there was Norman; he might
have turned round and said that at his age he could not
be troubled with a raw boy from the plough-tail, but

he was like a father to me and took no end of pains with me. When the old man died some years after, I stepped into his place, and now, of course, I have top wages and can lay by for a rainy day or a sunny day as it may happen, and Nelly is as happy as a bird. So you see, James, I am not the man that should turn up his nose at a little boy and vex a good, kind master. No, no! I shall miss you very much, James, but we shall pull through, and there's nothing like doing a kindness when 'tis put in your way, and I am glad I can do it."

"Then," said James, "you don't hold with that saying, ' Everybody look after himself, and take care of number one '."

"No, indeed," said John. "Where should I and Nelly have been if master and mistress and old Norman had only taken care of number one? Why—she in the workhouse and I hoeing turnips? Where would Black Beauty and Ginger have been if you had only thought of number one? Why, roasted to death! No, Jim, no! That is a selfish, heathenish saying whoever uses it, and any man who thinks he has nothing to do but take care of number one, why, it's a pity but what he had been drowned, like a puppy or a kitten, before he got his eyes open, that's what I think," said John, with a very decided jerk of his head.

James laughed at this; but there was a thickness in his voice when he said, " You have been my best friend except my mother; I hope you won't forget me."

"No, lad, no!" said John. "And if ever I can do you a good turn, I hope you won't forget me."

The next day Joe came to the stables to learn all he

could before James left. He learned to sweep the stable, to bring in the straw and hay; he began to clean the harness, and helped to wash the carriage. As he was quite too short to do anything in the way of grooming Ginger and me, James taught him upon Merrylegs, for he was to have full charge of him, under John. He was a nice little bright fellow and always came whistling to his work.

Merrylegs was a good deal put out at being " mauled about ", as he said, " by a boy who knew nothing "; but towards the end of the second week he told me confidentially that he thought the boy would turn out well.

At last the day came when James had to leave us; cheerful as he always was, he looked quite down-hearted that morning.

" You see," he said to John, " I am leaving a great deal behind—my mother and Betsy and you, and a good master and mistress, and then the horses, and my old Merrylegs. At the new place there will not be a soul that I shall know. If it were not that I shall get a higher place and be able to help my mother better, I don't think I should have made up my mind to it. It is a real pinch, John."

" Aye, James, lad, so it is, but I should not think much of you if you could leave your home for the first time and not feel it. Cheer up; you'll make friends there, and if you get on well—as I am sure you will— it will be a fine thing for your mother, and she will be proud enough that you have got into such a good place as that."

So John cheered him up, but every one was sorry to lose James; as for Merrylegs, he pined after him for several days and went quite off his appetite. So John took him out several mornings with a leading rein, when he exercised me, and trotting and galloping by my side, got up the little fellow's spirits again and he was soon all right.

Joe's father would often come in and give a little help, as he understood the work, and Joe took a great deal of pains to learn, and John was quite encouraged about him.

CHAPTER XVIII

GOING FOR THE DOCTOR

ONE night, a few days after James had left, I had eaten my hay and was laid down in my straw fast asleep, when I was suddenly awoke by the stable bell ringing very loud. I heard the door of John's house open and his feet running up to the Hall. He was back again in no time; he unlocked the stable door and came in, calling out, " Wake up, Beauty! You must go well now, if ever you did." And almost before I could think, he had got the saddle on my back and the bridle on my head; he just ran round for his coat, and then took me at a quick trot up to the Hall door. The Squire stood there with a lamp in his hand.

" Now, John," he said, " ride for your life—that is,

for your mistress's life; there is not a moment to lose. Give this note to Doctor White; give your horse a rest at the inn, and be back as soon as you can."

John said " Yes, sir," and was on my back in a minute. The gardener who lived at the lodge had heard the bell ring and was ready with the gate open, and away we went through the Park and through the village and down the hill till we came to the toll-gate. John called very loud and thumped upon the door, the man was soon out and flung open the gate.

" Now," said John, " do you keep your gate open for the Doctor; here's the money," and off we went again.

There was before us a long piece of level road by the river-side; John said to me, " Now, Beauty, do your best," and so I did. I wanted no whip nor spur, and for two miles I galloped as fast as I could lay my feet to the ground; I don't believe that my old grandfather who won the race at Newmarket could have gone faster. When we came to the bridge, John pulled me up a little and patted my neck. " Well done, Beauty! Good old fellow!" he said. He would have let me go slower, but my spirit was up and I was off again as before. The air was frosty, the moon was bright, it was very pleasant; we came through a village, then through a dark wood, then uphill, then downhill, till after an eight miles run we came to the town, through the streets and into the market place. It was all quite still except the clatter of my feet on the stones—everybody was asleep. The church clock struck three as we drew up at Doctor White's door. John rang the bell twice and then knocked at the door like thunder. A window was thrown up and Doctor White, in his nightcap, put his head out and said, " What do you want?"

" Mrs. Gordon is very ill, sir; master wants you to go at once; he thinks she will die if you cannot get there. Here is a note."

" Wait," he said. " I will come."

He shut the window and was soon at the door.

" The worst of it is," he said, " that my horse has been out all day and is quite done up; my son has just been sent for, and he has taken the other. What is to be done? Can I have your horse?"

" He has come at a gallop nearly all the way, sir, and I was to give him a rest here; but I think my master would not be against it if you think fit, sir."

" All right," he said, " I will soon be ready."

John stood by me and stroked my neck; I was very hot. The doctor came out with his riding whip.

" You need not take that, sir," said John; " Black Beauty will go till he drops. Take care of him, sir, if you can; I should not like any harm to come to him."

" No, no, John," said the doctor. " I hope not," and in a minute we had left John far behind.

I will not tell you about our way back; the doctor was a heavier man than John, and not so good a rider; however, I did my very best. The man at the toll-gate had it open. When we came to the hill, the doctor drew me up. " Now, my good fellow," he said, " take some breath." I was glad he did, for I was nearly spent, but that breathing helped me on and soon we were in the Park. Joe was at the lodge gate; my master was at the

Hall door, for he had heard us coming. He spoke not a word; the doctor went into the house with him, and Joe led me to the stable. I was glad to get home; my legs shook under me, and I could only stand and pant. I had not a dry hair on my body; the water ran down my legs, and I steamed all over, Joe used to say, like a pot on the fire. Poor Joe! He was young and small and as yet he knew very little, and his father, who would have helped him, had been sent to the next village; but I am sure he did the very best he knew. He rubbed my legs and my chest, but he did not put any warm cloth on me; he thought I was so hot I should not like it. Then he gave me a pail full of water to drink; it was cold and very good, and I drank it all; then he gave me some hay and some corn, and thinking he had done right, he went away. Soon I began to shake and tremble and turned deadly cold; my legs ached, my loins ached, and my chest ached, and I felt sore all over. Oh, how I wished for my warm thick cloth as I stood and trembled! I wished for John, but he had eight miles to walk, so I lay down in my straw and tried to go to sleep. After a long while I heard John at the door. I gave a low moan, for I was in great pain. He was at my side in a moment, stooping down by me. I could not tell him how I felt, but he seemed to know it all. He covered me up with two or three warm cloths, and then ran to the house for some hot water; he made me some warm gruel, which I drank, and then I think I went to sleep.

John seemed to be very much put out. I heard him say to himself, over and over again, "Stupid boy! Stupid boy! No cloth put on, and I dare say the water

was cold too. Boys are no good." But Joe was a good
boy after all.

I was now very ill; a strong inflammation had
attacked my lungs and I could not draw my breath
without pain. John nursed me night and day; he
would get up two or three times in the night to come to
me; my master, too, often came to see me.

"My poor Beauty," he said one day, "my good
horse, you saved your mistress's life, Beauty; yes, you
saved her life." I was very glad to hear that, for it
seems the doctor had said if we had been a little longer
it would have been too late. John told my master he
never saw a horse go so fast in his life; it seemed as if
the horse knew what was the matter. Of course I did,
though John thought not; at least I knew as much as
this, that John and I must go at the top of our speed
and that it was for the sake of the mistress.

CHAPTER XIX

ONLY IGNORANCE

I DO not know how long I was ill. Mr. Bond, the horse
doctor, came every day. One day he bled me; John
held a pail for the blood; I felt very faint after it and
thought I should die, and I believe they all thought so
too.

Ginger and Merrylegs had been moved into the
other stable so that I might be quiet, for the fever

made me very quick of hearing; any little noise seemed quite loud, and I could tell every one's footstep going to and from the house. I knew all that was going on. One night John had to give me a draught; Thomas Green came to help him. After I had taken it and John had made me as comfortable as he could, he said he would stay half an hour to see how the medicine settled. Thomas said he would stay with him, so they went and sat down on a bench that had been brought into Merrylegs's stall, and put down the lantern at their feet, that I might not be disturbed with the light.

For a while both men sat silent, and then Tom Green said in a low voice:

" I wish, John, you'd say a bit of a kind word to Joe; the boy is quite broken-hearted; he can't eat his meals and he can't smile. He says he knows it was all his fault, though he is sure he did the best he knew, and he says if Beauty dies no one will ever speak to him again. It goes to my heart to hear him. I think you might give him a just word; he is not a bad boy."

After a short pause John said slowly, " You must not be too hard on me, Tom. I know he meant no harm—I never said he did; I know he is not a bad boy, but you see I am sore myself. That horse is the pride of my heart, to say nothing of his being such a favourite with the master and mistress; and to think that his life may be flung away in this manner is more than I can bear; but if you think I am hard on the boy, I will try to give him a good word to-morrow—that is, I mean, if Beauty is better."

" Well, John, thank you. I knew you did not wish

to be too hard, and I am glad you see it was only ignorance."

John's voice almost startled me as he answered, " *Only* ignorance! Only *ignorance*! How can you talk about *only* ignorance? Don't you know that it is the worst thing in the world, next to wickedness?—and which does the most mischief, heaven only knows. If people can say, ' Oh! I did not know; I did not mean any harm,' they think it is all right. I suppose Martha Mulwash did not mean to kill that baby when she dosed it with Dalby and soothing syrups; but she did kill it, and was tried for manslaughter."

" And serve her right too," said Tom. " A woman should not undertake to nurse a tender little child without knowing what is good and what is bad for it."

" Bill Starkey," continued John, " did not mean to frighten his brother into fits when he dressed up like a ghost and ran after him in the moonlight; but he did; and that bright, handsome little fellow, that might have been the pride of any mother's heart, is just no better than an idiot, and never will be, if he live to be eighty years old. You were a good deal cut up yourself, Tom, two weeks ago, when those young ladies left your hothouse door open, with a frosty east wind blowing right in. You said it killed a good many of your plants."

" A good many!" said Tom. " There was not one of the tender cuttings that was not nipped off. I shall have to strike all over again, and the worst of it is that I don't know where to go to get fresh ones. I was nearly mad when I came in and saw what was done."

" And yet," said John, " I am sure the young ladies did not mean it; it was only ignorance!"

I heard no more of this conversation, for the medicine did well and sent me to sleep, and in the morning I felt much better; but I often thought of John's words when I came to know more of the world.

CHAPTER XX

JOE GREEN

JOE GREEN went on very well; he learned quickly, and was so attentive and careful that John began to trust him in many things; but, as I have said, he was small for his age and it was seldom that he was allowed to exercise either Ginger or me; but it so happened one morning that John was out with " Justice " in the luggage cart, and the master wanted a note to be taken immediately to a gentleman's house about three miles distant, and sent his orders for Joe to saddle me and take it; adding the caution that he was to ride carefully.

The note was delivered, and we were quietly returning till we came to the brickfield. Here we saw a cart heavily laden with bricks; the wheels had stuck fast in the stiff mud of some deep ruts and the carter was shouting and flogging the two horses unmercifully. Joe pulled up. It was a sad sight. There were the two horses straining and struggling with all their might to drag the cart out, but they could not move it; the sweat streamed from their legs and flanks, their sides heaved, and every muscle was strained, whilst the man, fiercely pulling at the head of the forehorse, swore and lashed most brutally.

"Hold hard!" said Joe. "Don't go on flogging the horses like that; the wheels are so stuck that they cannot move the cart." The man took no heed, but went on lashing.

"Stop! Pray stop," said Joe. "I'll help you to lighten the cart; they can't move it now."

"Mind your own business, you impudent young rascal, and I'll mind mine." The man was in a towering passion and the worse for drink, and laid on the whip again. Joe turned my head, and the next moment we were going at a round gallop towards the house of the master brickmaker. I cannot say if John would have approved of our pace, but Joe and I were both of one mind and so angry that we could not have gone slower.

The house stood close by the roadside. Joe knocked at the door and shouted, "Hulloa! Is Mr. Clay at home?" The door was opened and Mr. Clay himself came out.

"Hulloa, young man! You seem in a hurry. Any orders from the squire this morning?"

"No, Mr. Clay, but there's a fellow in your brick-yard flogging two horses to death. I told him to stop, and he wouldn't; I said I'd help him lighten the cart, and he wouldn't; so I have come to tell you. Pray, sir, go." Joe's voice shook with excitement.

"Thank ye, my lad," said the man, running in for his hat; then pausing a moment: "Will you give evidence of what you saw if I should bring the fellow up before a magistrate?"

"That I will," said Joe, "and glad too." The man was gone, and we were on our way home at a smart trot.

"Why, what's the matter with you, Joe? You look angry all over," said John as the boy flung himself from the saddle.

"I am angry all over, I can tell you," said the boy, and then in hurried excited words he told all that had happened. Joe was usually such a quiet, gentle little fellow that it was wonderful to see him so roused.

"Right, Joe! You did right, my boy, whether the fellow gets a summons or not. Many folks would have ridden by and said 'twas not their business to interfere. Now, I say, that with cruelty and oppression it is everybody's business to interfere when they see it. You did right, my boy."

Joe was quite calm by this time and proud that John approved of him, and he cleaned out my feet and rubbed me down with a firmer hand than usual.

They were just going home to dinner when the footman came down to the stable to say that Joe was wanted directly in master's private room; there was a man brought up for ill-using horses and Joe's evidence was wanted. The boy flushed up to his forehead and his eyes sparkled. "They shall have it," said he.

"Put yourself a bit straight," said John. Joe gave a pull at his necktie and a twitch at his jacket, and was off in a moment. Our master being one of the county magistrates, cases were often brought to him to settle or say what should be done. In the stable we heard no more for some time, as it was the men's dinner hour, but when Joe came next into the stable, I saw he was in high spirits. He gave me a good-natured slap and said, " We won't see such things done, will we, old fellow?" We heard afterwards that he had given his evidence so clearly, and the horses were in such an exhausted state, bearing marks of such brutal usage, that the carter was committed to take his trial and might possibly be sentenced to two or three months in prison.

It was wonderful what a change had come over Joe. John laughed and said he had grown an inch taller in that week, and I believe he had. He was just as kind and gentle as before, but there was more purpose and determination in all that he did—as if he had jumped at once from a boy into a man.

CHAPTER XXI

THE PARTING

I HAD now lived in this happy place three years, but sad changes were about to come over us. We heard from time to time that our mistress was ill. The doctor was often at the house, and the master looked grave and anxious. Then we heard that she must leave her home at once and go to a warm country for two or three years. The news fell upon the household like the tolling of a death-bell. Everybody was sorry; but the master began directly to make arrangements for breaking up his establishment and leaving England. We used to hear it talked about in our stable; indeed, nothing else was talked about.

John went about his work silent and sad, and Joe scarcely whistled. There was a great deal of coming and going; Ginger and I had full work.

The first of the party who went were Miss Jessie and Miss Flora with their governess. They came to bid us good-bye. They hugged poor Merrylegs like an old friend, and so indeed he was. Then we heard what had been arranged for us. Master had sold Ginger and me to his old friend, the Earl of W——, for he thought we should have a good place there. Merrylegs he had given to the Vicar, who was wanting a pony for Mrs. Blomefield, but it was on the condition that he should never be sold, and when he was past work that he should be shot and buried.

Joe was engaged to take care of him and to help in the house, so I thought that Merrylegs was well off. John had the offer of several good places, but he said he should wait a little and look round.

The evening before they left, the master came into the stable to give some directions and to give his horses the last pat. He seemed very low-spirited; I knew that by his voice. I believe we horses can tell more by the voice than many men can.

" Have you decided what to do, John?" he said. " I find you have not accepted any of those offers."

" No, sir. I have made up my mind that if I could get a situation with some first-rate colt-breaker and horse-trainer, that it would be the right thing for me. Many young animals are frightened and spoiled by wrong treatment which need not be, if the right man took them in hand. I always get on well with horses, and if I could help some of them to a fair start, I should feel as if I was doing some good. What do you think of it, sir?"

"I don't know a man anywhere," said master, "that I should think so suitable for it as yourself. You understand horses, and somehow they understand you, and in time you might set up for yourself; I think you could not do better. If in any way I can help you, write to me; I shall speak to my agent in London and leave your character with him."

Master gave John the name and address, and then he thanked him for his long and faithful service; but that was too much for John. "Pray don't, sir; I can't bear it. You and my dear mistress have done so much for me that I could never repay it; but we shall never forget you, sir, and please God we may some day see mistress back again like herself; we must keep up hope, sir." Master gave John his hand, but he did not speak, and they both left the stable.

The last sad day had come; the footman and the heavy luggage had gone off the day before, and there was only master and mistress and her maid. Ginger and I brought the carriage up to the Hall door for the last time. The servants brought out cushions and rugs and many other things, and when all were arranged, master came down the steps carrying the mistress in his arms (I was on the side next the house and could see all

that went on); he placed her carefully in the carriage,
while the house servants stood round crying.

"Good-bye again," he said. "We shall not forget
any of you," and he got in. "Drive on, John."

Joe jumped up, and we trotted slowly through the
Park and through the village where the people were
standing at their doors to have a last look and to say
"God bless them."

When we reached the railway station, I think mistress
walked from the carriage to the waiting-room. I heard
her say in her own sweet voice, "Good-bye, John.
God bless you." I felt the rein twitch, but John made
no answer, perhaps he could not speak. As soon as Joe
had taken the things out of the carriage, John called
him to stand by the horses, while he went on the platform. Poor Joe! He stood close up to our heads to hide
his tears. Very soon the train came puffing into the
station; then two or three minutes and the doors were
slammed to; the guard whistled and the train glided
away, leaving behind it only clouds of white smoke and
some very heavy hearts.

When it was quite out of sight, John came back.

"We shall never see her again," he said, "never."
He took the reins, mounted the box, and with Joe drove
slowly home; but it was not our home now.

PART II

CHAPTER XXII

EARLSHALL

THE next morning after breakfast Joe put Merrylegs into the mistress's low chaise to take him to the vicarage; he came first and said good-bye to us, and Merrylegs neighed to us from the yard. Then John put the saddle on Ginger and the leading rein on me, and rode us across the country about fifteen miles to Earlshall Park, where the Earl of W—— lived. There was a very fine house and a great deal of stabling; we went into the yard through a stone gateway, and John asked for Mr. York. It was some time before he came. He was a fine-looking, middle-aged man, and his voice said at once that he expected to be obeyed. He was very friendly and polite to John, and after giving us a slight look, he called a groom to take us to our boxes and invited John to take some refreshment.

We were taken to a light, airy stable and placed in boxes adjoining each other, where we were rubbed down and fed. In about half an hour John and Mr. York, who was to be our new coachman, came in to see us.

"Now, Mr. Manly," he said, after carefully looking at us both, "I can see no fault in those horses, but

we all know that horses have their peculiarities as well
as men, and that sometimes they need different treatment; I should like to know if there is anything
particular in either of these that you would like to
mention."

"Well," said John, "I don't believe there is a better
pair of horse in the country, and right grieved I am to
part with them, but they are not alike. The black one
is the most perfect temper I ever knew; I suppose he
has never known a hard word or a blow since he was
foaled, and all his pleasure seems to be to do what you
wish; but the chestnut, I fancy, must have had bad
treatment; we heard as much from the dealer. She
came to us snappish and suspicious, but when she found
what sort of place ours was it all went off by degrees; for
three years I have never seen the smallest sign of temper,
and if she is well treated there is not a better, more
willing animal than she is; but she is naturally a more
irritable constitution than the black horse; flies tease
her more; anything wrong in the harness frets her more;
and if she were ill-used or unfairly treated she would
not be unlikely to give tit for tat; you know that many
high-mettled horses will do so."

"Of course," said York, "I quite understand, but
you know it is not easy in stables like these to have all
the grooms just what they should be; I do my best and
there I must leave it. I'll remember what you have
said about the mare."

They were going out of the stable when John
stopped and said, "I had better mention that we have
never used the 'bearing rein' with either of them;

he black horse never had one on, and the dealer said
t was the gag-bit that spoiled the other's temper."

"Well," said York, "if they come here they must
wear the bearing rein. I prefer a loose rein myself,
and his lordship is always very reasonable about horses;
but my lady—that's another thing; she will have style;
and if her carriage horses are not reined up tight she
wouldn't look at them. I always stand out against the
gag-bit, and shall do so, but it must be tight up when
my lady rides!"

"I am sorry for it, very sorry," said John, "but I
must go now or I shall lose my train."

He came round to each of us to pat and speak to us
for the last time; his voice sounded very sad.

I held my face close to him; that was all I could do
to say good-bye; and then he was gone and I have
never seen him since.

The next day Lord W—— came to look at us; he
seemed pleased with our appearance.

"I have great confidence in these horses," he said,
"from the character my friend, Mr. Gordon, has given
me of them. Of course, they are not a match in colour,
but my idea is that they will do very well for the carriage
whilst we are in the country. Before we go to London I
must try to match Baron; the black horse, I believe, is
perfect for riding."

York then told him what John had said about us.

"Well," said he, "you must keep an eye to the mare
and put the bearing rein easy; I dare say they will do
very well with a little humouring at first. I'll mention
it to her ladyship."

7   (G 845)

In the afternoon we were harnessed and put in the carriage, and as the stable clock struck three we were led round to the front of the house. It was all very grand and three or four times as large as the old house at Birtwick, but not half as pleasant, if a horse may have an opinion. Two footmen were standing ready, dressed in drab livery, with scarlet breeches and white stockings. Presently we heard the rustling sound of silk as my lady came down the flight of stone steps. She stepped round to look at us; she was a tall, proud-looking woman, and did not seem pleased about something, but she said nothing and got into the carriage. This was the first time of wearing a bearing rein, and I must say, though it certainly was a nuisance not to be able to get my head down now and then, it did not pull my head higher than I was accustomed to carry it. I felt anxious about Ginger, but she seemed to be quiet and content.

The next day at three o'clock we were again at the door, and the footmen as before; we heard the silk dress rustle, and the lady came down the steps and in an imperious voice she said, " York, you must put those horses' heads higher; they are not fit to be seen."

York got down and said very respectfully, " I beg your pardon, my lady, but these horses have not been reined up for three years, and my lord said it would be safer to bring them to it by degrees; but if your lady-ship pleases, I can take them up a little more."

" Do so," she said.

York came round to our heads and shortened the rein himself, one hole, I think; every little makes a difference, be it for better or worse, and that day we had a steep hill to go up. Then I began to understand what I had heard of. Of course I wanted to put my head forward and take the carriage up with a will, as we had been used to do; but no, I had to pull with my head up now, and that took all the spirit out of me and the strain came on my back and legs. When we came in, Ginger said, " Now you see what it is like, but this is not bad, and if it does not get much worse than this I shall say nothing about it, for we are very well treated here; but if they strain me up tight, why, let 'em look out! I can't bear it, and I won't."

Day by day, hole by hole, our bearing reins were shortened, and instead of looking forward with pleasure to having any harness put on as I used to do, I began to dread it. Ginger, too, seemed restless, though she said very little. At last I thought the worst was over; for several days there was no more shortening, and I determined to make the best of it and do my duty, though it was now a constant harass instead of a pleasure, but the worst was not come.

CHAPTER XXIII

A STRIKE FOR LIBERTY

ONE day my lady came down later than usual, and the silk rustled more than ever.

" Drive to the Duchess of B——'s," she said, and

then, after a pause, " Are you never going to get those horses' heads up, York? Raise them at once and let us have no more of this humouring and nonsense."

York came to me first, whilst the groom stood at Ginger's head. He drew my head back and fixed the rein so tight that it was almost intolerable; then he went to Ginger, who was impatiently jerking her head up and down against the bit, as was her way now. She had a good idea of what was coming, and the moment York took the rein off the terret in order to shorten it, she took her opportunity and reared up so suddenly that York had his nose roughly hit and his hat knocked off; the groom was nearly thrown off his legs. At once they both flew to her head, but she was a match for them and went on plunging, rearing, and kicking in a most desperate manner; at last she kicked right over the carriage pole and fell down, after giving me a severe blow on my near quarter. There is no knowing what further mischief she might have done had not York promptly sat himself down flat on her head, to prevent her struggling, at the same time calling out, " Unbuckle the black horse! Run for the winch and unscrew the carriage pole; cut the trace here, somebody, if you can't unhitch it." One of the footmen ran for the winch and another brought a knife from the house. The groom soon set me free from Ginger and the carriage, and led me to my box. He just turned me in as I was, and ran back to York. I was much excited by what had happened, and if I had ever been used to kick or rear, I am sure I should have done it then; but I never had, and there I stood angry, sore in my leg, my head still strained up to the terret on the saddle and no power to get down. I was very miserable, and felt much inclined to kick the first person who came near me.

Before long, however, Ginger was led in by two grooms, a good deal knocked about and bruised. York came with her and gave his orders, and then came to look at me. In a moment he let down my head.

" Confound these bearing reins!" he said to himself. " I thought we should have some mischief soon—master will be sorely vexed; but there—if a woman's husband can't rule her, or course a servant can't; so I wash my hands of it, and if she can't get to the duchess's garden party, I can't help it."

York did not say this before the men; he always spoke respectfully when they were by. Now he felt me all over and soon found the place above my hock where I had been kicked. It was swelled and painful; he ordered it to be sponged with hot water, and then some lotion was put on.

Lord W—— was much put out when he learned what had happened; he blamed York for giving way to the mistress, to which he replied that in future he would much prefer to receive his orders only from his lordship; but I think nothing came of it, for things went on same as before. I thought York might have stood up better for his horses; but perhaps I am no judge.

Ginger was never put into the carriage again, but when she was well of her bruises, one of Lord W——'s younger sons said he should like to have her; he was sure she would make a good hunter. As for me, I was obliged still to go in the carriage and had a fresh partner called Max; he had always been used to the tight rein. I asked him how it was he bore it.

"Well," he said, "I bear it because I must, but it is shortening my life and it will shorten yours too, if you have to stick to it."

"Do you think," I said, "that our masters know how bad it is for us?"

"I can't say," he replied, "but the dealers and the horse doctors know it very well. I was at a dealer's once, who was training me and another horse to go as a pair; he was getting our heads up, as he said, a little higher and a little higher every day. A gentleman who was there asked him why he did so. 'Because,' said he, 'people won't buy them unless we do. The London people always want their horses to carry their heads high and to step high; of course, it is very bad for the horses, but then it is good for trade. The horses soon wear up, or get diseased, and they come for another pair.' That," said Max, " is what he said in my hearing and you can judge for yourself."

What I suffered with that rein for four long months in my lady's carriage it would be hard to describe; but I am quite sure that, had it lasted much longer, either my health or my temper would have given way. Before that I never knew what it was to foam at the mouth, but now the action of the sharp bit on my tongue and jaw, and the constrained position of my head and throat always caused me to froth at the mouth more or less. Some people think it very fine to see this, and say, "What fine, spirited creatures!" But it is just as unnatural for horses as for men to foam at the mouth;

it is a sure sign of some discomfort, and should be attended to. Besides this, there was a pressure on my windpipe, which often made my breathing very uncomfortable; when I returned from my work, my neck and chest were strained and painful, my mouth and tongue tender, and I felt worn and depressed.

In my old home I always knew that John and my master were my friends; but here, although in many ways I was well treated, I had no friend. York might have known, and very likely did know, how that rein harassed me; but I suppose he took it as a matter of course that could not be helped; at any rate, nothing was done to relieve me.

CHAPTER XXIV

THE LADY ANNE

EARLY in the spring Lord W—— and part of his family went up to London and took York with them. I and Ginger and some other horses were left at home for use, and the head groom was left in charge.

The Lady Harriet, who remained at the Hall, was a great invalid and never went out in the carriage, and the Lady Anne preferred riding on horseback with her brother or cousins. She was a perfect horsewoman, and as gay and gentle as she was beautiful. She chose me for her horse and named me " Black Auster ". I enjoyed these rides very much in the clear, cold air, sometimes with Ginger, sometimes with Lizzie. This

Lizzie was a bright bay mare, almost thoroughbred, and a great favourite with the gentlemen on account of her fine action and lively spirit; but Ginger, who knew more of her than I did, told me she was rather nervous.

There was a gentleman of the name of Blantyre staying at the Hall; he always rode Lizzie, and praised her so much that one day Lady Anne ordered the side-saddle to be put on her and the other saddle on me. When we came to the door, the gentleman seemed very uneasy.

" How is this?" he said. " Are you tired of your good Black Auster?"

" Oh no, not at all!" she replied, " but I am amiable enough to let you ride him for once, and I will try your charming Lizzie. You must confess that in size and appearance she is far more like a lady's horse than my own favourite."

" Do let me advise you not to mount her," he said. " She is a charming creature, but she is too nervous for a lady. I assure you she is not perfectly safe; let me beg you to have the saddles changed."

" My dear cousin," said Lady Anne, laughing, " pray do not trouble your good careful head about me; I have been a horsewoman ever since I was a baby, and have followed the hounds a good many times, though I do not approve of ladies hunting; but still that is the fact, and I intend to try this Lizzie that you gentlemen are all so fond of; so please help me to mount like a good friend, as you are."

There was no more to be said; he placed her carefully on the saddle, looked to the bit and curb, gave the reins gently into her hand, and then mounted me. Just as we were moving off a footman came out with a slip of paper and message from the Lady Harriet, " Would they ask this question for her at Dr. Ashley's and bring the answer?"

The village was about a mile off and the doctor's house was the last in it. We went along gaily enough till we came to his gate. There was a short drive up to the house between tall evergreens. Blantyre alighted at the gate and was going to open it for Lady Anne, but she said, " I will wait for you here, and you can hang Auster's rein on the gate."

He looked at her doubtfully. " I will not be five minutes," he said.

" Oh, do not hurry yourself; Lizzie and I shall not run away from you."

He hung my rein on one of the iron spikes and was soon hidden amongst the trees. Lizzie was standing quietly by the side of the road a few paces off with her back to me. My young mistress was sitting easily with a loose rein, humming a little song. I listened to my rider's footsteps until they reached the house, and heard him knock at the door. There was a meadow on the opposite side of the road, the gate of which stood open; just then, some cart horses and several young colts came trotting out in a very disorderly manner, whilst a boy behind was cracking a great whip. The colts were wild and frolicsome, and one of them bolted across the road and blundered up against Lizzie's hind legs; and whether it was the stupid colt, or the loud cracking of the whip, or both together, I cannot say, but she gave

a violent kick and dashed off into a headlong gallop.
It was so sudden that Lady Anne was nearly unseated;
but she soon recovered herself. I gave a loud shrill
neigh for help; again and again I neighed, pawing
the ground impatiently, and tossing my head to get
the rein loose. I had not long to wait. Blantyre came
running to the gate; he looked anxiously about, and
just caught sight of the flying figure, now far away on
the road. In an instant he sprang into the saddle. I
needed no whip or spur, for I was as eager as my
rider; he saw it and, giving me a free rein and leaning
a little forward, we dashed after them.

For about a mile and a half the road ran straight,
and then bent to the right, after which it divided into
two roads. Long before we came to the bend she was
out of sight. Which way had she turned? A woman was
standing at her garden gate, shading her eyes with
her hand and looking eagerly up the road. Scarcely
drawing the rein, Blantyre shouted, "Which way?"
"To the right," cried the woman, pointing with her
hand, and away we went up the right-hand road; then
for a moment we caught sight of her; another bend
and she was hidden again. Several times we caught
glimpses, and then lost them. We scarcely seemed to
gain ground upon them at all. An old road-mender was
standing hear a heap of stones—his shovel dropped
and his hands raised. As we came near he made a sign
to speak. Blantyre drew the rein a little. "To the
common, to the common, sir; she has turned off
there." I knew this common very well; it was for the
most part very uneven ground, covered with heather

and dark green furze bushes, with here and there a
scrubby old thorn tree; there were also open spaces of
fine short grass, with ant-hills amd mole turns everywhere; the worst place I ever knew for a headlong
gallop.

We had hardly turned on the common when we
caught sight again of the green habit flying on before us.
My lady's hat was gone and her long brown hair was
streaming behind her. Her head and body were
thrown back, as if she were pulling with all her
remaining strength and as if that strength were nearly
exhausted. It was clear that the roughness of the ground
had very much lessened Lizzie's speed, and there seemed
a chance that we might overtake her.

Whilst we were on the highroad, Blantyre had given
me my head; but now with a light hand and a practised eye he guided me over the ground in such a
masterly manner that my pace was scarcely slackened,
and we were decidedly gaining on them.

About half-way across the heath there had been a
wide dyke recently cut, and the earth from the cutting
was cast up roughly on the other side. Surely this would
stop them! But no; with scarcely a pause, Lizzie took
the leap, stumbled among the rough clods, and fell.
Blantyre groaned. " Now, Auster, do your best!" He
gave me a steady rein, I gathered myself well together,
and with one determined leap cleared both dyke and
bank.

Motionless among the heather, with her face to the
earth, lay my poor young mistress. Blantyre kneeled
down and called her name—there was no sound; gently

he turned her face upward, it was ghastly white and the eyes were closed. "Annie, dear Annie, do speak!" But there was no answer. He unbuttoned her habit, loosened her collar, felt her hands and wrists, then started up and looked wildly round him for help.

At no great distance there were two men cutting turf, who, seeing Lizzie running wild without a rider, had left their work to catch her.

Blantyre's halloo soon brought them to the spot. The foremost man seemed much troubled at the sight and asked what he could do.

"Can you ride?"

"Well, sir, I bean't much of a horseman, but I'd risk my neck for the Lady Anne; she was uncommon good to my wife in the winter."

"Then mount this horse, my friend; your neck will be quite safe, and ride to the doctor's and ask him to come instantly; then on to the Hall. Tell them all that you know, and bid them send me the carriage with Lady Anne's maid and help. I shall stay here."

"All right, sir, I'll do my best, and I pray God the dear young lady may open her eyes soon." Then seeing the other man, he called out, "Here, Joe, run for some water and tell my missis to come as quick as she can to the Lady Anne."

He then somehow scrambled into the saddle, and with a "Gee-up" and a clap on my sides with both his legs, he started on his journey, making a little circuit to avoid the dyke. He had no whip, which seemed to trouble him, but my pace soon cured that difficulty, and he found that the best thing he could do was to

stick to the saddle and hold me in, which he did man-
fully. I shook him as little as I could help, but once or
twice on the rough ground he called out " Steady!
Woah! Steady!" On the highroad we were all right;
and at the doctor's and the Hall he did his errand like
a good man and true. They asked him in to take a drop
of something. " No, no," he said, " I'll be back to 'em
again by a short cut through the fields, and be there
afore the carriage."

There was a great deal of hurry and excitement after
the news became known. I was just turned into my
box, and saddle and bridle were taken off and a cloth
thrown over me.

Ginger was saddled and sent off in great haste for
Lord George, and I soon heard the carriage roll out
of the yard.

It seemed a long time before Ginger came back
and before we were left alone; and then she told me
all that she had seen.

" I can't tell much," she said. " We went a gallop
nearly all the way and got there just as the doctor rode
up. There was a woman sitting on the ground with the
lady's head in her lap. The doctor poured something
into her mouth, but all that I heard was ' she is not
dead '. Then I was led off by a man to a little distance.
After awhile she was taken to the carriage and we came
home together. I heard my master say to a gentleman
who stopped him to inquire, that he hoped no bones
were broken, but that she had not spoken yet."

When Lord George took Ginger for hunting, York
shook his head; he said it ought to be a steady hand to

train a horse for the first season, and not a random rider like Lord George.

Ginger used to like it very much, but sometimes when she came back I could see that she had been very much strained, and now and then she gave a short cough. She had too much spirit to complain, but I could not help feeling anxious about her.

Two days after the accident Blantyre paid me a visit. He patted me and praised me very much; he told Lord George that he was sure the horse knew of Annie's danger as well as he did. " I could not have held him in if I would," said he. " She ought never to ride any other horse." I found by their conversation that my young mistress was now out of danger and would soon be able to ride again. This was good news to me and I looked forward to a happy life.

CHAPTER XXV

REUBEN SMITH

I MUST now say a little about Reuben Smith, who was left in charge of the stables when York went to London. No one more thoroughly understood his business than he did, and when he was all right there could not be a more faithful or valuable man. He was gentle and very clever in his management of horses, and could doctor them almost as well as a farrier, for he had lived two years with a veterinary surgeon. He was a first-rate driver; he could take a four-in-hand, or a tandem, as easily as a pair. He was a handsome man, a good scholar, and had very pleasant manners. I believe everybody liked him; certainly the horses did; the only wonder was that he should be in an under situation and not in the place of a head coachman like York; but he had one great fault, and that was the love of drink. He was not like some men, always at it; he used to keep steady for weeks or months together, and then he would break out and have a " bout " of it, as York called it, and be a disgrace to himself, a terror to his wife, and a nuisance to all that had to do with him. He was, however, so useful that two or three times York had hushed the matter up and kept it from the Earl's knowledge; but one night, when Reuben had to drive a party home from a ball, he was so drunk that he could not hold the reins, and a gentleman of the party had to mount the box and drive the ladies home. Of course this could not be hidden and Reuben was at once dismissed; his poor wife and little children had to turn out of the pretty cottage by the Park gate and go where they could. Old Max told me all this, for it happened a good while ago; but shortly before Ginger and I came Smith had been taken back again. York had interceded for him with the Earl, who was very kind-hearted, and the man had promised faithfully that he would never taste another drop as long as he lived there. He had kept his promise so well that York thought he might safely be trusted to fill his place whilst he was away, and he was so clever and honest that no one else seemed so well fitted for it.

It was now early in April and the family was expected

home some time in May. The light brougham was to
be freshly done up, and as Colonel Blantyre was obliged
to return to his regiment, it was arranged that Smith
should drive him to the town in it and ride back. For
this purpose he took the saddle with him and I was
chosen for the journey. At the station the colonel put
some money into Smith's hand and bid him good-bye,
saying, " Take care of your young mistress, Reuben,
and don't let Black Auster be hacked about by any
random young prig that wants to ride him—keep him
for the lady."

We left the carriage at the maker's, and Smith rode
me to the White Lion and ordered the ostler to feed me
well and have me ready for him at four o'clock. A nail
in one of my front shoes had started as I came along,
but the ostler did not notice it till just about four o'clock.
Smith did not come into the yard till five, and then he
said he should not leave till six, as he had met with
some old friends. The man then told him of the nail
and asked if he should have the shoe looked to.

" No," said Smith, " that will be all right till we get
home."

He spoke in a very loud, off-hand way, and I thought
it very unlike him not to see about loose nails in our
shoes. He did not come at six, nor seven, nor eight, and
it was nearly nine o'clock before he called for me, and
then it was with a loud, rough voice. He seemed in a
very bad temper and abused the ostler, though I could
not tell what for.

The landlord stood at the door and said, " Have a
care, Mr. Smith !" but he answered angrily with an

oath; and almost before he was out of the town he began to gallop, frequently giving me a sharp cut with his whip, though I was going at full speed. The moon had not yet risen and it was very dark. The roads were stony, having been recently mended; going over them at this pace, my shoe became looser, and when we were near the turnpike gate it came off.

If Smith had been in his right senses, he would have been sensible of something wrong in my pace; but he was too madly drunk to notice anything.

Beyond the turnpike was a long piece of road upon which fresh stones had just been laid—large sharp stones, over which no horse could be driven quickly without risk of danger. Over this road, with one shoe gone, I was forced to gallop at my utmost speed, my rider meanwile cutting into me with his whip and with wild curses urging me to go still faster. Of course my shoeless foot suffered dreadfully. The hoof was broken and split down to the very quick, and the inside was terribly cut by the sharpness of the stones.

This could not go on; no horse could keep his footing under such circumstances, the pain was too great. I stumbled and fell with violence on both my knees. Smith was flung off by my fall, and owing to the speed I was going at, he must have fallen with great force. I soon recovered my feet and limped to the side of the road, where it was free from stones. The moon had just risen above the hedge and by its light I could see Smith lying a few yards beyond me. He did not rise; he made one slight effort to do so and then there was a heavy groan. I could have groaned too, for I was suffering intense pain both from my foot and knees; but horses are used to bear their pain in silence. I uttered no sound, but I stood there and listened. One more heavy groan from Smith; but though he now lay in the full moonlight, I could see no motion. I could do nothing for him nor myself, but, oh! how I listened for the sound of horse, or wheels or footsteps. The road was not much frequented and at this time of the night we might stay for hours before help came to us. I stood watching and listening. It was a calm sweet April night; there were no sounds but a few low notes of a nightingale, and nothing moved but the white clouds near the moon and a brown owl that flitted over the hedge. It made me think of the summer nights long ago when I used to lie beside my mother in the green pleasant meadow at Farmer Grey's.

CHAPTER XXVI

HOW IT ENDED

It must have been nearly midnight when I heard at a great distance the sound of a horse's feet. Sometimes the sound died away, then it grew clearer again and nearer. The road to Earlshall led through plantations that belonged to the Earl; the sound came in that direction and I hoped it might be someone coming in search of us. As the sound came nearer and nearer, I was almost sure I could distinguish Ginger's step; a little nearer still and I could tell she was in the dogcart. I neighed loudly and was overjoyed to hear an answering neigh from Ginger, and men's voices. They came slowly over the stones and stopped at the dark figure that lay upon the ground.

One of the men jumped out and stooped down over it. "It is Reuben," he said, "and he does not stir!"

The other man followed and bent over him. "He's dead," he said. "Feel how cold his hands are."

They raised him up, but there was no life and his hair was soaked with blood. They laid him down again and came and looked at me. They soon saw my cut knees.

"Why, the horse has been down and thrown him! Who would have thought the black horse would have done that? Nobody thought he could fall. Reuben must have been lying here for hours! Odd, too, that the horse has not moved from the place."

Robert then attempted to lead me forward. I made a step, but almost fell again.

"Hallo! He's bad in his foot as well as his knees. Look here—his hoof is cut all to pieces; he might well come down, poor fellow! I tell you what, Ned, I'm afraid it hasn't been all right with Reuben! Just think of him riding a horse over these stones without a shoe! Why, if he had been in his right senses he would just as soon have tried to ride him over the moon. I'm afraid it has been the old thing over again. Poor Susan! She looked awfully pale when she came to my house to ask if he had not come home. She made believe she was not a bit anxious, and talked of a lot of things that might

have kept him. But for all that she begged me to go and
meet him—but what must we do? There's the horse to
get home as well as the body—and that will be no easy
matter."

Then followed a conversation between them, till it
was agreed that Robert as the groom should lead me
and Ned must take the body. It was a hard job to get
it into the dogcart, for there was no one to hold Ginger;
but she knew as well as I did what was going on, and
stood as still as a stone. I noticed that, because, if she
had a fault, it was that she was impatient in standing.

Ned started off very slowly with his sad load, and
Robert came and looked at my foot again; then he took
his handkerchief and bound it closely round, and so he
led me home. I shall never forget that night walk; it
was more than three miles. Robert led me on very
slowly, and I limped and hobbled on as well as I could
with great pain. I am sure he was sorry for me, for he
often patted and encouraged me, talking to me in a
pleasant voice.

At last I reached my own box and had some corn,
and after Robert had wrapped up my knees in wet
cloths, he tied up my foot in a bran poultice to draw
out the heat and cleanse it before the horse doctor saw
it in the morning, and I managed to get myself down
on the straw and slept in spite of the pain.

The next day, after the farrier had examined my
wounds, he said he hoped the joint was not injured,
and if so, I should not be spoiled for work, but I should
never lose the blemish. I believe they did their best to
make a good cure, but it was a long and painful one;

proud flesh, as they called it, came up in my knees and was burnt out with caustic, and when at last it was healed, they put a blistering fluid over the front of both knees to bring all the hair off; they had some reason for this, and I suppose it was all right.

As Smith's death had been so sudden and no one was there to see it, there was an inquest held. The landlord and ostler at the White Lion, with several other people, gave evidence that he was intoxicated when he started from the inn. The keeper of the tollgate said he rode at a hard gallop through the gate; and my shoe was picked up amongst the stones, so that the case was quite plain to them and I was cleared of all blame.

Everybody pitied Susan; she was nearly out of her mind; she kept saying over and over again, "Oh! He was so good—so good! It was all that cursed drink; why will they sell that cursed drink? Oh, Reuben, Reuben!" So she went on till after he was buried, and then, as she had no home or relations, she, with her six little children, were obliged once more to leave the pleasant home by the tall oak trees and go into that great gloomy Union House.

CHAPTER XXVII

RUINED, AND GOING DOWNHILL

As soon as my knees were sufficiently healed, I was turned into a small meadow for a month or two. No other creature was there, and though I enjoyed the liberty and the sweet grass, yet I had been so long used to society that I felt very lonely. Ginger and I had become fast friends and now I missed her company extremely. I often neighed when I heard horses' feet passing in the road, but I seldom got an answer; till one morning the gate was opened, and who should come in but dear old Ginger. The man slipped off her halter and left her there. With a joyful whinny I trotted up to her; we were both glad to meet, but I soon found that it was not for our pleasure that she was brought to be with me. Her story would be too long to tell, but the end of it was that she had been ruined by hard riding and was now turned off to see what rest would do.

Lord George was young and would take no warning; he was a hard rider and would hunt whenever he could get the chance, quite careless of his horse. Soon after I left the stable there was a steeplechase, and he determined to ride. Though the groom told him she was a little strained and was not fit for the race, he did not believe it, and on the day of the race urged Ginger to keep up with the foremost riders. With her high spirit, she strained herself to the utmost; she came in with the first three horses, but her wind was touched, beside which, he was too heavy for her and her back was strained. "And so," she said, "here we are— ruined in the prime of our youth and strength—you by a drunkard, and I by a fool; it is very hard." We both felt in ourselves that we were not what we had been. However, that did not spoil the pleasure we had in each other's company; we did not gallop about as we once did, but we used to feed and lie down together and stand for hours under one of the shady lime trees with our heads close to each other; and so we passed our time till the family returned from town.

One day we saw the Earl come into the meadow, and York was with him. Seeing who it was, we stood still under our lime tree and let them come up to us. They examined us carefully. The Earl seemed much annoyed.

"There is three hundred pounds flung away for no earthly use," said he; "but what I care most for is that these horses of my old friend, who thought they would find a home with me, are ruined. The mare shall have a twelvemonth's run, and we shall see what that will do for her; but the black one, he must be sold; 'tis a great pity, but I could not have knees like these in my stables."

"No, my lord, of course not," said York; "but he might get a place where appearance is not of much consequence, and still be well treated. I know a man in Bath, the master of some livery stables, who often wants a good horse at a low figure; I know he looks well after his horses. The inquest cleared the horse's character, and your lordship's recommendation, or mine, would be sufficient warrant for him."

"You had better write to him, York. I should be more particular about the place than the money he would fetch."

After this they left us.

"They'll soon take you away," said Ginger, "and I shall lose the only friend I have, and most likely we shall never see each other again. 'Tis a hard world!"

About a week after this, Robert came into the field with a halter, which he slipped over my head and led me away. There was no leave-taking of Ginger; we neighed to each other as I was led off, and she trotted anxiously along by the hedge calling to me as long as she could hear the sound of my feet.

Through the recommendation of York I was bought by the master of the livery stables. I had to go by train, which was new to me, and required a good deal of courage the first time; but as I found the puffing, rushing, whistling, and, more than all, the trembling of the horse box in which I stood did me no real harm, I soon took it quietly.

When I reached the end of my journey I found myself in a tolerably comfortable stable and well attended to. These stables were not so airy and pleasant as those I had been used to. The stalls were laid on a slope instead of being level, and as my head was kept tied to the manger, I was obliged always to stand on the slope, which was very fatiguing. Men do not seem to know yet that horses can do more work if they can stand comfortably and can turn about. However, I was

well fed and well cleaned, and, on the whole, I think
our master took as much care of us as he could. He kept
a good many horses and carriages of different kinds for
hire. Sometimes his own men drove them; at others
the horse and chaise were let to gentlemen or ladies who
drove themselves.

CHAPTER XXVIII

A JOB HORSE AND HIS DRIVERS

HITHERTO I had always been driven by people who at
least knew how to drive; but in this place I was to get
my experience of all the different kinds of bad and
ignorant driving to which we horses are subjected;
for I was a "job horse" and was let out to all sorts of
people who wished to hire me; and as I was good-
tempered and gentle, I think I was oftener let out to
the ignorant drivers than some of the other horses,
because I could be depended upon. It would take a
long time to tell of all the different styles in which I
was driven, but I will mention a few of them.

First, there were the tight-rein drivers—men who
seemed to think that all depended on holding the reins
as hard as they could, never relaxing the pull on the
horses' mouth or giving him the least liberty of movement. They are always talking about "keeping the
horse well in hand" and "holding a horse up", just as
if a horse was not made to hold himself up.

Some poor, broken-down horses, whose mouths have been made hard and insensible by just such drivers as these, may, perhaps, find some support in it; but for a horse who can depend upon its own legs and who has a tender mouth and is easily guided, it is not only torment- ing, but it is stupid.

Then there are the loose rein-drivers, who let the reins lie easily on our backs and their own hand rest lazily on their knees. Of course, such gentlemen have no control over a horse if anything happens suddenly. If a horse shies or starts or stumbles, they are nowhere and cannot help the horse or themselves till the mischief is done. Of course, for myself, I had no objection to it, as I was not in the habit either of starting or stumbling, and had only been used to depend on my driver for guidance and encouragement; still, one likes to feel the rein a little in going downhill, and likes to know that one's driver is not gone to sleep.

Besides, a slovenly way of driving gets a horse into bad and often lazy habits; and when he changes hands he has to be whipped out of them, with more or less pain and trouble. Squire Gordon always kept us to our best paces and our best manners. He said that spoiling a horse and letting him get into bad habits was just as cruel as spoiling a child, and both had to suffer for it afterwards.

Besides, these drivers are often careless altogether and will attend to anything else rather than their horses. I went out in the phaeton one day with one of them; he had a lady and two children behind. He flopped the reins about as we started, and of course gave me several unmeaning cuts with the whip, though I was fairly off. There had been a good deal of road-mending going on, and even where the stones were not freshly laid down there were a great many loose ones about. My driver was laughing and joking with the lady and the children, and talking about the country to the right and the left; but he never thought it worth while to keep an eye on his horse or to drive on the smoothest parts of the road; and so it easily happened that I got a stone in one of my forefeet.

Now, if Mr. Gordon or John or, in fact, any good driver had been there, he would have seen that something was wrong before I had gone three paces; or even if it had been dark, a practised hand would have felt by the rein that there was something wrong in the step, and they would have got down and picked out the stone. But this man went on laughing and talking, whilst at every step the stone became more firmly wedged between my shoe and the frog of my foot. The stone was sharp on the inside and round on the outside, which, as everyone knows, is the most dangerous kind that a horse can pick up, at the same time cutting his foot and making him most liable to stumble and fall.

Whether the man was partly blind or only very care-less, I can't say; but he drove me with that stone in my foot for a good half-mile before he saw anything. By that time I was going so lame with the pain that at last he saw it and called out, " Well, here's a go! Why, they have sent us out with a lame horse! What a shame!"

He then chucked the reins and flipped about with

the whip, saying, " Now, then, it's no use playing the old soldier with me; there's the journey to go and it's no use turning lame and lazy."

Just at this time a farmer came riding up on a brown cob; he lifted his hat and pulled up.

" I beg your pardon, sir," he said, " but I think there is something the matter with your horse; he goes very much as if he had a stone in his shoe. If you will allow me, I will look at his feet. These loose scattered stones are confounded dangerous things for the horses."

" He's a hired horse," said my driver. " I don't know what's the matter with him, but it's a great shame to send out a lame beast like this."

The farmer dismounted and, slipping his rein over his arm, at once took up my near foot.

" Bless me, there's a stone! Lame! I should think so !"

At first he tried to dislodge it with his hand, but as it was now very tightly wedged, he drew a stone-pick out of his pocket and, very carefully and with some trouble, got it out. Then holding it up, he said, " There, that's the stone your horse had picked up; it is a wonder he did not fall down and break his knees into the bargain !"

" Well, to be sure !" said my driver, " that is a queer thing ! I never knew that horses picked up stones before."

" Didn't you?" said the farmer, rather contemptuously. " But they do, though, and the best of them will do it and can't help it sometimes on such roads as these. And if you don't want to lame your horse, you must look sharp and get them out quickly. This foot is very much bruised," he said, setting it gently down and patting me. " If I might advise, sir, you had better drive him gently for a while; the foot is a good deal hurt and the lameness will not go off directly."

Then mounting his cob and raising his hat to the lady, he trotted off.

When he was gone, my driver began to flop the reins about and whip the harness, by which I understood that I was to go on, which of course I did, glad that the stone was gone, but still in a good deal of pain.

This was the sort of experience we job horses often came in for.

CHAPTER XXIX

COCKNEYS

THEN there is the steam-engine style of driving. These drivers were mostly people from towns, who never had a horse of their own and generally travelled by rail.

They always seem to think that a horse was something like a steam engine, only smaller. At any rate, they think that if only they pay for it, a horse is bound to go just as far, and just as fast, and with just as heavy a load as they please. And be the roads heavy and muddy, or dry and good; be they stony or smooth, uphill or downhill, it is all the same—on, on, on, one must go at the same pace, with no relief and no consideration.

These people never think of getting out to walk up a steep hill. Oh no; they have paid to ride and ride they will! The horse? Oh, he's used to it! What were horses made for if not to drag people uphill? Walk! A good joke indeed! And so the whip is plied and the rein is chucked and often a rough scolding voice cries out, "Go along, you lazy beast!" And then another slash of the whip, when all the time we are doing our very best to get along, uncomplaining and obedient, though often sorely harassed and downhearted.

This steam-engine style of driving wears us up faster than any other kind. I would far rather go twenty miles with a good considerate driver than I would go ten with some of these; it would take less out of me.

Another thing—they scarcely ever put on the drag, however steep the downhill may be, and thus bad accidents sometimes happen; or if they do put it on, they often forget to take it off at the bottom of the hill; and more than once I have had to pull half-way up the next hill with one of the wheels lodged fast in the drag-shoe, before my driver chose to think about it; and that is a terrible strain on a horse.

Then these Cockneys, instead of starting at an easy pace as a gentleman would do, generally set off at full speed from the very stable yard; and when they want to stop, they first whip us, and then pull up so suddenly that we are nearly thrown on our haunches and our mouths jagged with the bit; they call that pulling up with a dash! And when they turn a corner, they do it as sharply as if there were no right side or wrong side of the road.

I well remember one spring evening I and Rory had been out for the day. (Rory was the horse that mostly went with me when a pair was ordered, and a good honest fellow he was.) We had our own driver, and as he was always considerate and gentle with us, we had a very pleasant day. We were coming home at a good smart pace about twilight; our road turned sharp to the left; but as we were close to the hedge on our own side and there was plenty of room to pass, our driver did not pull us in. As we neared the corner, I heard a horse and two wheels coming rapidly down the hill towards us. The hedge was high and I could see nothing, but the next moment we were upon each other. Happily for me I was on the side next the hedge. Rory was on the right side of the pole and had not even a shaft to protect him. The man who was driving was making straight for the corner, and when he came in sight of us he had no time to pull over to his own side. The whole shock came upon Rory. The gig shaft ran right into the chest, making him stagger back with a cry that I shall never forget. The other horse was thrown upon his haunches, and one shaft broken. It turned out that it was a horse from our own stables, with the high-wheeled gig that the young men were so fond of.

The driver was one of those random, ignorant fellows who don't even know which is their own side of the road, or if they know, don't care. And there was poor Rory with his flesh torn open and bleeding and the blood streaming down. They said if it had been a little more to one side it would have killed him; and a good thing for him, poor fellow, if it had.

As it was, it was a long time before the wound healed, and then he was sold for coal carting; and what that is, up and down those steep hills, only horses know. Some of the sights I saw there, where a horse had to come downhill with a heavily loaded two-wheeled cart behind him, on which no drag could be placed, make me sad even now to think of.

After Rory was disabled, I often went in the carriage with a mare named Peggy, who stood in the next stall to mine. She was strong, well-made animal, of a bright dun-colour, beautifully dappled, and with a dark-brown mane and tail. There was no high breeding about her, but she was very pretty and remarkably sweet-tempered and willing. Still, there was an anxious look about her eye, by which I knew she had some trouble. The first time we went out together, I thought she had a very odd pace; she seemed to go partly in a trot, partly in a canter—three or four paces, and then to make a little jump forward.

It was very unpleasant for any horse who pulled with her, and made me quite fidgety. When we got home, I asked her what made her go in that odd, awkward way.

" Ah," she said in a troubled manner, " I know my paces are very bad, but what can I do? It really is not my fault; it is just because my legs are so short. I stand nearly as high as you, but your legs are a good three inches longer above your knees than mine, and, of course, you can take a much longer step, and go much faster. You see, I did not make myself; I wish I could have done so; I would have had long legs then; all my

roubles come from my short legs," said Peggy in a
lesponding tone.

" But how is it," I said, " when you are so strong and
good-tempered and willing?"

" Why, you see," said she, " men will go so fast,
and if one can't keep up to the other horses, it is nothing
but whip, whip, whip, all the time. And so I have had
to keep up as I could, and have got into this ugly,
shuffling pace. It was not always so; when I lived
with my first master I always went a good regular trot,
but then he was not in such a hurry. He was a young
clergyman in the country and a good kind master he
was. He had two churches a good way apart and a great
deal of work, but he never scolded or whipped me for
not going faster. He was very fond of me. I only wish
I was with him now; but he had to leave and go to a
large town, and then I was sold to a farmer.

" Some farmers, you know, are capital masters, but
I think this one was a low sort of man. He cared nothing about good horses, or good driving; he only cared
for going fast. I went as fast as I could, but that would
not do, and he was always whipping; so I got into this
way of making a spring forward to keep up. On market
nights he used to stay very late at the inn and then drive
home at a gallop.

" One dark night he was galloping home as usual,
when all on a sudden the wheel came against some great
heavy thing in the road and turned the gig over in a
minute. He was thrown out and his arm broken, and
some of his ribs, I think. At any rate, it was the end of
my living with him, and I was not sorry. But, you see, it

9   (G 845)

will be the same everywhere for me, if men *must* go so fast. I wish my legs were longer!"

Poor Peggy! I was very sorry for her, and I could comfort her, for I knew how hard it was upon slow-paced horses to be put with fast ones; all the whipping comes to their share and they can't help it.

She was often used in the phaeton and was very much liked by some of the ladies, because she was so gentle; and some time after this she was sold to two ladies who drove themselves and wanted a safe good horse.

I met her several times out in the country, going a good steady pace and looking as gay and contented as a horse could be. I was very glad to see her, for she deserved a good place.

After she left us another horse came in her stead. He was young and had a bad name for shying and start-ing, by which he had lost a good place. I asked him what made him shy.

" Well, I hardly know," he said. " I was timid when I was young, and was a good deal frightened several times, and if I saw anything strange I used to turn and look at it—you see, with our blinkers one can't see or understand what a thing is unless one looks round; and then my master always gave me a whipping, which, of course, made me start on and did not make me less afraid. I think if he would have let me just look at things quietly and see that there was nothing to hurt me, it would have been all right and I should have got used to them. One day an old gentleman was riding with him, and a large piece of white paper or rag blew across

st on one side of me; I shied and started forward; my
master as usual whipped me smartly, but the old man
ried out, ' You're wrong! You're wrong! You should
ever whip a horse for shying; he shies because he is
rightened, and you only frighten him more and make
he habit worse.' So I suppose all men don't do so. I
m sure I don't want to shy for the sake of it; but how
hould one know what is dangerous and what is not
f one is never allowed to get used to anything? I am
never afraid of what I know. Now I was brought up in
a park where there were deer; of course I knew them
as well as I knew a sheep or a cow, but they are not
common, and I know many sensible horses are frightened
at them and who kick up quite a shindy before they
will pass a paddock where there are deer."

I knew what my companion said was true, and I
wished that every young horse had as good a master
as Farmer Grey and Squire Gordon.

Of course we sometimes came in for good driving
here. I remember one morning I was put into the light
gig and taken to a house in Pulteney Street. Two
gentlemen came out; the taller of them came round to
my head, he looked at the bit and bridle, and just shifted
the collar with his hand to see if it fitted comfortably.

" Do you consider this horse wants a curb?" he said
to the ostler.

" Well," said the man, " I should say he would go
just as well without; he has an uncommon good mouth,
and though he has a fine spirit he has no vice; but we
generally find people like the curb."

" I don't like it," said the gentleman. " Be so good

as to take it off and put the rein in at the cheek. A easy mouth is a great thing on a long journey, is it not old fellow?" he said, patting my neck.

Then he took the reins and they both got up. I ca remember now how quickly he turned me round, and then with a light feel of the rein and drawing the whip gently across my back, we were off.

I arched my neck and set off at my best pace. found I had some one behind me who knew how a good horse ought to be driven. It seemed like old time again and made me feel quite gay.

This gentleman took a great liking to me, and after trying me several times with the saddle, he prevailed upon my master to sell me to a friend of his who wanted a safe pleasant horse for riding. And so it came to pass that in the summer I was sold to Mr. Barry.

CHAPTER XXX

A THIEF

My new master was an unmarried man. He lived at Bath and was much engaged in business. His doctor advised him to take horse exercise, and for this purpose he bought me. He hired a stable a short distance from his lodgings and engaged a man named Filcher as groom. My master knew very little about horses, but he treated me well, and I should have had a good and easy place but for circumstances of which he was gnorant. He ordered the best hay with plenty of oats, crushed beans and bran, with vetches or rye grass, as the man might think needful. I heard the master give the order, so I knew there was plenty of good food, and I thought I was well off.

For a few days all went on well; I found that my groom understood his business. He kept the stable clean and airy, and he groomed me thoroughly; and was never otherwise than gentle. He had been an ostler in one of the great hotels in Bath. He had given that up and now cultivated fruit and vegetables for the market; and his wife bred and fattened poultry and rabbits for sale. After a while it seemed to me that my oats came very short; I had the beans, but bran was mixed with them instead of oats, of which there were very few; certainly not more than a quarter of what there should have been. In two or three weeks this began to tell upon my strength and spirits. The grass food, though very good, was not the thing to keep up my condition without corn. However, I could not complain nor make known my wants. So it went on for about two months; and I wondered my master did not see that something was the matter. However, one afternoon he rode out into the country to see a friend of his—a gentleman farmer who lived on the road to Wells. This gentleman had a very quick eye for horses; and after he had welcomed his friend, he said, casting his eye over me:

" It seems to me, Barry, that your horse does not look so well as he did when you first had him. Has he been well?"

" Yes, I believe so," said my master, " but he is not nearly so lively as he was; my groom tells me that horses are always dull and weak in the autumn, and that I must expect it."

" Autumn! Fiddlesticks!" said the farmer. " Why, this is only August; and with your light work and good food he ought not to go down like this, even if it was autumn. How do you feed him?"

My master told him. The other shook his head slowly and began to feel me over.

" I can't say who eats your corn, my dear fellow, but I am much mistaken if your horse gets it. Have you ridden very fast?"

" No—very gently."

" Then just put your hand here," said he, passing his hand over my neck and shoulder. " He is as warm and damp as a horse just come up from grass. I advise you to look into your stable a little more. I hate to be suspicious, and, thank heaven, I have no cause to be, for I can trust my men, present or absent; but there are mean scoundrels, wicked enough to rob a dumb beast of his food. You must look into it." And turning to his man who had come to take me: " Give this horse a right good feed of bruised oats, and don't stint him."

" Dumb beasts!" Yes we are; but if I could have spoken I could have told my master where his oats went to. My groom used to come every morning about six o'clock, and with him a little boy, who always had a covered basket with him. He used to go with his father into the harness-room where the corn was kept, and I could see them, when the door stood ajar, fill a little bag with oats out of the bin and then he used to be off.

Five or six mornings after this, just as the boy had left the stable, the door was pushed open and a policeman walked in, holding the child tight by the arm; another policeman followed and locked the door on the inside, saying, " Show me the place where your father keeps his rabbits' food."

The boy looked very frightened and began to cry; but there was no escape, and he led the way to the corn-bin. Here the policeman found another empty bag like that which was found full of oats in the boy's basket.

Filcher was cleaning my feet at the time, but they soon saw him, and though he blustered a good deal, they walked him off to the " lock-up ", and his boy with him. I heard afterwards that the boy was not held to be guilty, but the man was sentenced to prison for two months.

CHAPTER XXXI

A HUMBUG

My master was not immediately suited, but in a few days my new groom came. He was a tall, good-looking fellow enough; but if ever there was a humbug in the shape of a groom, Alfred Smirk was the man. He was very civil to me and never used me ill; in fact, he did a great deal of stroking and patting when his master was there to see it. He always brushed my mane and tail with water and my hoofs with oil before he brought me to the door, to make me look smart; but as to cleaning my feet or looking to my shoes or grooming me thoroughly, he thought no more of that than if I had been a cow. He left my bit rusty, my saddle damp, and my crupper stiff.

Alfred Smirk considered himself very handsome; he spent a great deal of time about his hair, whiskers, and necktie before a little looking-glass in the harness room. When his master was speaking to him, it was always, " Yes, sir; yes, sir;" touching his hat at every word; and everyone thought he was a very nice man and that Mr. Barry was very fortunate to meet with him. I should say he was the laziest, most conceited fellow I ever came near. Of course, it was a great thing not to to be ill-used, but then a horse wants more than that. I had a loose box, and might have been very comfortable if he had not been to indolent to clean it out. He never took all the straw away, and the smell from what lay underneath was very bad; while the strong vapours that rose up made my eyes smart and inflame, and I did not feel the same appetite for my food.

One day his master came in and said, " Alfred, the stable smells rather strong. Should not you give that stall a good scrub and throw down plenty of water?"

" Well, sir," he said, touching his cap, " I'll do so if you please, sir, but it is rather dangerous, sir, throwing down water in a horse's box; they are very apt to take cold, sir. I should not like to do him an injury, but I'll do it if you please, sir."

" Well," said his master, " I should not like him to

take cold, but I don't like the smell of this stable. Do you think the drains are all right?"

"Well, sir, now you mention it, I think the drain does sometimes send back a smell; there may be something wrong, sir."

"Then send for the bricklayer and have it seen to," said his master.

"Yes, sir, I will."

The bricklayer came and pulled up a great many bricks and found nothing amiss; so he put down some lime and charged the master five shillings, and the smell in my box was as bad as ever; but that was not all; standing as I did on a quantity of moist straw my feet grew unhealthy and tender, and the master used to say:

"I don't know what is the matter with this horse; he goes very fumble-footed. I am sometimes afraid he will stumble."

"Yes, sir," said Alfred. "I have noticed the same myself when I have exercised him."

Now, the fact was that he hardly ever did exercise me, and when the master was busy I often stood for days together without stretching my legs at all and yet being fed just as high as if I were at hard work. This often disordered my health and made me sometimes heavy and dull, but more often restless and feverish. He never even gave me a meal of green meat or a bran mash, which would have cooled me, for he was altogether as ignorant as he was conceited; and then, instead of exercise or change of food, I had to take horse balls and draughts; which, beside the nuisance of having them poured down my throat, used to make me feel ill and uncomfortable.

One day my feet were so tender that trotting over some fresh stones with my master on my back, I made two such serious stumbles that, as he came down Lansdown into the city, he stopped at the farrier's and asked him to see what was the matter with me. The man took up my feet one by one and examined them; then standing up and dusting his hands one against the other, he said:

"Your horse has got the 'thrush', and badly too; his feet are very tender; it is fortunate that he has not been down. I wonder your groom has not seen to it before. This is the sort of thing we find in foul stables, where the litter is never properly cleared out. If you will send him here to-morrow, I will attend to the hoof, and I will direct your man how to apply the liniment which I will give him."

The next day I had my feet thoroughly cleansed and stuffed with tow, soaked in some strong lotion; and a very unpleasant business it was.

The farrier ordered all the litter to be taken out of my box day by day, and the floor kept very clean. Then I was to have bran mashes, a little green meat, and not so much corn, till my feet were well again. With this treatment I soon regained my spirits, but Mr. Barry was so much disgusted at being twice deceived by his grooms that he determined to give up keeping a horse and to hire when he wanted one. I was, therefore, kept till my feet were quite sound, and was then sold again.

PART III

CHAPTER XXXII

A HORSE FAIR

NO doubt a horse fair is a very amusing place to those who have nothing to lose; at any rate, there is plenty to see.

Long strings of young horses out of the country, fresh from the marshes; and droves of shaggy little Welsh ponies, no higher than Merrylegs; and hundreds of cart horses of all sorts, some of them with their long tails braided up and tied with scarlet cord; and a good many like myself, handsome and high-bred, but fallen into the middle class, through some accident or blemish, unsoundness of wind, or some other complaint. There were some splendid animals quite in their prime and fit for anything; they were throwing out their legs and showing off their paces in high style as they were trotted out with a leading rein, the groom running by the side. But round in the background there were a number of poor things, sadly broken down with hard work, with their knees knuckling over and their hind legs swinging out at every step; and there were some very dejected-looking old horses, with the under lip hanging down and the ears laying back heavily, as if there was no more pleasure in life and no more hope; there were some so thin you might see all their ribs, and some with old sores on their backs and hips; these were sad sights for a horse to look upon, who knows not but he may come to the same state.

There was a great deal of bargaining, or running up and beating down; and if a horse may speak his mind so far as he understands, I should say there were more lies told and more trickery at that horse fair than a clever man could give an account of. I was put with two or three other strong, useful-looking horses, and a good many people came to look at us. The gentlemen turned from me when they saw my broken knees, though the man who had me swore it was only a slip in the stall.

The first thing was to pull my mouth open, then to look at my eyes, then feel all the way down my legs, and give me a hard feel of the skin and flesh, and then try my paces. It was wonderful what a difference there was in the way these things were done. Some did it in a rough, off-hand way, as if one was only a piece of wood; while others would take their hands gently over one's body, with a pat now and then, as much as to say " by your leave ". Of course, I judged a good deal of the buyers by their manners to myself.

There was one man; I thought, if he would buy me, I should be happy. He was not a gentleman, nor yet one of the loud, flashy sort that called themselves so. He was rather a small man, but well made and quick in all his motions. I knew in a moment by the way he handled me that he was used to horses; he spoke gently, and his grey eye had a kindly, cheery look in it. It may seem strange to say—but it is true all the same—that the clean, fresh smell there was about him made me take to him; no smell of old beer and tobacco, which I hated, but a fresh smell as if he had come out of a hayloft. He offered twenty-three pounds for me; but that was refused and he walked away. I looked after him, but he was gone, and a very hard-looking, loud-voiced man came; I was dreadfully afraid he would have me; but he walked off. One or two more came who did not mean business. Then the hard-faced man came back again and offered twenty-three pounds. A very close bargain was being driven, for my salesman began to think he should not get all he asked and must come down; but just then the grey-eyed man came back again. I could not help reaching out my head towards him. He stroked my face kindly.

" Well, old chap," he said, " I think we should suit each other. I'll give twenty-four for him."

" Say twenty-five and you shall have him."

" Twenty-four ten," said my friend, in a very decided tone, " and not another sixpence—yes or no?"

" Done," said the salesman, " and you may depend upon it there's a monstrous deal of quality in that horse, and if you want him for cab work he's a bargain."

The money was paid on the spot, and my new master took my halter and led me out of the fair to an inn, where he had a saddle and bridle ready. He gave me a good feed of oats and stood by whilst I ate it, talking to himself and talking to me. Half an hour after we were on our way to London, through pleasant lanes and country roads, until we came into the great London thoroughfare, on which we travelled steadily till in the twilight we reached the great City. The gas lamps were already lighted; there were streets to the right and streets to the left, and streets crossing each other for mile upon mile. I thought we should never come to an end of them. At last, in passing through one, we came to a long cabstand, when my rider called out in a cheery voice, " Good-night, Governor!"

" Hallo!" cried a voice. " Have you got a good one?"

" I think so," replied my owner.

" I wish you luck with him."

" Thank ye, Governor," and he rode on. We soon turned up one of the side streets, and about half-way up that we turned into a very narrow street, with rather poor-looking houses on one side and what seemed to be coach-houses and stables on the other.

My owner pulled up at one of the houses and whistled. The door flew open, and a young woman, followed by a little girl and boy, ran out. There was a very lively greeting as my rider dismounted.

" Now, then, Harry, my boy, open the gates, and mother will bring us the lantern."

The next minute they were all standing round me in a small stable yard.

" Is he gentle, Father?"

" Yes, Dolly, as gentle as your own kitten. Come and pat him."

At once the little hand was patting about all over my shoulder without fear. How good it felt!

" Let me get him a bran mash while you rub him down," said the mother.

" Do, Polly; it's just what he wants, and I know you've got a beautiful mash ready for me."

CHAPTER XXXIII

A LONDON CAB HORSE

My new master's name was Jeremiah Barker, but as everyone called him Jerry, I shall do the same. Polly, his wife, was just as good a match as a man could have. She was a plump, trim, tidy little woman, with smooth dark hair, dark eyes, and a merry little mouth. The boy was nearly twelve years old—a tall, frank, good-tempered lad; and little Dorothy (Dolly they called her) was her mother over again, at eight years old. They were all wonderfully fond of each other; I never knew such a happy, merry family before or since. Jerry had a cab of his own, and two horses which he drove and attended to himself. His other horse was a tall, white, rather large-boned animal, called Captain; he was old now, but when he was young he must have been splendid; he had still a proud way of holding his head and arching his neck; in fact, he was a high-bred, fine-mannered, noble old horse, every inch of him. He told me that in his early youth he went to the Crimean War; he belonged to an officer in the cavalry and used to lead the regiment; I will tell more of that hereafter.

The next morning, when I was well groomed, Polly and Dolly came into the yard to see me and make friends. Harry had been helping his father since the

10   (G 845)

early morning, and had stated his opinion that I should turn out " a regular brick ". Polly brought me a slice of apple, and Dolly a piece of bread, and made as much of me as if I had been the " Black Beauty " of olden times. It was a great treat to be petted again and talked to in a gentle voice, and I let them see as well as I could that I wished to be friendly. Polly thought I was very handsome and a great deal too good for a cab, if it was not for the broken knees.

" Of course, there's no one to tell us whose fault that was," said Jerry, " and as long as I don't know I shall give him the benefit of the doubt; for a firmer, neater stepper I never rode. We'll call him ' Jack ', after the old one, shall we, Polly?"

" Do," she said, " for I like to keep a good name going."

Captain went out in the cab all the morning. Harry came in after school to feed me and give me water. In the afternoon I was put into the cab. Jerry took as much pains to see if the collar and bridle fitted comfortably, as if he had been John Manly over again. When the crupper was let out a hole or two, it all fitted well. There was no bearing rein—no curb—nothing but a plain ring snaffle. What a blessing that was!

After driving through the side street we came to the large cabstand where Jerry had said " Good-night ". On one side of this wide street were high houses with wonderful shop fronts, and on the other was an old church and churchyard surrounded by iron palisades. Alongside these iron rails a number of cabs were drawn up, waiting for passengers; bits of hay were lying about on the ground; some of the men were standing together, some were sitting on their boxes reading the newspaper, and one or two were feeding their horses with bits of hay and a drink of water. We pulled up in the rank at the back of the last cab. Two or three men came round and began to look at me and pass their remarks.

" Very good for a funeral," said one.

" Too smart-looking," said another, shaking his head in a very wise way. " You'll find out something wrong one of these fine mornings, or my name isn't Jones."

" Well," said Jerry pleasantly, " I suppose I need not find it out till it finds me out, eh? And if so, I'll keep up my spirits a little longer."

Then came up a broad-faced man, dressed in a great grey coat with great grey capes and great white buttons, a grey hat, and a blue comforter loosely tied round his neck; his hair was grey too, but he was a jolly-looking fellow and the other men made way for him. He looked me all over as if he had been going to buy me; and then straightening himself up with a grunt, he said, " He's the right sort for you, Jerry; I don't care what you gave for him, he'll be worth it." Thus my character was established on the stand.

This man's name was Grant, but he was called " Grey Grant ", or " Governor Grant ". He had been the longest on that stand of any of the men, and he took it upon himself to settle matters and stop disputes. He was generally a good-humoured, sensible man; but if his temper was a little out, as it was sometimes when he had drunk too much, nobody liked to come too near his fist, for he could deal a very heavy blow.

The first week of my life as a cab horse was very trying; I had never been used to London, and the noise, the hurry, the crowds of horses, carts, and carriages that I had to make my way through, made me feel anxious and harassed; but I soon found that I could perfectly trust my driver, and then I made myself easy and got used to it.

Jerry was as good a driver as I had ever known; and, what was better, he took as much thought for his horses as he did for himself. He soon found out that I was willing to work and do my best; and he never laid the whip on me unless it was gently drawing the end of it over my back when I was to go on; but generally I knew this quite well by the way in which he took up the reins; and I believe his whip was more frequently stuck up by his side than in his hand.

In a short time I and my master understood each other as well as horse and man can do. In the stable, too, he did all that he could for our comfort. The stalls were the old-fashioned style, too much on the slope; but he had two movable bars fixed across the back of our stalls, so that at night and when we were resting, he just took off our halters and put up the bars, and thus we could turn about and stand whichever way we pleased, which is a great comfort.

Jerry kept us very clean, and gave us as much change of food as he could and always plenty of it; and not only that, but he always gave us plenty of clean fresh water, which he allowed to stand by us both night and day, except, of course, when we came in warm. Some people say that a horse ought not to drink all he likes;

but I know if we are allowed to drink when we want it, we drink only a little at a time, and it does us a great deal more good than swallowing down half a bucketful at a time, because we have been left without till we are thirsty and miserable. Some grooms will go home to their beer and leave us for hours with our dry hay and oats and nothing to moisten them; then, of course, we gulp down too much at once, which helps to spoil our breathing and sometimes chills our stomachs. But the best thing that we had here was our Sundays for rest; we worked so hard in the week that I do not think we could have kept up to it but for that day; besides, we had then time to enjoy each other's company. It was on these days that I learned my companion's history.

CHAPTER XXXIV

AN OLD WAR HORSE

CAPTAIN had been broken in and trained for an army horse; his first owner was an officer of cavalry going out to the Crimean War. He said he quite enjoyed the training with all the other horses, trotting together, turning together to the right hand or to the left, halting at the word of command, or dashing forward at full speed at the sound of the trumpet or signal of the officer. He was, when young, a dark, dappled iron-grey, and considered very handsome. His master, a young, high-spirited gentleman, was very fond of him and treated him from the first with the greatest care and kindness. He told me he thought the life of an army horse was very pleasant; but when he came to being sent abroad, over the sea in a great ship, he almost changed his mind.

"That part of it," said he, "was dreadful! Of course we could not walk off the land into the ship, so they were obliged to put strong straps under our bodies, and then we were lifted off our legs in spite of our struggles, and were swung through the air over the water to the deck of the great vessel. There we were placed in small close stalls, and never for a long time saw the sky or were able to stretch our legs. The ship sometimes rolled about in high winds, and we were knocked about and felt bad enough. However, at last it came to an end, and we were hauled up and swung over again to the land; we were very glad, and snorted and neighed for joy when we once more felt firm ground under our feet.

"We soon found that the country we had come to was very different to our own, and that we had many hardships to endure besides the fighting; but many of the men were so fond of their horses that they did everything they could to make them comfortable, in spite of snow, wet, and all things out of order."

"But what about the fighting?" said I. "Was not that worse than anything else?"

"Well," said he, "I hardly know; we always liked to hear the trumpet sound and to be called out, and were impatient to start off, though sometimes we had to stand for hours waiting for the word of command; and when the word was given, we used to spring forward

as gaily and eagerly as if there were no cannon balls,
bayonets, or bullets. I believe so long as we felt our
rider in the saddle and his hand steady on the bridle,
not one of us gave way to fear, not even when the terrible
bombshells whirled through the air and burst into a
thousand pieces.

" I, with my noble master, went into many actions
together without a wound; and though I saw horses
shot down with bullets, pierced through with lances,
and gashed with fearful sabre-cuts; though we left
them dead on the field or dying in the agony of their
wounds, I don't think I feared for myself. My master's
cheery voice, as he encouraged his men, made me feel
as if he and I could not be killed. I had such perfect
trust in him that whilst he was guiding me I was ready
to charge up to the very cannon's mouth. I saw many
brave men cut down, many fall mortally wounded
from their saddles. I had heard the cries and groans of
the dying, I had cantered over ground slippery with
blood, and frequently had to turn aside to avoid
trampling on wounded man or horse; but, until one
dreadful day, I had never felt terror; that day I shall
never forget."

Here old Captain paused for a while and drew a long
breath. I waited, and he went on:

" It was one autumn morning, and, as usual, an
hour before daybreak our cavalry had turned out,
ready caparisoned for the day's work, whether it might
be fighting or waiting. The men stood by their horses
waiting, ready for orders. As the light increased there
seemed to be some excitement among the officers; and

before the day was well begun we heard the firing of the enemy's guns.

"Then one of the officers rode up and gave the word for the men to mount, and in a second every man was in his saddle and every horse stood expecting the touch of the rein or the pressure of his rider's heels, all animated, all eager; but still we had been trained so well that, except by the champing of our bits and the restive tossing of our heads from time to time, it could not be said that we stirred.

"My dear master and I were at the head of the line, and as all sat motionless and watchful, he took a little stray lock of my mane which had turned over on the wrong side, laid it over on the right, and smoothed it down with his hand; then patting my neck, he said, 'We shall have a day of it to-day, Bayard, my beauty; but we'll do our duty as we have done.' He stroked my neck that morning, more, I think, than he had ever done before; quietly on and on, as if he were thinking of something else. I loved to feel his hand on my neck, and arched my crest proudly and happily; but I stood very still, for I knew all his moods, and when he liked me to be quiet and when gay.

"I cannot tell all that happened on that day, but I will tell of the last charge that we made together: it was across a valley right in front of the enemy's cannon. By this time we were well used to the roar of heavy guns, the rattle of musket fire, and the flying of shot near us; but never had I been under such a fire as we rode through on that day. From the right, from the left, and from the front, shot and shell poured in upon us.

Many a brave man went down, many a horse fell, flinging his rider to the earth; many a horse without a rider ran wildly out of the ranks: then, terrified at being alone with no hand to guide him, came pressing in amongst his old companions, to gallop with them to the charge.

"Fearful as it was, no one stopped, no one turned back. Every moment the ranks were thinned, but as our comrades fell we closed in to keep them together; and instead of being shaken or staggered in our pace, our gallop became faster and faster as we neared the cannon, all clouded in white smoke, while the red fire flashed through it.

"My master, my dear master, was cheering on his comrades with his right arm raised on high, when one of the balls, whizzing close to my head, struck him. I felt him stagger with the shock, though he uttered no cry. I tried to check my speed, but the sword dropped from his right hand, the rein fell loose from the left, and sinking backward from the saddle he fell to the earth; the other riders swept past us, and by the force of their charge I was driven from the spot where he fell.

"I wanted to keep my place by his side and not leave him under that rush of horses' feet, but it was in vain; and now, without a master or a friend, I was alone on that great slaughter ground; then fear took hold on me and I trembled as I had never trembled before; and I too, as I had seen other horses do, tried to join in the ranks and gallop with them; but I was beaten off by the swords of the soldiers. Just then a soldier whose horse had been killed under him caught at my bridle and mounted me; and with this new master I was again going forward. But our gallant company was cruelly overpowered, and those who remained alive after the fierce fight for the guns came galloping back over the same ground. Some of the horses had been so badly wounded that they could scarcely move from the loss of blood; other noble creatures were trying on three legs to drag themselves along, and others were struggling to rise on their forefeet, when their hind legs had been shattered by shot. Their groans were piteous to hear, and the beseeching look in their eyes as those who escaped passed by and left them to their fate, I shall never forget. After the battle the wounded men were brought in and the dead buried."

"And what about the wounded horses?" I said. "Were they left to die?"

"No, the army farriers went over the field with their pistols and shot all that were ruined; some that had only slight wounds were brought back and attended to, but the greater part of the noble willing creatures that went out that morning never came back! In our stables there was only about one in four that returned.

"I never saw my dear master again. I believe he fell dead from the saddle. I never loved any other master so well. I went into many other engagements, but was only once wounded, and then not seriously; and when the war was over I came back again to England, as sound and strong as when I went out."

I said, "I have heard people talk about war as if it was a very fine thing."

" Ah!" said he, " I should think they never saw it.
No doubt it is very fine when there is no enemy, when
it is just exercise and parade and sham-fight.   Yes,
it is very fine then; but when thousands of good brave
men and horses are killed or crippled for life it has a
very different look."

" Do you know what they fought about?" said I.

" No," he said, " that is more than a horse can
understand, but the enemy must have been awfully
wicked people if it was right to go all that way over the
sea on purpose to kill them."

CHAPTER XXXV

JERRY BARKER

I NEVER knew a better man than my new master: he
was kind and good and as strong for the right as John
Manly; and so good-tempered and merry that very
few people could pick a quarrel with him. He was very
fond of making little songs and singing them to himself.
One he was very fond of was this:

> Come, father and mother,
> And sister and brother,
> Come, all of you, turn to
> And help one another.

And so they did. Harry was as clever at stablework
as a much older boy, and always wanted to do what he
could.   Then Polly and Dolly used to come in the

morning to help with the cab—to brush and beat the
cushions and rub the glass, while Jerry was giving u
a cleaning in the yard and Harry was rubbing the har
ness. There used to be a great deal of laughing and
fun between them, and it put Captain and me in much
better spirits than if we had heard scolding and hard
words. They were always early in the morning, for
Jerry would say:

> If you in the morning
>   Throw minutes away,
> You can't pick them up
>   In the course of the day.
> You may hurry and skurry,
> And flurry and worry,
> You've lost them for ever,
>   For ever and aye.

He could not bear any careless loitering and waste of
time; and nothing was so near making him angry as
to find people who were always late, wanting a cab
horse to be driven hard to make up for their idleness.

One day, two wild-looking young men came out of
a tavern close by the stand and called Jerry:

"Here, cabby, look sharp! We are rather late.
Put on the steam, will you, and take us to the Victoria
in time for the one o'clock train? You shall have a
shilling extra."

"I will take you at the regular pace, gentlemen;
shillings don't pay for putting on the steam like that."

Larry's cab was standing next to ours. He flung open
the door and said, "I'm your man, gentlemen! Take
my cab; my horse will get you there all right;" and

s he shut them in, with a wink towards Jerry, said, " It's against his conscience to go beyond a jog-trot." Then, slashing his jaded horse, he set off as hard as he could. Jerry patted me on the neck. " No, Jack, a shilling would not pay for that sort of thing, would it, ld boy?"

Although Jerry was determinedly set against hard driving to please careless people, he always went a good fair pace, and was not against putting on the team, as he said, if only he knew *why*.

I well remember one morning, as we were on the stand waiting for a fare, that a young man, carrying a heavy portmanteau, trod on a piece of orange peel which lay on the pavement and fell down with great force.

Jerry was the first to run and lift him up. He seemed much stunned, and as they led him into a shop he walked as if he were in great pain. Jerry, of course, came back to the stand, but in about ten minutes one of the shopmen called him, so he drew up to the pavement.

" Can you take me to the South-Eastern Railway?" said the young man. " This unlucky fall has made me late, I fear; but it is of great importance that I should not lose the twelve o'clock train. I should be most thankful if you could get me there in time, and will gladly pay you an extra fare."

" I'll do my very best," said Jerry heartily, " if you think you are well enough, sir," for he looked dreadfully white and ill.

" I *must* go," he said earnestly. " Please to open the door and let us lose no time."

The next minute Jerry was on the box, with a cheer
chirrup to me and a twitch of the rein that I wel
understood.

"Now then, Jack my boy," said he, "spin along
we'll show them how we can get over the ground if w
only know why."

It is always difficult to drive fast in the city in th
middle of the day when the streets are full of traffic
but we did what could be done; and when a goo
driver and a good horse, who understand each other
are of one mind, it is wonderful what they can do.
had a very good mouth—that is, I could be guided b
the slightest touch of the rein, and that is a great thin
in London, amongst carriages, omnibuses, carts, vans
trucks, cabs and great wagons creeping along at
walking pace; some going one way, some another
some going slowly, others wanting to pass them; omni
buses stopping short every few minutes to take up
passenger, obliging the horse that is coming behind t
pull up too, or to pass, and get before them. Perhap
you try to pass, but just then something else come
dashing in through the narrow opening and you hav
to keep in behind the omnibus again. Presently yo
think you see a chance and manage to get to the front
going so near the wheels on each side that half an incl
nearer and they would scrape. Well, you get along fo
a bit, but soon find yourself in a long train of carts anc
carriages all obliged to go at a walk; perhaps you
come to a regular block-up, and have to stand still fo
minutes together till something clears out into a sid
street or the policeman interferes. You have to be

ady for any chance—to dash forward if there be an
pening, and be quick as a rat dog to see if there be
oom and if there be time, lest you get your own wheels
cked or smashed or the shaft of some other vehicle run
to your chest or shoulder. All this is what you have
o be ready for. If you want to get through London
st in the middle of the day, it wants a deal of practice.

Jerry and I were used to it, and no one could beat us
t getting through when we were set upon it. I was
uick and bold and could always trust my driver;
erry was quick and patient at the same time, and
ould trust his horse, which was a great thing too. He
ery seldom used the whip; I knew by his voice and
is " click click " when he wanted to get on fast, and
y the rein where I was to go, so there was no need for
whipping; but I must go back to my story.

The streets were very full that day, but we got on
retty well as far as the bottom of Cheapside, where
here was a block for three or four minutes. The young
nan put his head out and said anxiously, " I think I
ad better get out and walk; I shall never get there
f this goes on."

" I'll do all that can be done, sir," said Jerry. " I
hink we shall be in time. This block-up cannot last
nuch longer, and your luggage is very heavy for you
o carry, sir."

Just then the cart in front of us began to move on,
nd then we had a good turn. In and out, in and out
ve went, as fast as horseflesh could do it, and for a
wonder had a good clear time on London Bridge, for
here was a whole train of cabs and carriages, all going

our way at a quick trot, perhaps wanting to catch the very train. At any rate, we whirled into the station with many more, just as the great clock pointed to eight minutes to twelve o'clock.

"Thank God, we are in time!" said the young man. "And thank you too, my friend, and your good horse. You have saved me more than money can ever pay for. Take this extra half-crown."

"No, sir, no; thank you all the same. So glad we hit the time, sir; but don't stay now, sir; the bell is ringing. Here, porter! Take this gentleman's luggage—Dover line—twelve o'clock—that's it," and without waiting for another word, Jerry wheeled me round to make room for other cabs that were dashing up at the last minute, and drew up on one side till the crush was past.

"'So glad!' he said, 'so glad!' Poor young fellow! I wonder what it was that made him so anxious!"

Jerry often talked to himself quite loud enough for me to hear, when we were not moving.

On Jerry's return to the rank there was a good deal of laughing and chaffing at him for driving hard to the train for an extra fare, as they said, all against his principles; and they wanted to know how much he had pocketed.

"A good deal more than I generally get," said he, nodding slyly. "What he gave me will keep me in little comforts for several days."

"Gammon!" said one.

"He's a humbug," said another, "preaching to us, and then doing the same himself."

" Look here, mates," said Jerry, " the gentleman offered me half a crown extra, but I didn't take it; 'twas quite pay enough for me to see how glad he was to catch that train; and if Jack and I choose to have a quick run now and then, to please ourselves, that's our business and not yours."

" Well," said Larry, " *you'll* never be a rich man."

" Most likely not," said Jerry; " but I don't know that I shall be the less happy for that. I have heard the Commandments read a great many times and I never noticed that any of them said, ' Thou shalt be rich '; and there are a good many curious things said in the New Testament about rich men that I think would make me feel rather queer if I was one of them."

" If you ever do get rich," said Governor Grant, looking over his shoulder across the top of his cab, " you'll deserve it, Jerry, and you won't find a curse come with your wealth. As for you, Larry, you'll die poor; you spend too much on whipcord."

" Well," said Larry, " what is a fellow to do if his horse won't go without it?"

" You never take the trouble to see if he will go without it; your whip is always going as if you had the St. Vitus' dance in your arm; and if it does not wear you out, it wears your horse out; you know you are always changing your horses, and why? Because you never give them any peace or encouragement."

" Well, I have not had good luck," said Larry. " That's where it is."

" And you never will," said the Governor. " Good Luck is rather particular who she rides with, and

11   (G 845)

mostly prefers those who have got common sense and a good heart; at least, that is my experience."

Governor Grant turned round again to his newspaper, and the other men went to their cabs.

CHAPTER XXXVI

THE SUNDAY CAB

ONE morning, as Jerry had just put me into the shafts and was fastening the traces, a gentleman walked into the yard. " Your servant, sir," said Jerry.

" Good-morning, Mr. Barker," said the gentleman. " I should be glad to make some arrangements with you for taking Mrs. Briggs regularly to church on Sunday mornings. We go to the new church now and that is rather farther than she can walk."

" Thank you, sir," said Jerry, " but I have only taken out a six days' licence, and therefore I could not take a fare on a Sunday; it would not be legal."

" Oh!" said the other. " I did not know yours was a six days' cab; but, of course, it would be very easy to alter your licence. I would see that you did not lose by it; the fact is, Mrs. Briggs very much prefers you to drive her."

" I should be glad to oblige the lady, sir, but I had a seven days' licence once, and the work was too hard

AUTHOR'S NOTE.—*Six days' licence.* A few years since the annual charge for a cab licence was very much reduced, and the difference between the six and seven days' cabs was abolished.

for me and too hard for my horses. Year in and year out, not a day's rest, and never a Sunday with my wife and children, and never able to go to a place of worship, which I had always been used to do before I took to the driving box; so for the last five years I have only taken a six days' licence, and I find it better all the way round."

"Well, of course," replied Mr. Briggs, "it is very proper that every person should have rest and be able to go to church on Sundays, but I should have thought you would not have minded such a short distance for the horse, and only once a day; you would have all the afternoon and evening for yourself, and we are very good customers, you know."

"Yes, sir, that is true, and I am grateful for all favours, I am sure, and anything that I could do to oblige you or the lady, I should be proud and happy to do; but I can't give up my Sundays, sir, indeed I can't. I read that God made man, and He made horses and all other beasts, and as soon as He had made them, He made a day of rest and bade that all should rest one day in seven; and I think, sir, He must have known what was good for them, and I am sure it is good for me. I am stronger and healthier altogether now that I have a day of rest; the horses are fresh, too, and do not wear up nearly so fast. The six-day drivers all tell me the same, and I have laid by more money in the Savings Bank than ever I did before. And as for the wife and children, sir—why, heart alive! they would not go back to the seven days for all they could see."

"Oh, very well," said the gentleman. "Don't

trouble yourself, Mr. Barker, any further. I will inquire somewhere else." And he walked away.

"Well," says Jerry to me, "we can't help it, Jack, old boy; we must have our Sundays."

"Polly!" he shouted. "Polly! Come here."

She was there in a minute.

"What is it all about, Jerry?"

"Why, my dear, Mr. Briggs wants me to take Mrs. Briggs to church every Sunday morning. I say, ' I have only a six days' licence.' He says, ' Get a seven days' licence and I'll make it worth your while '; and you know, Polly, they are very good customers to us. Mrs. Briggs often goes out shopping for hours or making calls, and then she pays down fair and honourable like a lady; there's no beating down or making three hours into two hours and a half, as some folks do; and its easy work for the horses—not like tearing along to catch trains for people that are always a quarter of an hour too late; and if I don't oblige her in this matter, it is very likely we shall lose them altogether. What do you say, little woman?"

"I say, Jerry," says she, speaking very slowly, "I say, if Mrs. Briggs would give you a sovereign every Sunday morning, I would not have you a seven days' cabman again. We have known what it was to have no Sundays; and now we know what it is to call them our own. Thank God, you earn enough to keep us, though it is sometimes close work to pay for all the oats and hay, the licence, and the rent besides. But Harry will soon be earning something, and I would rather struggle on harder than we do than go back to those horrid times,

hen you hardly had a minute to look at your own
hildren, and we never could go to a place of worship
ogether or have a happy, quiet day. God forbid that
e should ever turn back to those times; that's what I
ay, Jerry."

"And that is just what I told Mr. Briggs, my dear,"
aid Jerry, "and what I mean to stick to, so don't go
nd fret yourself, Polly" (for she had begun to cry). "I
vould not go back to the old times if I earned twice as
auch, so that is settled, little woman. Now, cheer up,
nd I'll be off again to the stand."

Three weeks had passed away after this conversation,
nd no order had come from Mrs. Briggs, so there was
othing but taking jobs from the stand. Jerry took it to
eart a good deal, for, of course, the work was harder
or horse and man; but Polly would always cheer him
p and say, "Never mind, father; never mind:

> Do your best,
> And leave the rest;
> 'Twill all come right
> Some day or night."

It soon became known that Jerry had lost his best
ustomer, and for what reason; most of the men said
e was a fool, but two or three took his part.

"If working men don't stick to their Sunday," said
Truman, "they'll soon have none left; it is every man's
ight and every beast's right. By God's law we have a
ay of rest, and by the law of England we have a day of
est; and I say we ought to hold to the rights these laws
ive us, and keep them for our children."

"All very well for you religious chaps to talk so,"

said Larry, " but I'll turn a shilling when I can. I don'
believe in religion, for I don't see that your religiou
people are any better than the rest."

" If they are not better," put in Jerry, " it is becaus
they are *not* religious. You might as well say that ou
country's laws are not good because some people brea
them. If a man gives way to his temper and speaks evi
of his neighbour and does not pay his debts, he is n
religious; I don't care how much he goes to church
If some men are shams and humbugs, that does no
make religion untrue. Real religion is the best and th
truest thing in the world, and the only thing that ca
make a man really happy or make the world an
better."

" If religion was good for anything," said Jones
" it would prevent your religious people from makin
us work on Sundays as you know many of them do
and that's why I say religion is nothing but a sham
Why, if it was not for the church and chapel-goers i
would be hardly worth while our coming out on a Sun
day; but they have their privileges, as they call them
and I go without. I shall expect them to answer for m
soul, if I can't get a chance of saving it."

Several of the men applauded this, till Jerry said:

" That may sound well enough, but it won't do
every man must look after his own soul; you can't la
it down at another man's door like a foundling and
expect him to take care of it. And don't you see, if yo
are always sitting on your box waiting for a fare, the
will say, ' If we don't take him, someone else will, an
he does not look for any Sunday.' Of course they don'

go to the bottom of it, or they would see if they never came for a cab it would be no use your standing there; but people don't always like to go to the bottom of things; it may not be convenient to do it; but if you Sunday drivers would all strike for a day of rest, the thing would be done."

"And what would all the good people do if they could not get to their favourite preachers?" said Larry.

" 'Tis not for me to lay down plans for other people," said Jerry, " but if they can't walk so far, they can go to what is nearer; and if it should rain, they can put on their mackintoshes as they do on a week-day. If a thing is right, it *can* be done, and if it is wrong, it *can be done without*; and a good man will find a way; and that is as true for us cabmen as it is for the churchgoers."

CHAPTER XXXVII

THE GOLDEN RULE

Two or three weeks after this, as we came into the yard rather late in the evening, Polly came running across the road with the lantern (she always brought it to him if it was not very wet).

" It has all come right, Jerry; Mrs. Briggs sent her servant this afternoon to ask you to take her out to-morrow at eleven o'clock. I said, ' Yes, I thought so, but we supposed she employed some one else now.'

" ' Well,' says he, ' the real fact is, master was put out because Mr. Barker refused to come on Sundays, and he has been trying other cabs, but there's some-

thing wrong with them all; some drive too fast and
some too slow, and the mistress says there is not one
of them so nice and clean as yours, and nothing will
suit her but Mr. Barker's cab again.' "

Polly was almost out of breath, and Jerry broke out
into a merry laugh:

" ' All come right, some day or night.' You were
right, my dear; you generally are. Run in and get the
supper, and I'll have Jack's harness off and make him
snug and happy in no time."

After this, Mrs. Briggs wanted Jerry's cab quite as
often as before—never, however, on a Sunday; but
there came a day when we had Sunday work, and this
was how it happened. We had all come home on
Saturday night very tired and very glad to think that
the next day would be all rest; but so it was not to be.

On Sunday morning Jerry was cleaning me in the
yard, when Polly stepped up to him, looking very full
of something.

" What is it?" said Jerry.

" Well, my dear," she said, " poor Dinah Brown
has just had a letter brought to say that her mother is
dangerously ill, and that she must go directly if she
wishes to see her alive. The place is more than ten
miles away from here, out in the country, and she says
if she takes the train she should still have four miles to
walk; and so weak as she is, and the baby only four
weeks old, of course that would be impossible; and
she wants to know if you would take her in your cab,
and she promises to pay you faithfully as she can get
the money."

" Tut, tut, we'll see about that. It was not the money I was thinking about, but of losing our Sunday; the horses are tired, and I am tired too—that's where it pinches."

" It pinches all round, for that matter," said Polly, " for it's only half Sunday without you, but you know we should do to other people as we should like they should do to us; and I know very well what I should like if my mother was dying; and, Jerry dear, I am sure it won't break the Sabbath; for if pulling a poor beast or donkey out of a pit would not spoil it, I am quite sure taking poor Dinah would not do it."

" Why, Polly, you are as good as the minister, and so, as I've had my Sunday morning sermon early to-day, you may go and tell Dinah that I'll be ready for her as the clock strikes ten. But stop—just step round to butcher Braydon's with my compliments and ask him if he would lend me his light trap; I know he never uses it on the Sunday, and it would make a wonderful difference to the horse."

Away she went and soon returned, saying that he could have the trap and welcome.

" All right," said he. " Now put me up a bit of bread and cheese, and I'll be back in the afternoon as soon as I can."

" And I'll have the meat pie ready for an early tea instead of for dinner," said Polly; and away she went, whilst he made his preparations to the tune of " Polly, the woman and no mistake ", of which tune he was very fond.

I was selected for the journey, and at ten o'clock we

started in a light, high-wheeled gig, which ran so easily that, after the four-wheeled cab, it seemed like nothing.

It was a fine May day, and as soon as we were out of the town, the sweet air, the smell of the fresh grass, and the soft country roads were as pleasant as they used to be in the old times, and I soon began to feel quite fresh.

Dinah's family lived in a small farmhouse up a green lane, close by a meadow with some fine shady trees; there were two cows feeding in it. A young man asked Jerry to bring his trap into the meadow, and he would tie me up in the cowshed; he wished he had a better stable to offer.

" If your cows would not be offended," said Jerry, " there is nothing my horse would like so well as to have an hour or two in your beautiful meadow; he's quiet, and it would be a rare treat for him."

" Do, and welcome," said the young man. " The best we have is at your service for your kindness to my sister. We shall be having some dinner in an hour and I hope you'll come in, though with mother so ill we are all out of sorts in the house."

Jerry thanked him kindly, but said as he had some dinner with him there was nothing he should like so well as walking about in the meadow.

When my harness was taken off, I did not know what I should do first—whether to eat the grass, or roll over on my back, or lie down and rest, or have a gallop across the meadow out of sheer spirits at being free; and I did all by turns. Jerry seemed to be quite as happy as I was; he sat down by a bank under a shady tree and listened to the birds; then he sang himself and read out of the little brown book he is so fond of; then wandered round the meadow and down by a little brook, where he picked the flowers and the hawthorn and tied them up with long sprays of ivy; then he gave me a good feed of oats which he had brought with him; but the time seemed all too short—I had not been in a field since I left poor Ginger at Earlshall.

We came home gently, and Jerry's first words were as we came into the yard, "Well, Polly, I have not lost my Sunday after all, for the birds were singing hymns in every bush and I joined in the service; and as for Jack, he was like a young colt."

When he handed Dolly the flowers, she jumped about for joy.

CHAPTER XXXVIII

DOLLY AND A REAL GENTLEMAN

THE winter came in early, with a great deal of cold and wet. There was snow or sleet or rain almost every day for weeks, changing only for keen driving winds or sharp frosts. The horses all felt it very much. When it is a dry cold, a couple of good thick rugs will keep the warmth in us; but when it is soaking rain they soon get wet through and are no good. Some of the drivers had a waterproof cover to throw over, which was a fine thing; but some of the men were so poor that they could not protect either themselves or their horses and many of them suffered very much that winter. When

we horses had worked half the day, we went to our dry
stables, and could rest; whilst they had to sit on their
boxes, sometimes staying out as late as one or two
o'clock in the morning if they had a party to wait for.

When the streets were slippery with frost or snow,
that was the worst of all for us horses; one mile of such
travelling, with a weight to draw and no firm footing,
would take more of us than four on a good road; every
nerve and muscle of our bodies is on the strain to keep
our balance; and, added to this, the fear of falling is
more exhausting than anything else. If the roads are
very bad indeed, our shoes are roughed, but that makes
us feel nervous at first.

When the weather was very bad, many of the men
would go and sit in the tavern close by, and get some one
to watch for them; but they often lost a fare in that
way, and could not, as Jerry said, be there without
spending money. He never went to the " Rising Sun ";
there was a coffee-shop near, where he now and then
went; or he bought of an old man who came to our
rank with tins of hot coffee and pies. It was his
opinion that spirits and beer made a man colder
afterwards, and that dry clothes, good food, cheer-
fulness, and a comfortable wife at home were the
best things to keep a cabman warm. Polly always sup-
plied him with something to eat when he could not
get home, and sometimes he would see little Dolly
peeping from the corner of the street to make sure if
" father " was on the stand. If she saw him, she would
run off at full speed and soon come back with something
in a tin or basket—some hot soup or pudding that

Polly had ready. It was wonderful how such a little thing could get safely across the street, often thronged with horses and carriages; but she was a brave little maid and felt it quite an honour to bring " father's first course", as he used to call it. She was a general favourite on the stand, and there was not a man who would not have seen her safely across the street, if Jerry had not been able to do it.

One cold windy day, Dolly had brought Jerry a basin of something hot and was standing by him whilst he ate it. He had scarcely begun when a gentleman, walking towards us very fast, held up his umbrella. Jerry touched his hat in return, gave the basin to Dolly, and was taking off my cloth, when the gentleman hastened up, cried out, " No, no, finish your soup, my friend; I have not much time to spare, but I can wait till you have done and set your little girl safe on the pavement." So saying, he seated himself in the cab. Jerry thanked him kindly and came back to Dolly.

" There, Dolly, that's a gentleman; that's a real gentleman, Dolly; he has got time and thought for the comfort of a poor cabman and a little girl."

Jerry finished his soup, set the child across, and then took his orders to drive to " Clapham Rise ". Several times after that the same gentleman took our cab. I think he was very fond of dogs and horses, for whenever we took him to his own door, two or three dogs would come bounding out to meet him. Sometimes he came round and patted me, saying in his quiet, pleasant way, " This horse has got a good master and he deserves it." It was a very rare thing for any one to notice the horse that had been working for him. I have known ladies do it now and then, and this gentleman and one or two others have given me a pat and a kind word; but ninety-nine out of a hundred would as soon think of patting the steam-engine that drew the train.

This gentleman was not young, and there was a forward stoop in his shoulders as if he was always going at something. His lips were thin and close shut, though they had a very pleasant smile; his eye was keen, and there was something in his jaw and the motion of his head that made one think he was very determined in anything he set about. His voice was pleasant and kind; any horse would trust that voice, though it was just as decided as everything else about him.

One day he and another gentleman took our cab; they stopped at a shop in R—— Street, and whilst his friend went in, he stood at the door. A little ahead of us on the other side of the street a cart with two very fine horses was standing before some wine vaults; the carter was not with them, and I cannot tell how long they had been standing, but they seemed to think they had waited long enough and began to move off. Before they had gone many paces the carter came running out and caught them. He seemed furious at their having moved, and with whip and rein punished them brutally, even beating them about the head. Our gentleman saw it all and, stepping quickly across the street, said in a decided voice:

" If you don't stop that directly, I'll have you summoned for leaving your horses and for brutal conduct."

The man, who had clearly been drinking, poured

forth some abusive language, but he left off knocking the horses about and, taking the reins, got into his cart. Meantime our friend had quietly taken a notebook from his pocket and, looking at the name and address painted on the cart, he wrote something down.

" What do you want with that?" growled the carter, as he cracked his whip and was moving on. A nod and a grim smile was the only answer he got.

On returning to the cab our friend was joined by his companion, who said laughingly, " I should have thought, Wright, you had enough business of your own to look after without troubling yourself about other people's horses and servants."

Our friend stood still for a moment, and throwing his head a little back, " Do you know why this world is as bad as it is?"

" No," said the other.

" Then I'll tell you. It is because people think *only* about their own business, and won't trouble themselves to stand up for the oppressed nor bring the wrongdoer to light. I never see a wicked thing like this without doing what I can, and many a master has thanked me for letting him know how his horses have been used."

" I wish there were more gentlemen like you, sir," said Jerry, " for they are wanted badly enough in this city."

After this we continued our journey, and as they got out of the cab our friend was saying, " My doctrine is this, that if we see cruelty or wrong that we have the power to stop and do nothing, we make ourselves sharers in the guilt."

CHAPTER XXXIX

SEEDY SAM

I should say that, for a cab horse, I was very well off indeed. My driver was my owner, and it was his interest to treat me well and not overwork me, even had he not been so good a man as he was; but there were a great many horses which belonged to the large cab owners who let them out to their drivers for so much money a day. As the horses did not belong to these men, the only thing they thought of was how to get their money out of them—first to pay the master, and then to provide for their own living; and a dreadful time some of these horses had of it. Of course I understood but little, but it was often talked over on the stand, and the Governor, who was a kind-hearted man and fond of horses, would sometimes speak up if one came in very much jaded or ill-used.

One day a shabby, miserable-looking driver, who went by the name of " Seedy Sam ", brought in his horse looking dreadfully beat, and the Governor said:

" You and your horse look more fit for the police station than for this rank."

The man flung his tattered rug over the horse, turned full round upon the Governor, and said in a voice that sounded almost desperate:

" If the police have any business with the matter, it ought to be with the masters who charge us so much or with the fares that are fixed so low. If a man has to pay eighteen shillings a day for the use of a cab and two horses, as many of us have to do in the season, and must make that up before we earn a penny for ourselves, I say, 'tis more than hard work—nine shillings a day to get out of each horse before you begin to get your own living; you know that's true, and if the horses don't work we must starve, and I and my children have known what that is before now. I've six of 'em, and only one earns anything; I am on the stand fourteen or sixteen hours a day and I haven't had a Sunday these ten or twelve weeks; you know, Skinner never gives a day if he can help it, and if I don't work hard, tell me who does! I want a warm coat and a mackintosh, but with so many to feed how can a man get it? I had to pledge my clock a week ago to pay Skinner, and I shall never see it again."

Some of the other drivers stood round nodding their heads and saying he was right. The man went on:

" You that have your own horses and cabs, or drive for good masters, have a chance of getting on and a chance of doing right; I haven't. We can't charge more than sixpence a mile after the first, within the four-mile radius. This very morning I had to go a clear six miles and only took three shillings. I could not get a return fare and had to come all the way back; there's twelve miles for the horse and three shillings for me. After that I had a three-mile fare, and there were bags and boxes enough to have brought in a good many twopences if they had been put outside; but you know how people do; all that could be piled up inside on the front seat were put in, and three heavy boxes went on

12

the top; that was sixpence, and the fare one and sixpence; then I got a return for a shilling. Now that makes eighteen miles for the horse and six shillings for me; there's three shillings still for that horse to earn, and nine shillings for the afternoon horse before I touch a penny. Of course it is not always as bad as that, but you know it often is, and I say 'tis a mockery to tell a man that he must not overwork his horse, for when a beast is downright tired there's nothing but the whip that will keep his legs agoing; you can't help yourself— you must put your wife and children before the horse; the masters must look to that—we can't. I don't ill-use my horse for the sake of it; none of you can say I do. There's wrong lays somewhere—never a day's rest, never a quiet hour with the wife and children. I often feel like an old man, though I'm only forty-five. You know how quick some of the gentry are to suspect us of cheating and over-charging; why, they stand with their purses in their hands, counting it over to a penny and looking at us as if we were pickpockets. I wish some of 'em had got to sit on my box sixteen hours a day and get a living out of it, and eighteen shillings beside, and that in all weathers; they would not be so uncommon particular never to give us sixpence over, or to cram all the luggage inside. Of course, some of 'em tip us pretty handsome now and then, or else we could not live, but you can't *depend* upon that."

The men who stood round much approved this speech and one of them said, " It is desperate hard, and if a man sometimes does what is wrong it is no wonder; and if he gets a dram too much, who's to blow him up?"

Jerry had taken no part in this conversation, but I never saw his face look so sad before. The Governor had stood with both his hands in his pockets; now he took his handkerchief out of his hat and wiped his forehead.

"You've beaten me, Sam," he said, "for it's all true and I won't cast it up to you any more about the police; it was the look in that horse's eye that come over me. It is hard lines for man and it is hard lines for beast, and who's to mend it I don't know; but any way you might tell the poor beast that you were sorry to take it out of him in that way. Sometimes a kind word is all we can give 'em, poor brutes, and 'tis wonderful what they do understand."

A few mornings after this talk a new man came on the stand with Sam's cab.

"Hallo!" said one. "What's up with Seedy Sam?"

"He's ill in bed," said the man. "He was taken last night in the yard and could scarcely crawl home. His wife sent a boy this morning to say his father was in a high fever and could not get out, so I'm here instead."

The next morning the same man came again.

"How is Sam?" inquired the Governor.

"He's gone," said the man.

"What, gone? You don't mean to say he's dead?"

"Just snuffed out," said the other; "he died at four o'clock this morning. All yesterday he was raving —raving about Skinner and having no Sundays. 'I never had a Sunday's rest,'—these were his last words."

No one spoke for awhile, and then the Governor said, "I tell you what, mates, this is a warning for us."

CHAPTER XL

POOR GINGER

ONE day, whilst our cab and many others were waiting outside one of the parks where a band was playing, a shabby old cab drove up beside ours. The horse was an old worn-out chestnut, with an ill-kept coat and bones that showed plainly through it; the knees knuckled over and the forelegs were very unsteady. I had been eating some hay, and the wind rolled a little lock of it that way, and the poor creature put out her long, thin neck and picked it up, and then turned round and looked about for more. There was a hopeless look in the dull eye that I could not help noticing, and then, as I was thinking where I had seen that horse before, she looked full at me and said, " Black Beauty, is that you?"

It was Ginger! But how changed! The beautifully arched and glossy neck was now straight and lank and fallen in; the clean, straight legs and delicate fetlocks were swelled; the joints were grown out of shape with hard work; the face that was once so full of spirit and life was now full of suffering, and I could tell by the heaving of her sides and her frequent cough how bad her breath was.

Our drivers were standing a little way off, so I sidled up to her a step or two that we might have a little quiet talk. It was a sad tale that she had to tell.

After a twelvemonth's run off at Earlshall, she was considered to be fit for work again and was sold to a gentleman. For a little while she got on very well, but after a longer gallop than usual the old strain returned, and after being rested and doctored she was again sold. In this way she changed hands several times, but always getting lower down.

" And so at last," said she, " I was bought by a man who keeps a number of cabs and horses and lets them out. You look well off, and I am glad of it, but I could not tell you what my life has been. When they found out my weakness, they said I was not worth what they gave for me, and that I must go into one of the low cabs and just be used up; that is what they are doing, whipping and working with never one thought of what I suffer; they paid for me and must get it out of me, they say. The man who hires me now pays a deal of money to the owner every day, and so he has to get it out of me too; and so it's all the week round and round, with never a Sunday rest."

I said, " You used to stand up for yourself if you were ill-used."

" Ah !" she said. " I did once, but it's no use; men are strongest, and if they are cruel and have no feeling there is nothing that we can do but just bear it, bear it on and on to the end. I wish the end was come; I wish I was dead. I have seen dead horses, and I am sure they do not suffer pain. I wish I may drop down dead at my work and not be sent off to the knacker's."

I was very much troubled and I put my nose up to hers, but I could say nothing to comfort her. I think she was pleased to see me, for she said, " You are the only friend I ever had."

Just then her driver came up and, with a tug at her mouth, backed her out of the line and drove off, leaving me very sad indeed.

A short time after this a cart with a dead horse in it passed our cabstand. The head hung out of the cart tail, the lifeless tongue was slowly dropping with blood; and the sunken eyes! But I can't speak of them—the sight was too dreadful. It was a chestnut horse with a long, thin neck. I saw a white streak down the forehead; I believe it was Ginger; I hoped it was, for then her troubles would be over. Oh! If men were more merciful, they would shoot us before we came to such misery.

CHAPTER XLI

THE BUTCHER

I saw a great deal of trouble amongst the horses in London, and much of it that might have been prevented by a little common sense. We horses do not mind hard work if we are treated reasonably, and I am sure there are many driven by quite poor men who have a happier life than I had when I used to go in the Countess of W——'s carriage, with my silver-mounted harness and high feeding.

It often went to my heart to see how the little ponies were used, straining along with heavy loads or staggering under heavy blows from some low, cruel boy. Once I saw a little grey pony with a thick mane and a pretty head, and so much like Merrylegs that if

I had not been in harness I should have neighed to him. He was doing his best to pull a heavy cart, while a strong rough boy was cutting him under the belly with his whip and chucking cruelly at his little mouth. Could it be Merrylegs? It was just like him; but then Mr. Blomefield was never to sell him, and I think he would not do it; but this might have been quite as good a little fellow and had as happy a place when he was young.

I often noticed the great speed at which butchers' horses were made to go, though I did not know why it was so till one day when we had to wait some time in " St. John's Wood ". There was a butcher's shop next door and, as we were standing, a butcher's cart came dashing up at a great pace. The horse was hot and much exhausted; he hung his head down, while his heaving sides and trembling legs showed how hard he had been driven. The lad jumped out of the cart and was getting the basket when the master came out of the shop much displeased. After looking at the horse, he turned to the lad: " How many times shall I tell you not to drive in this way? You ruined the last horse and broke his wind, and you are going to ruin this in the same way. If you were not my own son, I would dismiss you on the spot; it is a disgrace to have a horse brought to the shop in a condition like that. You are liable to be taken up by the police for such driving, and if you are, you need not look to me for bail, for I have spoken to you till I am tired; you must look out for yourself."

During this speech the boy had stood by, sullen and dogged, but when his father ceased, he broke out angrily.

It wasn't his fault and he wouldn't take the blame; he was only going by orders all the time.

"You always say, ' Now be quick! Now look sharp!' And when I go to the houses, one wants a leg of mutton for an early dinner and I must be back with it in a quarter of an hour; another cook had forgotten to order the beef; I must go and fetch it and be back in no time or the mistress will scold; and the housekeeper says they have company coming unexpectedly and must have some chops sent up directly; and the lady at No. 4 in the Crescent *never* orders her dinner till the meat comes in for lunch, and it's nothing but hurry, hurry, all the time. If the gentry would think of what they want and order their meat the day before, there need not be this blow up!"

"I wish to goodness they would," said the butcher. "'Twould save me a wonderful deal of harass, and I could suit my customers much better if I knew beforehand. But there—what's the use of talking? Who ever thinks of a butcher's convenience or a butcher's horse? Now then, take him in and look to him well; mind he does not go out again to-day, and if anything else is wanted, you must carry it yourself in the basket." With that he went in and the horse was led away.

But all boys are not cruel. I have seen some as fond of their pony or donkey as if it had been a favourite dog, and the little creatures have worked away as cheerfully and willingly for their young drivers as I work for Jerry. It may be hard work sometimes, but a friend's hand and voice make it easy.

There was a young coster-boy who came up our street

with greens and potatoes; he had an old pony, not very handsome but the cheerfullest and pluckiest little thing I ever saw, and to see how fond those two were of each other was a treat. The pony followed his master like a dog and, when he got into his cart, would trot off without a whip or a word and rattle down the street as merrily as if he had come out of the Queen's stables. Jerry liked the boy and called him " Prince Charlie ", for he said he would make a king of drivers some day.

There was an old man, too, who used to come up our street with a little coal cart; he wore a coal-heaver's hat and looked rough and black. He and his old horse used to plod together along the street, like two good partners who understood each other; the horse would stop of his own accord at the doors where they took coal of him; he used to keep one ear bent toward his master. The old man's cry could be heard up the street long before he came near. I never knew what he said, but the children called him " Old Ba-a ar Hoo ", for it sounded like that. Polly took her coal of him and was very friendly, and Jerry said it was a comfort to think how happy an old horse *might* be in a poor place.

CHAPTER XLII

THE ELECTION

As we came into the yard one afternoon, Polly came out. " Jerry! I've had Mr. B—— here asking about your vote, and he wants to hire your cab for the election. He will call for an answer."

" Well, Polly, you may say that my cab will be otherwise engaged; I should not like to have it pasted over with their great bills, and as to make Jack and Captain race about to the public-houses to bring up half-drunken voters, why I think 'twould be an insult to the horses. No, I shan't do it."

" I suppose you'll vote for the gentleman? He said he was of your politics."

" So he is in some things, but I shall not vote for him, Polly; you know what his trade is?"

" Yes."

" Well, a man who gets rich by that trade may be all very well in some ways, but he is blind as to what working men want; I could not in my conscience send him up to make the laws. I dare say they'll be angry, but every man must do what he thinks to be the best for his country."

On the morning before the election Jerry was putting me into the shafts, when Dolly came into the yard sobbing and crying, with her little blue frock and white pinafore spattered all over with mud.

" Why, Dolly, what is the matter?"

" Those naughty boys," she sobbed, " have thrown the dirt all over me, and called me a little ragga—ragga——"

" They called her a little blue raggamuffin, Father," said Harry, who ran in looking very angry; " but I have given it to them; they won't insult my sister again. I have given them a thrashing they will remember—a set of cowardly, rascally, orange blackguards!"

Jerry kissed the child and said, " Run in to Mother,

my pet, and tell her I think you had better stay at home to-day and help her."

Then turning gravely to Harry:

" My boy, I hope you will always defend your sister and give anybody who insults her a good thrashing— that is as it should be; but mind, I won't have any election blackguarding on my premises. There are as many blue blackguards as there are orange, and as many white as there are purple or any other colour, and I won't have any of my family mixed up with it. Even women and children are ready to quarrel for the sake of a colour, and not one in ten of them knows what it is about."

" Why, Father, I thought blue was for Liberty."

" My boy, Liberty does not come from colours; they only show party, and all the liberty you can get out of them is liberty to get drunk at other people's expense, liberty to ride to the poll in a dirty old cab, liberty to abuse any one that does not wear your colour and to shout yourself hoarse at what you only half understand —that's your liberty!"

" Oh, Father, you are laughing."

" No, Harry, I am serious, and I am ashamed to see how men go on that ought to know better. An election is a very serious thing; at least it ought to be, and every man ought to vote according to his conscience and let his neighbour do the same."

CHAPTER XLIII

A FRIEND IN NEED

AT last came the election day; there was no lack of work for Jerry and me. First came a stout puffy gentleman with a carpet bag; he wanted to go to the Bishopsgate station; then we were called by a party who wished to be taken to the Regent's Park; and next we were wanted in a side street where a timid, anxious old lady was waiting to be taken to the bank. There we had to stop to take her back again, and just as we had set her down, a red-faced gentleman with a handful of papers came running up out of breath, and before Jerry could get down, he had opened the door, popped himself in, and called out, " Bow Street Police Station, quick!" So off we went with him, and when after another turn or two we came back, there was no other cab on the stand. Jerry put on my nose-bag, for, as he said, " We must eat when we can on such days as these, so munch away, Jack, and make the best of your time, old boy."

I found I had a good feed of crushed oats wetted up with a little bran; this would be a treat any day, but was specially refreshing then. Jerry was so thoughtful and kind—what horse would not do his best for such a master? Then he took out one of Polly's meat pies and, standing near me, he began to eat it. The streets were very full, and the cabs with the Candidates' colours on them were dashing about through the crowd as if life and limb were of no consequence; we saw two people knocked down that way, and one was a woman. The horses were having a bad time of it, poor things, but the voters inside thought nothing of that; many of them were half drunk, hurrahing out of the cab windows if their own party came by. It was the first election I had seen and I don't want to be in another, though I have heard things are better now.

Jerry and I had not eaten many mouthfuls before a poor young woman, carrying a heavy child, came along the street. She was looking this way and that way, and seemed quite bewildered. Presently she made her way up to Jerry, and asked if he could tell her the way to St. Thomas's Hospital and how far it was to get there. She had come from the country that morning, she said, in a market cart; she did not know about the election and was quite a stranger in London. She had got an order for the Hospital for her little boy. The child was crying with a feeble pining cry.

" Poor little fellow!" she said. " He suffers a deal of pain; he is four years old and can't walk any more than a baby, but the doctor said if I could get him into the Hospital, he might get well. Pray, sir, how far is it? And which way is it?"

" Why, missus," said Jerry, " you can't get there walking through crowds like this! Why, it is three miles away and that child is heavy."

" Yes, bless him, he is; but I am strong, thank God, and if I knew the way, I think I should get on somehow. Please tell me the way."

" You can't do it," said Jerry. " You might be knocked down and the child run over. Now, look here,

just get into this cab and I'll drive you safe to the Hospital. Don't you see the rain is coming on?"

"No, sir, no, I can't do that, thank you; I have only
just money enough to get back with. Please tell me the
way."

"Look you here, missus," said Jerry, "I've got a
wife and dear children at home, and I know a father's
feelings. Now get you into that cab and I'll take you
there for nothing; I'd be ashamed of myself to let a
woman and a sick child run a risk like that."

"Heaven bless you!" said the woman, and burst into
tears.

"There, there, cheer up, my dear; I'll soon take
you there. Come, let me put you inside."

As Jerry went to open the door, two men, with
colours in their hats and button-holes, ran up, calling
out "Cab!"

"Engaged," cried Jerry, but one of the men, pushing
past the woman, sprang into the cab, followed by the
other. Jerry looked as stern as a policeman. "This
cab is already engaged, gentlemen, by that lady."

"Lady!" said one of them. "Oh, she can wait!
Our business is very important. Besides we were in first,
it is our right and we shall stay in."

A droll smile came over Jerry's face as he shut the
door upon them. "All right, gentlemen; pray stay in
as long as it suits you; I can wait whilst you rest your-
selves." And turning his back upon them, he walked
up to the young woman who was standing near me.
"They'll soon be gone," he said, laughing. "Don't
trouble yourself, my dear."

And they soon were gone, for when they understood
erry's dodge they got out, calling him all sorts of bad
ames and blustering about his number and getting
. summons. After this little stoppage we were soon on
ur way to the Hospital, going as much as possible
hrough by-streets. Jerry rung the great bell and helped
he young woman out.

"Thank you a thousand times," she said. "I could
never have got here alone."

"You're kindly welcome, and I hope the dear child
vill soon be better."

He watched her go in at the door and gently he said
o himself, "Inasmuch as ye have done to one of the
east of these." Then he patted my neck, which was
always his way when anything pleased him.

The rain was now coming down fast, and just as we
were leaving the Hospital the door opened again and
he porter called out "Cab!" We stopped and a lady
came down the steps. Jerry seemed to know her at once;
he put back her veil and said, "Barker! Jeremiah
Barker! Is it you? I am very glad to find you here;
you are just the friend I want, for it is very difficult to
get a cab in this part of London to-day."

"I shall be proud to serve you, ma'am; I am right
glad I happened to be here. Where may I take you
to, ma'am?"

"To the Paddington Station, and then if we are in
good time, as I think we shall be, you shall tell me all
about Mary and the children."

We got to the station in good time and, being under
shelter, the lady stood a good while talking to Jerry.

I found she had been Polly's mistress, and after many inquiries about her she said:

"How do you find the cab-work suit you in winter? I know Mary was rather anxious about you last year."

"Yes, ma'am, she was; I had a bad cough that followed me up quite into the warm weather, and when I am kept out late she does worry herself a good deal. You see, ma'am, it is all hours and all weathers and that does try a man's constitution; but I am getting on pretty well and I should feel quite lost if I had not horses to look after. I was brought up to it, and I am afraid I should not do so well at anything else."

"Well, Barker," she said, "it would be a great pity that you should seriously risk your health in this work, not only for your own, but for Mary and the children's sake; there are many places where good drivers or good grooms are wanted, and if ever you think you ought to give up this cab-work, let me know." Then sending some kind messages to Mary, she put something into his hand, saying, "There is five shillings each for the two children; Mary will know how to spend it."

Jerry thanked her and seemed much pleased, and turning out of the station, we at last reached home, and I at least, was tired.

CHAPTER XLIV

OLD CAPTAIN AND HIS SUCCESSOR

CAPTAIN and I were great friends. He was a noble old fellow and he was very good company. I never thought that he would have to leave his home and go down the hill, but his turn came; and this was how it happened. I was not there, but I heard all about it.

He and Jerry had taken a party to the great railway station over London Bridge, and were coming back, somewhere between the Bridge and the Monument, when Jerry saw a brewer's empty dray coming along, drawn by two powerful horses. The drayman was lashing his horses with his heavy whip; the dray was light and they started off at a furious rate; the man had no control over them and the street was full of traffic; one young girl was knocked down and run over, and the next moment they dashed up against our cab; both the wheels were torn off and the cab was thrown over. Captain was dragged down, the shafts splintered, and one of them ran into his side. Jerry, too, was thrown but was only bruised; nobody could tell how he escaped; he always said 'twas a miracle. When poor Captain was got up, he was found to be very much cut and knocked about. Jerry led him home gently, and a sad sight it was to see the blood soaking into his white coat and dropping from his side and shoulder. The drayman was proved to be very drunk and was fined, and the brewer had to pay damages to our master; but there was no one to pay damages to poor Captain.

The farrier and Jerry did the best they could to ease his pain and make him comfortable. The fly had to be mended, and for several days I did not go out and Jerry earned nothing. The first time we went to the stand after the accident, the Governor came up to hear how Captain was.

"He'll never get over it," said Jerry, "at least not for my work, so the farrier said this morning. He says he may do for carting and that sort of work. It has put me out very much. Carting indeed! I've seen what horses come to at that work round London. I only wish all the drunkards could be put in a lunatic asylum, instead of being allowed to run foul of sober people. If they would break their *own* bones and smash their *own* carts and lame their *own* horses, that would be their own affair and we might let them alone, but it seems to me that the innocent always suffer; and then they talk about compensation! You can't make compensation—there's all the trouble and vexation and loss of time, besides losing a good horse that's like an old friend—it's nonsense talking of compensation! If there's one devil that I should like to see in the bottomless pit more than another, it's the drink devil."

"I say, Jerry," said the Governor, "you are treading pretty hard on my toes, you know; I'm not so good as you are, more shame for me; I wish I was."

"Well," said Jerry, "why don't you cut with it,

Governor? You are too good a man to be the slave of such a thing."

" I'm a great fool, Jerry; but I tried once for two days and I thought I should have died. How did you do?"

" I had hard work at it for several weeks; you see, I never did get drunk, but I found that I was not my own master, and that when the craving came on it was hard work to say ' no '. I saw that one of us must knock under—the drink devil or Jerry Barker, and I said that it should not be Jerry Barker, God helping me. But it was a struggle, and I wanted all the help I could get, for till I tried to break the habit I did not know how strong it was; but then Polly took such pains that I should have good food, and when the craving came on, I used to get a cup of coffee or some peppermint or read a bit in my book, and that was a help to me. Sometimes I had to say over and over to myself, ' Give up the drink or lose your soul? Give up the drink or break Polly's heart?' But thanks be to God and my dear wife, my chains were broken, and now for ten years I have not tasted a drop and never wish for it."

" I've a great mind to try it," said Grant, " for 'tis a poor thing not to be one's own master."

" Do, Governor. You'll never repent it, and what a help it would be to some of the poor fellows in our rank if they saw you do without it. I know there's two or three would like to keep out of that tavern if they could."

At first Captain seemed to do well, but he was a very old horse, and it was only his wonderful constitution and Jerry's care that had kept him up at the cab-work so long; now he broke down very much. The farrier said he might mend up enough to sell for a few pounds, but Jerry said, no! A few pounds got by selling a good old servant into hard work and misery would canker all the rest of his money, and he thought the kindest thing he could do for the fine old fellow would be to put a sure bullet through his heart, and then he would never suffer more; for he did not know where to find a kind master for the rest of his days.

The day after this was decided, Harry took me to the forge for some new shoes; when I returned, Captain was gone. I and the family felt it all very much.

Jerry had now to look for another horse, and he soon heard of one through an acquaintance who was under-groom in a nobleman's stables. He was a valuable young horse, but he had run away, smashed into another carriage, flung his lordship out, and so cut and blemished himself that he was no longer fit for a gentleman's stables, and the coachman had orders to look round and sell him as well as he could.

" I can do with high spirits," said Jerry, " if a horse is not vicious or hard-mouthed."

" There is not a bit of vice in him," said the man. " His mouth is very tender and I think myself that was the cause of the accident. You see, he had just been clipped and the weather was bad, and he had not had exercise enough, and when he did go out, he was as full of spring as a balloon. Our governor (the coachman, I mean) had him harnessed in as tight and strong as he could, with the martingale, and the bearing rein, a very sharp curb, and the reins put in at the bottom bar; it is my belief that it made the horse mad, being tender in the mouth and so full of spirits."

" Likely enough. I'll come and see him," said Jerry.

The next day, Hotspur—that was his name—came home; he was a fine brown horse, without a white hair on him, as tall as Captain, with a very handsome head and only five years old. I gave him a friendly greeting by way of good fellowship, but did not ask him any questions. The first night he was very restless; instead of lying down, he kept jerking his halter rope up and down through the ring, and knocking the block about against the manger so that I could not sleep. However, the next day, after five or six hours in the cab, he came in quiet and sensible. Jerry patted and talked to him a good deal, and very soon they understood each other, and Jerry said that with an easy bit and plenty of work, he would be as gentle as a lamb; and that it was an ill wind that blew nobody good, for if his lordship had lost a hundred-guinea favourite, the cabman had gained a good horse with all his strength in him.

Hotspur thought it a great comedown to be a cab horse and was disgusted at standing in the rank, but he confessed to me at the end of the week that an easy mouth and a free hand made up for a great deal, and after all, the work was not so degrading as having one's head and tail fastened to each other at the saddle. In fact, he settled in well and Jerry liked him very much.

CHAPTER XLV

JERRY'S NEW YEAR

CHRISTMAS and the New Year are very merry times for some people; but for cabmen and cabmen's horses it is no holiday, though it may be a harvest. There are so many parties, balls, and places of amusement open, that the work is hard and often late. Sometimes driver and horse have to wait for hours in the rain or frost, shivering with cold, whilst the merry people within are dancing to the music. I wonder if the beautiful ladies ever think of the weary cabman waiting on his box, and his patient beast standing till his legs get stiff with cold.

I had now most of the evening work, as I was well accustomed to standing and Jerry was also more afraid of Hotspur taking cold. We had a great deal of late work in the Christmas week, and Jerry's cough was bad; but however late we were, Polly sat up for him and came out with the lantern to meet him, looking anxious and troubled.

On the evening of the New Year we had to take two gentlemen to a house in one of the West End squares. We set them down at nine o'clock and were told to come again at eleven. "But," said one of them, "as it is a card party you may have to wait a few minutes, but don't be late."

As the clock struck eleven we were at the door, for

Jerry was always punctual. The clock chimed the quarters—one, two, three, and then struck twelve, but the door did not open.

The wind had been very changeable, with squalls or rain during the day, but now it came on a sharp driving sleet which seemed to come all the way round; it was very cold and there was no shelter. Jerry got off his box and came and pulled one of my cloths a little more over my neck; then he took a turn or two up and down, stamping his feet; then he began to beat his arms, but that set him off coughing; so he opened the cab door and sat at the bottom with his feet on the pavement, and was a little sheltered. Still the clock chimed the quarters and no one came. At half-past twelve, he rang the bell and asked the servant if he would be wanted that night.

" Oh, yes! You'll be wanted safe enough," said the man. " You must not go. It will soon be over." And again Jerry sat down, but his voice was so hoarse I could hardly hear him.

At a quarter past one the door opened and the two gentlemen came out; they got into the cab without a word and told Jerry where to drive—that was nearly two miles. My legs were numb with cold and I thought I should have stumbled. When the men got out, they never said they were sorry to have kept us waiting so long, but were angry at the charge: however, as Jerry never charged more than was his due, so he never took less, and they had to pay for the two hours and a quarter waiting; but it was hard-earned money to Jerry.

At last we got home; he could hardly speak and his

cough was dreadful. Polly asked no questions, but opened the door and held the lantern for him.

" Can't I do something?" she said.

" Yes; get Jack something warm, and then boil me some gruel."

This was said in a hoarse whisper. He could hardly get his breath, but he gave me a rub down as usual and even went up into the hayloft for an extra bundle of straw for my bed. Polly brought me a warm mash that made me comfortable, and then they locked the door.

It was late the next morning before any one came, and then it was only Harry. He cleaned us and fed us and swept out the stalls, then he put the straw back again as if it was Sunday. He was very still and neither whistled nor sang. At noon he came again and gave us our food and water: this time Dolly came with him; she was crying, and I could gather from what they said that Jerry was dangerously ill and the doctor said it was a bad case. So two days passed and there was great trouble indoors. We only saw Harry and sometimes Dolly. I think she came for company, for Polly was always with Jerry and he had to be kept very quiet.

On the third day whilst Harry was in the stable, a tap came at the door and Governor Grant came in.

" I wouldn't go to the house, my boy," he said, " but I want to know how your father is."

" He is very bad," said Harry. " He can't be much worse; they call it ' bronchitis '; the doctor thinks it will turn one way or another to-night."

" That's bad, very bad!" said Grant, shaking his head. " I know two men who died of that last week; it takes 'em off in no time; but while there's life there's hope, so you must keep up your spirits."

" Yes," said Harry quickly, " and the doctor said that Father had a better chance than most men, because he didn't drink. He said yesterday the fever was so high that if Father had been a drinking man it would have burnt him up like a piece of paper; but I believe he thinks he will get over it. Don't you think he will, Mr. Grant?"

The Governor looked puzzled.

" If there's any rule that good men should get over these things, I am sure he will, my boy; he's the best man I know. I'll look in early to-morrow."

Early next morning he was there.

" Well?" said he.

" Father is better," said Harry. " Mother hopes he will get over it."

" Thank God!" said the Governor. " And now you must keep him warm and keep his mind easy, and that brings me to the horses. You see, Jack will be all the better for the rest of a week or two in a warm stable, and you can easily take him a turn up and down the street to stretch his legs; but this young one, if he does not get work, he will soon be all up on end, as you may say, and will be rather too much for you; and when he does go out, there'll be an accident."

" It is like that now," said Harry. " I have kept him short of corn, but he's so full of spirit I don't know what to do with him."

"Just so," said Grant. "Now look here, will you tell your mother that if she is agreeable, I will come for him every day till something is arranged, and take him for a good spell of work; and whatever he earns I'll bring your mother half of it, and that will help with the horses' feed. Your father is in a good club, I know, but that won't keep the horses and they'll be eating their heads off all this time. I'll come at noon and hear what she says." And, without waiting for Harry's thanks, he was gone.

At noon I think he went and saw Polly, for he and Harry came to the stable together, harnessed Hotspur, and took him out.

For a week or more he came for Hotspur, and when Harry thanked him or said anything about his kindness, he laughed it off, saying it was all good luck for him, for his horses were wanting a little rest which they would not otherwise have had.

Jerry grew better steadily, but the doctor said that he must never go back to the cab work again if he wished to be an old man. The children had many consultations together about what Father and Mother would do and how they could help to earn money.

One afternoon Hotspur was brought in very wet and dirty.

"The streets are nothing but slush," said the Governor. "It will give you a good warming, my boy, to get him clean and dry."

"All right, Governor," said Harry. "I shall not leave him till he is; you know I have been trained by my father."

" I wish all the boys had been trained like you," said the Governor.

While Harry was sponging off the mud from Hotspur's body and legs, Dolly came in, looking very full of something.

" Who lives at Fairstowe, Harry? Mother has got a letter from Fairstowe; she seemed so glad and ran upstairs to Father with it."

" Don't you know? Why, it is the name of Mrs. Fowler's place—mother's old mistress, you know—the lady that father met last summer, who sent you and me five shillings each."

" Oh, Mrs. Fowler!—Of course I know all about her. I wonder what she is writing to mother about."

" Mother wrote to her last week," said Harry. " You know she told Father if ever he gave up the cab work she would like to know. I wonder what she says. Run in and see, Dolly."

Harry scrubbed away at Hotspur with a huish! huish! like any old ostler.

In a few minutes Dolly came dancing into the stable.

" Oh, Harry, there never was anything so beautiful! Mrs. Fowler says we are all to go and live near her. There is a cottage now empty that will just suit us, with a garden and a henhouse and apple trees and everything! And her coachman is going away in the spring, and then she will want Father in his place; and there are good families round, where you can get a place in the garden or the stable or as a page-boy; and there's a good school for me; and Mother is laughing and crying by turns and Father does look so happy!"

"That's uncommon jolly," said Harry, "and just the right thing, I should say; it will suit Father and Mother both. But I don't intend to be a page-boy with tight clothes and rows of buttons; I'll be a groom or a gardener."

It was quickly settled that as soon as Jerry was well enough they should remove to the country, and that the cab and horses should be sold as soon as possible.

This was heavy news for me, for I was not young now and could not look for any improvement in my conditions. Since I left Birtwick I had never been so happy as with my dear master, Jerry; but three years of cab work, even under the best conditions, will tell on one's strength, and I felt that I was not the horse that I had been.

Grant said at once that he would take Hotspur, and there were men on the stand who would have bought me; but Jerry said I should not go to cab work again with just anybody, and the Governor promised to find a place for me where I should be comfortable.

The day came for going away. Jerry had not been allowed to go out yet, and I never saw him after New Years' Eve. Polly and the children came to bid me good-bye. "Poor old Jack! Dear old Jack! I wish we could take you with us," she said, and then, laying her hand on my mane, she put her face close to my neck and kissed me. Dolly was crying and kissed me too. Harry stroked me a great deal, but said nothing, only he seemed very sad; and I was led away to my new place.

PART IV

CHAPTER XLVI

JAKES AND THE LADY

I WAS sold to a corn dealer and baker whom Jerry knew and with him he thought I should have good food and fair work. In the first he was quite right, and if my master had always been on the premises I do not think I should have been overloaded; but there was a foreman who was always hurrying and driving every one, and frequently when I had quite a full load he would order something else to be taken on. My carter, whose name was Jakes, often said it was more than I ought to take, but the other always overruled him: "'Twas no use going twice when once would do, and he chose to get business forward."

Jakes, like the other carters, always had the bearing rein up, which prevented me from drawing easily, and by the time I had been there three or four months I found the work telling very much on my strength.

One day I was loaded more than usual and part of the road was a steep uphill. I used all my strength, but could not get on and was obliged continually to stop. This did not please my driver and he laid his whip on badly. "Get on, you lazy fellow," he said, "or I'll make you."

Again I started the heavy load and struggled on a

few yards; again the whip came down and again
struggled forward. The pain of that great cart whi
was sharp, but my mind was hurt quite as much as m
poor sides. To be punished and abused when I wa
doing my very best was so hard it took the heart o
me. A third time he was flogging me cruelly when
lady stepped quickly up to him and said in a swee
earnest voice:

"Oh, pray do not whip your good horse any more
I am sure he is doing all he can and the road is ver
steep. I am sure he is doing his best."

"If doing his best won't get this load up, he must d
something more than his best—that's all I know
ma'am," said Jakes.

"But is it not a very heavy load?" she said.

"Yes, yes, too heavy," he said, "but that's not m
fault. The foreman came just as we were starting, an
would have three hundredweight more put on to sav
him trouble, and must get on with it as well as I can.

He was raising the whip again when the lady said:

"Pray, stop. I think I can help you if you will le
me."

The man laughed.

"You see," she said, "you do not give him a fai
chance; he cannot use all his power with his head hel
back as it is with that bearing rein; if you would take i
off I am sure he would do better. *Do* try it," she sai
persuasively. "I should be very glad if you would."

"Well, well," said Jakes, with a short laugh, "any
thing to please a lady, of course. How far would yo
wish it down, ma'am?"

" Quite down; give him his head altogether."

The rein was taken off and in a moment I put my head down to my very knees. What a comfort it was! Then I tossed it up and down several times to get the aching stiffness out of my neck.

" Poor fellow! That is what you wanted," said she, patting and stroking me with her gentle hand. " And now if you will speak kindly to him and lead him on, I believe he will be able to do better."

Jakes took the rein, " Come on, Blackie." I put down my head and threw my whole weight against the collar; I spared no strength. The load moved on, and I pulled it steadily up the hill and then stopped to take breath.

The lady had walked along the footpath and now came across into the road. She stroked and patted my neck as I had not been patted for many a long day.

" You see, he was quite willing when you gave him the chance; I am sure he is a fine-tempered creature and I dare say has known better days. You won't put that rein on again, will you?" for he was just going to hitch it up on the old plan.

" Well, ma'am, I can't deny that having his head has helped him up the hill and I'll remember it another time, and thank you, ma'am; but if he went without a bearing rein I should be the laughing-stock of all the carters. It is the fashion, you see."

" Is it not better," she said, " to lead a good fashion than to follow a bad one? A great many gentlemen do not use bearing reins now; our carriage horses have not worn them for fifteen years and work with much

14

less fatigue than those who have them. Besides," sh
added in a very serious voice, " we have no right t
distress any of God's creatures without a very goo
reason; we call them dumb animals, and so they ar
for they cannot tell us how they feel, but they do no
suffer less because they have no words. But I must no
detain you now; I thank you for trying my plan witl
your good horse, and I am sure you will find it far bette
than the whip. Good-day." And with another sof
pat on my neck she stepped lightly across the path an
I saw her no more.

" That was a real lady, I'll be bound for it," said Jake
to himself. " She spoke just as polite as if I was a gentle
man, and I'll try her plan—uphill, at any rate." An
I must do him the justice to say that he let my rein ou
several holes, and going uphill after that he alway
gave me my head; but the heavy loads went on. Goo
feed and fair rest will keep up one's strength under ful
work, but no horse can stand against overloading; an
I was getting so thoroughly pulled down from this caus
that a younger horse was bought in my place. I ma
as well mention here that I suffered at this time fron
another cause. I had heard horses speak of it, but ha
never myself had experience of the evil; this was
badly lighted stable; there was only one very smal
window at the end and the consequence was that th
stalls were almost dark.

Besides the depressing effect this had on my spirits
it very much weakened my sight, and when I wa
suddenly brought out of the darkness into the glare o
daylight it was very painful to my eyes. Several time

stumbled over the threshold and could scarcely see
where I was going.

I believe, had I stayed there very long, I should have
become purblind, and that would have been a great
misfortune, for I have heard men say that a stone-blind
horse was safer to drive than one which had imperfect
sight, as it generally makes them very timid. However,
I escaped without any permanent injury to my sight
and was sold to a large cab owner.

CHAPTER XLVII

HARD TIMES

I SHALL never forget my new master; he had black
eyes and a hooked nose, his mouth was as full of teeth
as a bulldog's, and his voice was as harsh as the grinding
of cartwheels over gravel stones. His name was Nicho-
las Skinner, and I believe he was the same man that
poor Seedy Sam drove for.

I have heard men say that seeing is believing, but
I should say that *feeling* is believing, for much as I had
seen before, I never knew till now the utter misery of
a cab horse's life.

Skinner had a low set of cabs and a low set of drivers;
he was hard on the men and the men were hard on the
horses. In this place we had no Sunday rest and it was
in the heat of summer.

Sometimes on a Sunday morning a party of fast men
would hire the cab for the day; four of them inside

and another with the driver, and I had to take them ten or fifteen miles out into the country and back again; never would any of them get down to walk up a hill, let it be ever so steep or the day ever so hot—unless, indeed, when the driver was afraid I should not manage it; and sometimes I was so fevered and worn that I could hardly touch my food. How I used to long for the nice bran mash with nitre in it that Jerry used to give us on Saturday nights in hot weather, that used to cool us down and make us so comfortable. Then we had two nights and a whole day for unbroken rest, and on Monday morning we were as fresh as young horses again; but here there was no rest and my driver was just as hard as his master. He had a cruel whip with something so sharp at the end that it sometimes drew blood, and he would even whip me under the belly and flip the lash out at my head. Indignities like these took the heart out of me terribly, but still I did my best and never hung back; for, as poor Ginger said, it was no use; men are the strongest.

My life was now so utterly wretched that I wished I might, like Ginger, drop down dead at my work and be out of my misery; and one day my wish very nearly came to pass.

I went on the stand at eight in the morning, and had done a good share of work when we had to take a fare to the railway. A long train was just expected in, so my driver pulled up at the back of some of the outside cabs, to take the chance of a return fare. It was a very heavy train, and as all the cabs were soon engaged, ours was called for. There was a party of four: a noisy, blustering man with a lady, a little boy and a young girl, and a great deal of luggage. The lady and the boy got into the cab, and while the man ordered about the luggage, the young girl came and looked at me.

" Papa," she said, " I am sure this poor horse cannot take us and all our luggage so far, he is so very weak and worn out. Do look at him."

" Oh, he's all right, miss," said my driver. " He's strong enough."

The porter, who was pulling about some heavy boxes, suggested to the gentleman, as there was so much luggage, whether he would not take a second cab.

" Can your horse do it or can't he?" said the blustering man.

" Oh, he can do it all right, sir. Send up the boxes, porter; he could take more than that." And he helped to haul up a box so heavy that I could feel the springs go down.

" Papa, papa, do take a second cab," said the young girl in a beseeching tone. " I am sure we are wrong; I am sure it is very cruel."

" Nonsense, Grace! Get in at once and don't make all this fuss; a pretty thing it would be if a man of business had to examine every cab horse before he hired it—the man knows his own business of course. There, get in and hold your tongue!"

My gentle friend had to obey, and box after box was dragged up and lodged on the top of the cab or settled by the side of the driver. At last all was ready, and with his usual jerk at the rein and slash of the whip he drove out of the station.

The load was very heavy and I had had neither food nor rest since the morning; but I did my best as I always had done, in spite of cruelty and injustice.

I got along fairly well till we came to Ludgate Hill but there the heavy load and my own exhaustion were too much. I was struggling to keep on, goaded by constant chucks of the rein and use of the whip, when in a single moment—I cannot tell how—my feet slipped from under me and I fell heavily to the ground on my side; the suddenness and the force with which I fell seemed to beat all the breath out of my body. I lay perfectly still; indeed, I had no power to move and I thought now I was going to die. I heard a sort of confusion round me, loud angry voices and the getting down of the luggage, but it was all like a dream. I thought I heard that sweet, pitiful voice saying, " Oh, that poor horse! It is all our fault." Some one came and loosened the throat strap of my bridle, and undid the traces which kept the collar so tight upon me. Someone said, " He's dead; he'll never get up again." Then I could hear a policeman giving orders, but I did not even open my eyes; I could only draw a gasping breath now and then. Some cold water was thrown over my head, and some cordial was poured into my mouth and something was covered over me. I cannot tell how long I lay there, but I found my life coming back, and a kind-voiced man was patting me and encouraging me to rise. After some more cordial had been given me, and after one or two attempts, I staggered to my feet and was gently led to some stables which were close by. Here I was put into a well-littered stall, and some warm gruel was brought to me, which I drank thankfully.

In the evening I was sufficiently recovered to be led back to Skinner's stables, where I think they did the best they could for me. In the morning Skinner came with a farrier to look at me. He examined me very closely and said:

" This is a case of overwork more than disease, and if you could give him a run off for six months, he would be able to work again; but now there is not an ounce of strength in him."

" Then he must just go to the dogs," said Skinner. " I have no meadows to nurse sick horses in; he might get well or he might not—that sort of thing don't suit my business. My plan is to work 'em as long as they'll go and then sell 'em for what they'll fetch, at the knacker's or elsewhere."

" If he was broken-winded," said the farrier, " you had better have him killed out of hand, but he is not. There is a sale of horses coming off in about ten days; if you rest him and feed him up he may pick up, and you may get more than his skin is worth, at any rate."

Upon this advice Skinner rather unwillingly, I think, gave orders that I should be well fed and cared for, and the stable man, happily for me, carried out the orders with a much better will than his master had in giving them. Ten days of perfect rest, plenty of good oats, hay, bran mashes, with boiled linseed mixed in them, did more to get up my condition than anything else could have done; those linseed mashes were delicious, and I began to think, after all, it might be better to live than

go to the dogs. When the twelfth day after the accident
came, I was taken to the sale, a few miles out of London.
I felt that any change from my present place must be
an improvement, so I held up my head and hoped for
the best.

CHAPTER XLVIII

FARMER THOROUGHGOOD AND HIS
GRANDSON WILLIE

AT this sale, of course, I found myself in company with
the old broken-down horses—some lame, some broken-
winded, some old, and some that I am sure it would
have been merciful to shoot.

The buyers and sellers too, many of them, looked
not much better off than the poor beasts they were
bargaining about. There were poor old men, trying
to get a horse or pony for a few pounds, that might drag
about some little wood or coal cart. There were poor
men trying to sell a worn-out beast for two or three
pounds rather than have the greater loss of killing them.
Some of them looked as if poverty and hard times had
hardened them all over; but there were others that I
would have willingly used the last of my strength in
serving—poor and shabby, but kind and human, with
voices that I could trust. There was one tottering old
man that took a great fancy to me, and I to him, but
I was not strong enough. It was an anxious time! Coming from the better part of the fair, I noticed a man

who looked like a gentleman farmer, with a young boy
by his side; he had a broad back and round shoulders, a
kind, ruddy face, and he wore a broad-brimmed hat.
When he came up to me and my companions, he stood
still and gave a pitiful look round upon us. I saw his
eye rest on me; I had still my good mane and tail,
which did something for my appearance. I pricked my
ears and looked at him.

"There's a horse, Willie, that has known better
days."

"Poor old fellow!" said the boy. "Do you think,
grandpa, he was ever a carriage horse?"

"Oh, yes, my boy," said the farmer, coming closer.
"He might have been anything when he was young.
Look at his nostrils and his ears, the shape of his neck
and shoulder; there's a deal of breeding about that
horse." He put out his hand and gave me a kind pat
on the neck. I put out my nose in answer to his kindness; the boy stroked my face.

"Poor old fellow! See, grandpa, how well he understands kindness. Could not we buy him and make him
young again, as you did with Ladybird?"

"My dear boy, I can't make all old horses young;
besides, Ladybird was not so very old as she was run
down and badly used."

"Well, grandpa, I don't believe that this one is old;
look at his mane and tail. I wish you would look into
his mouth and then you could tell; though he is so very
thin, his eyes are not sunk like some old horses'."

The old gentleman laughed. "Bless the boy! He is
as horsey as his old grandfather."

"But do look at his mouth, grandpa, and ask the price. I am sure he would grow young in our meadows."

The man who had brought me for sale now put in his word.

"The young gentleman is a real knowing one, sir. Now the fact is, this 'ere hoss is just pulled down with overwork in the cabs; he's not an old one, and I heerd as how the vetenary should say that a six months' run off would set him right up, being as how his wind was not broken. I've had the tending of him these ten days past, and a gratefuller, pleasanter animal I never met with, and 'twould be worth a gentleman's while to give a five-pound note for him and let him have a chance. I'll be bound he'd be worth twenty pounds next spring."

The old gentleman laughed and the little boy looked up eagerly.

"Oh, grandpapa, did you not say the colt sold for five pounds more than you expected? You would not be poorer if you did buy this one."

The farmer slowly felt my legs, which were much swelled and strained; then he looked at my mouth: "Thirteen or fourteen, I should say; just trot him out, will you?"

I arched my poor thin neck, raised my tail a little, and threw out my legs as well as I could, for they were very stiff.

"What is the lowest you will take for him?" said the farmer as I came back.

"Five pounds, sir; that was the lowest price my master set."

" 'Tis a speculation," said the old gentleman, shaking his head, but at the same time slowly drawing out his purse, " quite a speculation! Have you any more business here?" he said, counting the sovereigns into his hand.

" No, sir. I can take him for you to the inn, if you please."

" Do so; I am now going there."

They walked forward and I was led behind. The boy could hardly control his delight, and the old gentleman seemed to enjoy his pleasure. I had a good feed at the inn, and was then gently ridden home by a servant of my new master's and turned into a large meadow with a shed in one corner of it.

Mr. Thoroughgood, for that was the name of my benefactor, gave orders that I should have hay and oats every night and morning and the run of the meadow during the day, and " You, Willie," said he, " must take the oversight of him; I give him in charge to you."

The boy was proud of his charge and undertook it in all seriousness. There was not a day when he did not pay me a visit, sometimes picking me out from amongst the other horses and giving me a bit of carrot or something good, or sometimes standing by me whilst I ate my oats. He always came with kind words and caresses, and of course I grew very fond of him. He called me Old Crony, as I used to come to him in the field and follow him about. Sometimes he brought his grandfather, who always looked closely at my legs:

" This is our point, Willie," he would say; " but he

is improving so steadily that I think we shall see a change for the better in the spring.

The perfect rest, the good food, the soft turf, and gentle exercise soon began to tell on my condition and my spirits. I had a good constitution from my mother, and I was never strained when I was young, so that I had a better chance than many horses who have worked before they came to their full strength. During the winter my legs improved so much that I began to feel quite young again. The spring came round and one day in March, Mr. Thoroughgood determined that he would try me in the phaeton. I was well pleased, and he and Willie drove me a few miles. My legs were not stiff now and I did the work with perfect ease.

" He's growing young, Willie. We must give him a little gentle work now, and by midsummer he will be as good as Ladybird. He has a beautiful mouth and good paces; they can't be better."

" Oh, grandpapa, how glad I am you bought him !"

" So am I, my boy, but he has to thank you more than me. We must now be looking out for a quiet, genteel place for him, where he will be valued."

CHAPTER XLIX

MY LAST HOME

ONE day during this summer the groom cleaned and dressed me with such extraordinary care that I thought some new change must be at hand; he trimmed my fetlocks and legs, passed the tarbrush over my hoofs, and even parted my forelock. I think the harness had an extra polish. Willie seemed half anxious, half merry as he got into the chaise with his grandfather.

" If the ladies take to him," said the old gentleman, " they'll be suited and he'll be suited; we can but try."

At the distance of a mile or two from the village we came to a pretty, low house, with a lawn and shrubbery at the front and a drive up to the door. Willie rang the bell and asked if Miss Blomefield or Miss Ellen was at home. Yes, they were. So, whilst Willie stayed with me, Mr. Thoroughgood went into the house. In about ten minutes he returned, followed by three ladies; one tall, pale lady, wrapped in a white shawl, leaned on a younger lady, with dark eyes and a merry face; the other, a very stately-looking person, was Miss Blomefield. They all came and looked at me and asked questions. The younger lady—that was Miss Ellen—took to me very much; she said she was sure she should like me— I had such a good face. The tall, pale lady said that she should always be nervous in riding behind a horse that had once been down, as I might come down again, and if I did she should never get over the fright.

" You see, ladies," said Mr. Thoroughgood, " many first-rate horses have had their knees broken through the carelessness of their drivers, without any fault of their own, and from what I see of this horse I should say that is his case: but of course I do not wish to influence you. If you incline, you can have him on trial, and then your coachman will see what he thinks of him."

" You have always been such a good adviser to us about our horses," said the stately lady, " that your recommendation would go a long way with me, and if my sister Lavinia sees no objection, we will accept your offer of a trial with thanks."

It was then arranged that I should be sent for the next day.

In the morning a smart-looking young man came for me. At first he looked pleased, but when he saw my knees, he said in a disappointed voice:

" I didn't think, sir, you would have recommended my ladies a blemished horse like that."

" Handsome is that handsome does," said my master. " You are only taking him on trial, and I am sure you will do fairly by him, young man, and if he is not as safe as any horse you ever drove, send him back."

I was led home, placed in a comfortable stable, fed, and left to myself. The next day, when my groom was cleaning my face, he said:

" That is just like the star that Black Beauty had; he is much the same height too. I wonder where he is now."

A little further on he came to the place in my neck where I was bled and where a little knot was left in the skin. He almost started, and began to look me over carefully, talking to himself.

" White star in the forehead, one white foot on the off side, this little knot just in that place." Then, looking at the middle of my back: " And as I am alive, there is that little patch of white hair that John used to call 'Beauty's threepenny bit'. It *must* be Black Beauty! Why, Beauty! Beauty, do you know me? Little Joe Green that almost killed you?" And he began patting and patting me as if he was quite overjoyed.

I could not say that I remembered him, for now he was a fine-grown young fellow, with black whiskers and a man's voice, but I was sure he knew me and that he was Joe Green, and I was very glad. I put my nose up to him and tried to say that we were friends. I never saw a man so pleased.

" Give you a fair trial! I should think so indeed! I wonder who the rascal was that broke your knees, my old beauty! You must have been badly served out somewhere. Well, well, it won't be my fault if you haven't good times of it now. I wish John Manly was here to see you."

In the afternoon I was put into a low Park chair and brought to the door. Miss Ellen was going to try me and Green went with her. I soon found that she was a good driver, and she seemed pleased with my paces. I heard Joe telling her about me, and that he was sure I was Squire Gordon's old Black Beauty.

When we returned, the other sisters came out to hear how I behaved myself. She told them what she had just heard, and said:

" I shall certainly write to Mrs. Gordon and tell her that her favourite horse has come to us. How pleased she will be!"

After this I was driven every day for a week or so, and as I appeared to be quite safe, Miss Lavinia at last ventured out in the small close carriage. After this it was quite decided to keep me and call me by my old name of " Black Beauty ".

I have now lived in this happy place a whole year. Joe is the best and kindest of grooms. My work is easy and pleasant, and I feel my strength and spirits all coming back again. Mr. Thoroughgood said to Joe the other day:

" In your place he will last till he is twenty years old —perhaps more."

Willie always speaks to me when he can, and treats me as his special friend. My ladies have promised that I shall never be sold, and so I have nothing to fear; and here my story ends. My troubles are all over and I am at home; and often before I am quite awake, I fancy I am still in the orchard at Birtwick, standing with my old friends under the apple trees.

Nancy Drew
in
Password to Larkspur Lane

KU-206-698

This Armada book belongs to:

Other Nancy Drew Mystery Stories available in Armada

The Secret of Shadow Ranch
The Mystery of the 99 Steps
Mystery at the Ski Jump
The Spider Sapphire Mystery
The Clue in the Crossword Cipher
The Quest of the Missing Map
The Clue in the Old Stagecoach
The Clue of the Broken Locket
The Message in the Hollow Oak
The Invisible Intruder
The Ghost of Blackwood Hall

The Nancy Drew Mystery Stories

Password to Larkspur Lane

Carolyn Keene

First published in the U.K. in 1972 by William Collins
Sons & Co. Ltd., London and Glasgow. First published
in Armada in 1976 by William Collins Sons & Co. Ltd.,
14 St. James's Place, London SW1A 1PF

© MCMLXVI Grosset & Dunlap Inc. All rights reserved
under International and Pan-American copyright conventions.
Published pursuant to agreement with Grosset & Dunlap
Inc., New York, N.Y., U.S.A.

© 1972 in Great Britain and The British Commonwealth (except
Canada) by William Collins Sons & Co. Ltd.

Printed in Great Britain by
Love & Malcomson Ltd., Brighton Road,
Redhill, Surrey

CONDITIONS OF SALE:
This book is sold subject to the condition that
it shall not, by way of trade or otherwise, be lent
re-sold, hired out or otherwise circulated without
the publisher's prior consent in any form of
binding or cover other than that in which it is
published and without a similar condition
including this condition being imposed on the
subsequent purchaser.

"The blue flame again!" Mr Corning gasped

CONTENTS

CHAPTER		PAGE
1	SINGING HORSES	9
2	A GOLDEN CLUE	15
3	A CHASE	23
4	FRIGHTENED GRANDPARENTS	30
5	BLUE FIRE	37
6	MYSTERIOUS MORGAN	47
7	UNFRIENDLY KEEPER	55
8	OVER THE WALL!	64
9	SURPRISES	73
10	AN UNWELCOME GIFT	80
11	A HAZARDOUS DROP	89
12	THE CRYSTAL GARDEN	95
13	BAITING A THIEF	102
14	THE MATCHING NECKLACE	109
15	DARING PLANS	117
16	SLEUTHING	125
17	ATTIC HIDEOUT	132
18	THE UNDERGROUND CELL	141
19	CAUGHT!	147
20	THE SP	154

·1·

Singing Horses

"If this were two thousand years ago—!"

Nancy Drew paused on the flagstone path of her garden in front of a border of beautiful larkspur. For a moment the attractive red-haired girl of eighteen watched the tall blue plumes waving in the breeze. Then she turned to the middle-aged woman behind her.

"I must select the very best for the flower show, Hannah," she said.

The Drews' housekeeper and Nancy paused to look up at a passing aeroplane. They were startled to hear its engines cut out. As Nancy and Hannah watched in alarm, a wounded bird plummeted down and landed amongst the flowers.

"A homing pigeon!" Nancy exclaimed, seeing the tiny metal tube attached to its leg. "Maybe the bird's carrying a message!"

Hannah Gruen's eyes were on the plane. "Oh, Nancy!" she gasped. "It's going to crash!"

Nancy gazed upward and saw that the twin-engine craft was flying very low. The plane was tan colour and had a curious design outlined in black on the fuselage.

"It looks like a winged horse," Nancy thought, but

9

she could not be sure, since the sun was shining in her eyes.

Suddenly the coughing engines roared to life and the plane nosed upward, then zoomed away.

"Whew!" Hannah exclaimed. "I thought that thing was going to fall right onto our house!"

"I wonder if the plane hit this pigeon," Nancy said, and once more turned her attention to the bird, which was panting feebly.

"You poor dear!" she said, picking it up. Gently Nancy felt for broken bones, but found none. "The pigeon may only be stunned," she said.

"What a miracle that it's alive!" Hannah said.

Nancy nodded. "I'd better see if the pigeon's carrying a message. It might be something important that we ought to report to the bird's owner."

While the housekeeper held the pigeon, Nancy removed the top of the capsule on its leg and slid out a thin piece of paper. She unrolled the message and read aloud:

"'*Trouble here. After five o'clock blue bells will be singing horses. Come tonight.*'"

Nancy and Hannah looked at each other in puzzlement. "It's a strange message," the housekeeper said. "What in the world does that mean?"

"I wish I knew," Nancy replied, "but it sounds urgent—and mysterious." She slipped the message into her pocket. "I'll wire the International Federation of American Homing Pigeon Fanciers and give them the number stamped on the bird's leg ring. All homing pigeons are registered by number so the owners can be traced."

She examined the ring containing the digits 2-21-12-12,

then hurried off to phone the telegram. By the time she returned, Hannah had placed the bird in a cardboard box lined with cotton.

Nancy brought an eye-dropper and with it gave the pigeon water. Then she put some wild-bird seed in the box. "Do get well," she said softly.

"How are pigeons trained to carry messages?" Hannah asked as Nancy placed the box on a garage shelf.

"They have a home loft. No matter where the birds are released, they always fly back there."

"Did you ever hear how fast they can fly?"

"I read about some pigeons who raced from Mexico City to New York, averaging a mile a minute." Nancy glanced at her watch. "I'd better hurry or I won't get to the flower show on time."

She continued snipping prize larkspurs and putting them in a basket.

"Before all the excitement began," said Hannah, "you were saying, 'If this were two thousand years ago—,' but you didn't finish. What did you mean?"

Nancy smiled. "I was thinking that if I had lived two thousand years ago I might have been a Grecian maiden. And in that case, I might be praying right now in the Temple of Apollo at Delphi. I always imagine flowers there. Maybe delphinium—that's another name for larkspur."

"What would you be asking for?" said Hannah.

"That my father's olive groves would bear extra well, that his vines would be loaded with grapes and his nets heavy with fish every morning."

Hannah laughed heartily at the thought of her employer, Carson Drew, the well-known lawyer, picking olives or hauling in a fish-filled net.

While talking, Nancy and Hannah had been cutting stalks with the finest flowers and before long they had a basketful. Nancy took it into the kitchen and carefully fashioned an exquisite arrangement in an old English vase. She carried it to her convertible parked in the circular drive.

She thought, "My car was a good-looking one until that horrid man ran into it last week." Ruefully she surveyed the dent.

"Good luck with your entry," Mrs Gruen said. "Hope it wins a prize!"

"Hannah, you're a darling!" Nancy exclaimed and kissed her. The two had a deep affection for each other. The girl's mother had died when Nancy was very young and the housekeeper had helped Mr Drew bring up his only child.

As Nancy drove across the town of River Heights, she mulled over the strange message on the homing pigeon. Was it a code? Suddenly it occurred to Nancy that the pigeon might have been released from the plane which accidentally struck it. She wondered what the reply would be from the Homing Pigeon Fanciers association.

"Maybe," she thought excitedly, "I've stumbled upon a new mystery!"

By this time she had reached the Blenheim estate on the outskirts of River Heights. The broad tree-shadowed lawn was filled with women setting up displays for the annual charity flower show. Nancy had been assigned a spot in the greenhouse behind the mansion.

As she set her larkspur arrangement in place, the chairman came up to her. "My, Nancy, your delphiniums are gorgeous," Mrs Winsor said.

"Thank you," Nancy replied.

"I just adore larkspur," the woman said. "Such a lovely old-fashioned flower. My grandmother had them in her garden. She always had hollyhocks and bluebells, too."

Bluebells! Nancy's mind leaped to the mysterious message. Could the *blue bells* in it mean flowers?

Aloud she said, "Mrs Winsor, I hope the judges like my flowers as much as you do!"

Nancy hurried back to the convertible. She was eager to get home and see if a reply to her telegram had come.

To make better time, Nancy turned off the main highway on to a little-travelled shortcut. As she drove down the narrow road, Nancy saw an old black saloon parked along one side.

The dusty leaves of some sprawling bushes lay across the top of the car and hung down over the windscreen and other windows. It was impossible to see inside.

"That's really an old-timer," Nancy thought, and wondered if anyone were inside it.

After she had passed the car, her eyes shifted to the rear-view mirror. Slowing up, she studied the licence number plate, which was so mud-splattered that only four digits showed: 2-21-1.

Nancy's interest quickened at once. These were the first four numbers on the pigeon's leg band! Was there a connection?

She gave the licence number plate another fleeting glance and noted by the colour that it was from another state, but she could not see the identifying initials.

A moment later an oncoming car passed her. The driver raised a hand and called, "Hello, Nancy!"

"Dr Spire!" she exclaimed.

The famous bone specialist, a friend of the Drew family, was often called out on local emergencies. Glancing back again, Nancy was surprised to see Dr Spire pull up behind the old saloon.

Wondering if she could be of help, Nancy stopped at the side of the road and watched as the physician walked towards the parked car carrying his black bag. As he reached the saloon, a rear door swung open. Dr Spire put one foot inside and leaned forward. With a sudden movement he vanished into the car and it roared away.

"That was strange!" Nancy said aloud. "It seemed as if someone jerked him into the back seat. He may have been kidnapped!"

On a hunch, Nancy backed her convertible to the physician's car, then braked and leaped out. Dr Spire had locked his car and the keys were gone.

"I guess he expected to be met," Nancy told herself. "He probably jumped into the old saloon. But the whole thing is peculiar."

When Nancy reached home, Mrs Gruen opened the front door "It's here. Came a few minutes ago." She handed over a telegram.

Nancy tore open the envelope. The telegram was from the Pigeon Fanciers association. It read:

LOCAL REPRESENTATIVE WILL CALL. BIRD NOT REGISTERED. SUSPECT TROUBLE. KEEP MESSAGE SECRET

·2·

A Golden Clue

"ANOTHER strange message!" remarked Hannah Gruen. "What do you think now, Nancy?"

"That a real mystery has dropped into my lap." Nancy grinned. "And about time! I've been longing for one. I can't wait to tell Dad about this!"

Carson Drew had always been close to his daughter, and often discussed his cases with her, because she grasped the issues so clearly and quickly.

Nancy re-read the telegram and said to Mrs Gruen, "The pigeon isn't registered. That's so its messages can't be traced to the sender."

Hannah replied, "Well, it takes all kinds of folks to make a world. What's more, pigeons, planes and telegrams aren't getting tonight's dinner ready. We're having a chicken casserole, one of your father's favourites."

"And mine," said Nancy.

"Mr Drew likes sweet pickles too," Hannah added. "I'll go down to the cellar and get a jar."

Nancy's thoughts returned to the odd message which had been attached to the pigeon's leg. She took the note from her pocket and studied it again. The words were neatly printed in black ink.

For safe-keeping, Nancy slipped the note and the

15

telegram into her handbag, and set it on the hall table. At that moment she heard a thumping noise and a cry from the cellar.

"Hannah!" she called. There was no answer.

Nancy dashed to the kitchen and looked down the cellar stairs. A huddled figure lay on the floor.

"Oh!" Nancy exclaimed and ran down the steps.

The housekeeper managed to sit up. "I slipped," she said shakily. "Oh, my back!"

"Hannah!" Nancy exclaimed anxiously. "Are you badly hurt?"

"No," the housekeeper replied. "I can get up, I'm sure. Just give me a hand."

Nancy put one arm round Hannah and helped the woman to her feet. Mrs Gruen stood still a few moments to catch her breath, then said:

"I guess I didn't break anything, thank goodness. But I'm afraid I've strained my back."

"I'll drive you to Dr Spire's," Nancy said, "and let him examine you." With the girl's help, the house-keeper slowly climbed the stairs.

"I have to get dinner," Hannah announced.

"That can wait," Nancy said firmly. "We'll leave a note telling Dad where we've gone."

As they drove towards the doctor's residence and office, Nancy hoped that he was back from his mys-terious call. When they reached the house, Mrs Spire told them her husband was out.

"Is he still on that case out near the Blenheim estate?" Nancy asked. "I passed him on my way home from the flower show."

"Yes, he is, but he should be home soon." She and Nancy helped Hannah to a couch in the office. Then

Mrs Spire excused herself to get dinner, and asked Nancy to answer the office phone if it should ring. Twenty minutes later it buzzed.

Nancy lifted the receiver, but before she could say "Hello", a muffled voice asked if Dr Spire had returned. When Nancy said No, the caller directed her to write down a message.

As she wrote, a strange expression crossed her face. At the end of the message, the speaker abruptly hung up.

"Can I believe my eyes?" Nancy wondered as she looked at the message she had jotted down.

"If you say blue bells, you will get into trouble, for they are no longer used here."

"Blue bells again!" Nancy told herself. Was Dr Spire somehow involved in the mystery of the message attached to the pigeon's leg? Could it be more than coincidence that the numbers on the licence number plate of the black saloon matched the first four digits on the bird's leg band? Her suspicion that the doctor had been pulled forcibly into the saloon came flooding back.

Nancy was about to tell Hannah what the anonymous caller had said, when brisk footsteps were heard outside the door. Dr Spire, a lanky, balding man, strode into the office. Although he looked worried, his thin, intense face lighted with a smile.

"Well, Nancy, we meet again!"

Hiding her surprise and relief at seeing him safe, Nancy replied with a cheerful greeting.

The physician turned to Hannah. "Mrs Gruen, my wife has told me of your accident. I'm sorry to hear about it. I'll take a look at you now."

Fifteen minutes later the doctor announced that she had a strained back. "Rest in bed a few days. I'll write a prescription for you. In ten days you'll be feeling like your old self."

"I'll see that she rests," Nancy promised.

She helped Hannah to the car and settled her comfortably in the front seat. Then she excused herself and hurried back inside. The doctor was seated at his desk, gazing into space. He looked at Nancy inquiringly.

"I jotted down this phone message for you," she said. "It is important that I ask you something about it."

The doctor's lips tightened as he read the message.

"Does it make sense to you?" Nancy asked.

"Yes," he said grimly.

Dr Spire stood up and strode across the room. Then he turned and faced Nancy. "I need help in solving a strange mystery. There's nobody with whom I'd rather discuss it than you and your father. Will you help me?"

"Of course," Nancy replied.

"Then will you both come back later?"

Nancy agreed. "I'm eager to hear your story. I think the mystery may be linked to one I'm working on."

The doctor looked amazed, but before he could ask what she meant, Mrs Spire came to tell him that dinner was ready. Nancy quickly excused herself.

When she and Hannah reached home, Carson Drew, a tall, distinguished-looking man, was eagerly waiting for them. He was sorry to hear what had happened to the housekeeper and helped her upstairs. After Mrs Gruen was settled in bed, Nancy brought her a tray of food, then prepared dinner for her father and herself.

While they ate, Nancy told him about the strange

occurrences. Mr Drew shook his head and chuckled. "You attract mystery like nectar in a flower attracts a bee, Nancy."

She grinned. "In this case, I'll be the blossom and hope the villain will come my way!"

"I'll go with you tonight," he agreed, "and I'll do anything I can to help."

With a twinkle in her eyes Nancy said, "Then you can start clearing the table. I'll scrape the dishes and put them in the dish-washer."

Carson Drew laughed. "You caught me that time, young lady!"

But he was Nancy's willing helper and it did not take the father-daughter team long to tidy the kitchen. Then they set off for Dr Spire's office. He greeted them cordially and indicated deep leather armchairs.

Mr Drew said quietly, "Suppose you tell us what's worrying you, Richard."

"It's a strange story," the physician said. "I almost can't believe it myself. This afternoon I had a phone call saying that a patient of mine, Mrs Manning Smith, had been in a minor car accident on Hollow Hill Road. She wanted me to meet her there and if necessary take her to the hospital.

"The caller—a man—told me to look for an old black saloon. Since I know Mrs Smith has such a car, I thought nothing of it. After passing you on the road, Nancy, I spotted the car, parked, and went up to it. The back door swung open. As I leaned forward to look inside, my shoulders were seized and I was yanked to the floor. Before I could move, a hood was dropped over my head and a man on each side held me firmly."

"How far did you travel?" Nancy asked.

"A long time—about an hour. Not a word was spoken during the trip."

"Where did they take you?" Mr Drew asked.

"I don't know. But some of the roads were bumpy. I think we were out in the country. When the hood was finally removed I found myself in what appeared to be a hospital room."

"Was there a patient?" Nancy asked eagerly.

"Yes, but not Mrs Smith. Someone explained a clerk had made a mistake. I didn't learn the patient's name. She was an elderly woman, suffering from a dislocated shoulder. There was just one other person in the room—a nurse. She was a large, hard-faced woman and warned me not to talk to the patient."

"Did you try?" Mr Drew queried.

"No, but all the time I was working, it seemed as if she wanted to tell me something. Her eyes kept flashing signals which I could not understand. Then, while I was taking her pulse, the nurse turned for a moment and the woman slipped this into my hand."

Dr Spire reached into his pocket and held out a thin, gold-chain bracelet with a small gold shield dangling from it.

"How dainty!" Nancy exclaimed as she took the bracelet to examine it. Set into the bangle was a garnet.

"There's an inscription over the jewel," she said. " 'To my darling Mary from Joe.' " Nancy turned the shield over. "On the other side is a coat of arms. Perhaps we could trace it and find out the woman's name. If she's being held against her will, we ought to rescue her!"

"It's worth a try," her father agreed.

"Keep the bracelet, Nancy," the doctor said, "and see what you can learn about it." Then he continued his story. "When I finished, two men came in and replaced the hood. Then I was driven back to my car. A couple of times when I tried to resist, they got rough."

"How dreadful!" Nancy burst out. "Dr Spire, do you think the woman was able to talk, but had been ordered not to?"

"Yes, I do."

"Did you see or hear anything that would help us find the place?"

Dr Spire smiled. "I learned the password to the place."

"Marvellous!" said Nancy. "What was it?"

He replied, "As we turned into a driveway—I could tell by the creak of gates—the driver said 'Bluebells' and someone answered 'Pass'."

Nancy's eyes sparkled with excitement. "This is where my story comes in, Dr Spire." Quickly she told him about the pigeon, the plane, and the telegram. "Whoever is holding the woman prisoner must have been afraid you had heard the password. So he decided to change it."

"Yes, that would have been just about five o'clock, as the pigeon message said," the physician agreed. "The phone call here was to warn me not to try finding the place again or using the password to get in if I did."

Carson Drew spoke up. "Richard, you must report this to the police."

Just then the telephone rang. When the physician finished the call, he said, "Emergency at the hospital.

I'll have to go. Carson, will you and Nancy report the incident to the police for me?"

"We'll stop at headquarters," the lawyer replied.

As the Drews left the house, Nancy noticed a shadowy figure across the street. "Are we being watched?" the young sleuth wondered.

While driving into town Nancy noted a pair of headlights reflected in her mirror. One was dimmer than the other. The uneven lights stayed close behind all the way to police headquarters. Nancy slowed down in front of the building, and the car, a sleek black saloon, went past.

"No place to park here, Dad," she said. "Suppose you hop out and start telling your story. I'll join you as soon as I find a parking space."

Mr Drew got out, and a few minutes later Nancy pulled into the far side of a car park at the corner. When she stepped out of the car, a hulky figure emerged from the nearby shadows.

A feeling of apprehension swept over Nancy, and she tried to dart past the man. But a powerful hand seized her arm and jerked her back.

"Not so fast!" the stranger growled in a deep voice.

·3·

A Chase

"LET me go or I'll scream!" Nancy cried out.

Instantly the man released her arm, but he swiftly stepped in front of her. "Wait a minute," he commanded. "You want to help your father, don't you?"

"I don't know what you're talking about," Nancy said warily. She studied the husky, broad-shouldered man. He had heavy brows, deep-set eyes, and a cruel mouth.

"You're Nancy Drew, aren't you?"

Nancy hesitated, afraid he might be trying to find her father to harm him. "Are you sure you're talking to the right person?" she asked.

"Okay," the man said bitterly, "play it smart. It's been years since I saw Drew, and maybe I'm wrong. But I could be right, so you take a message."

Nancy did not reply, and the stranger went on, "Tell Carson Drew to mind his own business or he's in for a bad shock."

"If you're through," Nancy said coldly, "I'll go now."

The man stepped aside and she hurried from the car park, her heart pounding. As she reached the pavement Nancy came face to face with two friends.

"Why, Nancy Drew!" exclaimed Jean Moss. "I

haven't seen you for weeks!" Her escort, Bill Wright, added, "Been solving any mysteries lately?"

Nancy's heart sank. Had the man in the car park heard them? She managed to talk pleasantly with the couple for a few minutes but she was worried.

As Jean and Bill moved off, Nancy heard a soft laugh from the shadows. A moment later a deep voice said mockingly, "Good night, Miss Drew." The speaker melted into the darkness.

Biting her lip in vexation, Nancy ran to police head-quarters. The officer on duty directed her to the Detective Bureau. Here Mr Drew was conferring with Lieutenant Mulligan, a red-faced, brawny man with thinning hair. He knew the Drews only by reputation.

Once again Nancy told her story. The detective jotted down the partial licence number of the suspicious car.

When Nancy handed him the bracelet, he said, "Hmm. Has an inscription, but it's old. Mary and Joe could have been dead for years. No last name or dates, either. Afraid it won't be much use to us."

"If you don't mind," Nancy said, "I'd like to see if I can trace the owner."

"Go ahead," the lieutenant said and gave it back. "We'll check out the car's licence number, but probably the kidnappers are using phoney plates."

As Nancy and her father walked back to the car park, she told him about the stranger who had accosted her there and the warning message.

Mr Drew frowned. "I don't know who he could be. Some crank, I suppose."

Cars were closely parked on either side of Nancy's convertible, so she gave her full attention to pulling out of the tight space. Soon after she had driven into the street and turned towards home, headlights appeared in her mirror. The right one was dim!

"Dad, the same car that followed us before is behind us," Nancy said tensely. "I'm afraid the driver's the man who wants to harm you! Let's try to shake him."

Keeping within the speed limit, Nancy drove into the residential section of the city, taking every short cut and winding street she knew. Meanwhile Mr Drew watched the car behind, which continued to follow.

"It seems useless to try getting away," he said finally. "I'd like to get a good look at the driver."

"All right," Nancy replied.

She increased her speed, widening the distance between the two cars, until she approached an intersection where there was a bright overhead light. She swung round, her tyres squealing on the asphalt, and stopped short, facing her pursuer.

When he came abreast of them, Carson Drew gasped. "Follow him!" the lawyer ordered as the driver zoomed off.

Nancy turned again and pursued the saloon. Just as she was about to overtake it, the traffic light ahead turned red. The driver rode straight through, rounded a corner, and disappeared.

Nancy sighed. "We'll never find him now."

"Never mind," said Mr Drew. "It was a good try. Let's go home."

"Who was that man, Dad?" Nancy asked.

"Adam Thorne, an escaped convict. Thank goodness, he didn't hurt you."

Nancy shuddered. "What was he jailed for?"

"Thorne was given ten years for embezzling the

assets of an estate. While in jail he became very bitter and at times violent."

"But what's his interest in you?" Nancy queried.

Mr Drew explained that Thorne had been a River Heights lawyer. "He was disbarred prior to his trial and I was in charge of gathering the evidence against him."

"I see," said Nancy. "Dad, I have a hunch Adam Thorne is involved in the bluebell mystery. He must have been spying outside Dr Spire's house and recognized you. Probably he's not only looking for revenge, but wants to keep us from working on the case."

"I'm afraid you're right. For Pete's sake be careful, Nancy."

"You too, Dad."

A few minutes later the Drews reached home. While Nancy checked on Hannah, who was asleep, Mr Drew called Lieutenant Mulligan and reported his daughter's encounter with Adam Thorne and the resultant, unsuccessful chase.

"If Thorne's tied in with Dr Spire's kidnapping," said Mulligan, "he'll stop at nothing. I'll broadcast a bulletin immediately."

The next morning Nancy was up early and went to talk to Hannah Gruen.

"I have good news for you," the housekeeper said. "My niece Effie has offered to come here and work while I'm laid up."

"Good. Effie's fun."

"And scatter-brained sometimes," Hannah remarked.

After breakfast Nancy drove off to get Effie Schneider. When she rang the bell of the small timber cottage, the door was opened by Effie's mother.

"Hello, Mrs Schneider," said Nancy. "How are you?"

"Fine thanks. Please come in. Effie isn't dressed yet. She's been reading a movie magazine instead of putting on her clothes . . . Effie!" she called.

"Here I am, Mum," a high-pitched voice replied. "Hi, Nancy!" said the girl as she walked into the living-room munching a banana.

"Hello, Effie," Nancy greeted the thin, seventeen-year-old girl.

Effie had light-blonde hair, which she wore close-cropped with a feathery fringe over her forehead. She was dressed in a Chinese-style pink kimono, with high-heeled satin mules.

"This outfit is like the one Ling Su wore in the movie, 'The Chinese Wall Mystery'," Effie remarked, making an Oriental bow.

Nancy grinned, but Mrs Schneider said tartly, "Hurry up and put on street clothes, Effie." As her daughter went off, Mrs Schneider turned to Nancy. "Once Effie stops mooning about movie stars and singers, she's really a good worker and a fine cook."

Nancy had her doubts about this, but later was agreeably surprised when Effie prepared a delicious luncheon of chicken salad, hot rolls, and iced tea. She would not let Nancy help her.

"Aunt Hannah told me you're working on a mystery," Effie said. "That's exciting. You keep your mind on the case. I'll do the work around the house. I once read a mystery about a circus girl who was shot out of a cannon and disappeared. It took three detectives a whole month to find her. Bet you can't guess where."

Nancy grinned. "Inside the cannon?"

"Oh gee, how'd you know? Effie said. "You must have read the story.

"No, I didn't."

Bewildered, Effie shook her head and walked off. After eating lunch, Nancy decided to start tracing the owner of the bracelet. Half an hour later she walked into Butler and Stone's jewellery shop and asked for Mr Stone, who was a personal friend.

"Well, Nancy, what can I do for you?" the jeweller asked cordially. "Are you interested in a diamond-studded detective badge today?" he teased.

Nancy laughed. "Do you sell them?" she countered.

"Oh sure. To the police," the jeweller replied with a grin.

Nancy took the bracelet from her purse. "Mr Stone, could you trace this coat of arms?"

The jeweller held the bracelet towards the window to get a better look at the heraldic design on the shield. As he did so, Nancy noticed a large woman in a pink butterfly-print dress looking through the plate-glass window.

"Just a moment," Nancy said quickly to Mr Stone. "Is there some other place—"

The jeweller understood at once. "Another mystery?" he asked.

When Nancy nodded, he motioned to a private office at the back of the shop. Once again Mr Stone examined the bracelet. "This was made in Victorian times," he announced. "I doubt if it was designed round here. Hmm, an attractive coat of arms. Three mullets dexter and a Maltese cross sinister; crest, a falcon's head embattled, with the motto '*Esse quam videre*'.

"Every authentic coat of arms is a matter of record," Mr Stone explained. "It will take time, but we will be able to trace the family, if not the individual owner. May I keep the bracelet temporarily?"

Nancy hesitated. "It doesn't belong to me," she said. "Could you make a copy of the crest?"

"Certainly. Please take a seat." Mr Stone excused himself and went out. In fifteen minutes he returned, gave the bracelet to Nancy, and said he would send the tracing to a Mr Abelard de Gotha, an expert on coats of arms.

"Thank you. I'll stop by in a couple of days to see if you've heard about it," Nancy said.

As the young detective left the store her thoughts turned to the sick woman who had given the bracelet to Dr Spire.

"I wonder who she is, poor thing."

At the corner Nancy waited with a group of people for the light to change. As the walk signal came on, someone pushed roughly past her and darted out into the street. Nancy recognized the pink butterfly-print dress and at the same moment realized that her arm felt strangely light.

"My handbag!" Nancy gasped. "It's gone!"

The woman was hurrying ahead of the crowd. Nancy was sure she had stolen the bag and sprinted after her.

"Stop!" Nancy shouted, but the woman broke into a run.

Nancy put on a spurt of speed and caught up with her on the far pavement. "Give me back my—"

The big woman whirled and gave Nancy a powerful push that sent her reeling. She fell backwards off the pavement!

·4·

Frightened Grandparents

SEVERAL quick-acting pedestrians caught Nancy just before she hit the road.

"Are you hurt?" exclaimed a middle-aged woman as she helped the girl to her feet. "I saw that awful woman push you. Were you trying to catch her?"

Nancy took a deep breath and said, "Yes. She has stolen my handbag," then added, "I'm all right. Thanks so much."

Suddenly Nancy spotted the thief hurrying into Brent's Department Store down the street. She dashed after her and hastened through the revolving doors.

Looking round quickly, Nancy saw a flash of pink near the lifts. By the time she reached them, the woman had gone up in one of the lifts.

Nancy darted to the nearby escalator and rushed up, two steps at a time. On the second floor she sped to the lifts but saw by the indicator light that the one she wanted had already left. The woman was not in sight.

"What luck!" Nancy murmured, darting back to the escalator.

A few moments later she arrived breathless on the third floor. As Nancy looked towards the lift, the door was starting to close. No one was inside. The woman she was after must have stepped off here!

"May I help you?" asked a salesgirl. "We have some lovely—"

"No, no!" Nancy panted. "I'm after a thief! A woman in a pink print dress. Did you see her get off the elevator?"

The girl's eyes grew wide. "A thief!" she exclaimed. "Why, yes, I did see her, but I don't know where she went. What did she take?"

"My handbag," said Nancy.

"I'll get my supervisor," said the salesgirl.

Nancy glanced round the third floor, where many customers were examining racks of dresses. Where could the woman be hiding?

"Dressing-rooms," Nancy decided. She saw that the Autumn Clothes Department had fewer customers than the others. "I'll start there."

She hastened across the floor and peered through an archway into a narrow aisle. There was a row of curtained cubicles along one wall.

Quietly Nancy peeked into the first room. Empty! In the next a stout woman was struggling into a tight dress. She did not see Nancy. Quickly the young detective moved along the row of dressing-rooms. In the fifth room she found the thief!

The woman was leaning against the wall, panting. Nancy's open handbag lay on a shelf beside her and in one hand the woman clutched the gold-chain bracelet.

"I'll take that!" Nancy said, stepping into the cubicle.

The woman froze in amazement for a moment, then swiftly seized the handbag and hurled it at Nancy. As the girl ducked, the contents scattered and the woman tried to dash past. Nancy seized her wrist and caught hold of the bracelet.

"Help! Thief!" she shouted.

Instantly the woman let go of the gold chain, broke free, and raced into the corridor, with Nancy at her heels. The thief darted through the arch, but as Nancy reached it, two saleswomen arrived, blocking the way.

"What happened?" one asked.

"That woman in pink!" Nancy exclaimed. "I must stop her!" She darted round the salesladies and ran towards the lifts.

Too late! She saw the thief board a lift just before the door closed.

How to stop her? Suddenly Nancy spotted a store telephone behind a nearby counter. She hurried to it and picked up the receiver.

"Operator, this is an emergency! Ring the phone nearest the entrance on Main Street, please!"

In a second a voice said, "Silverware!"

"Listen carefully," Nancy said tersely. "A large woman in a pink print dress will probably come rushing towards you any minute now, heading for the door. Stop her! She's a thief!"

"Just a moment," said the girl. There was a pause, then the speaker said, "The woman you described passed my counter as we were talking. I ran after her, but she hopped into a taxi and it sped off. Shall I notify the store detective?"

"No, thanks," said Nancy. "It's too late."

Disappointed, she hung up, as a voice behind her said, "What's going on?"

Nancy turned round. It was Mr Mahoney, the store manager. He was surrounded by salesladies. One gave

Nancy her handbag with all the contents restored.

"Oh, hello, Nancy," said Mr Mahoney. "What's this about a thief in the store?"

Nancy took him aside and explained briefly. "I don't think the woman is an ordinary bag snatcher. She's probably mixed up in a case I'm working on."

"Well, I hope you catch her," Mr Mahoney said. He waved goodbye and walked off.

Nancy examined her handbag. The strap had been cut. "I doubt if that woman knew I had the bracelet with me before she saw it through the jeweller's window." The young detective suspected that Adam Thorne had engaged the thief to follow her.

"I believe she recognized the bracelet," Nancy told herself, "and she'll tell Thorne about it. I hope the old lady who owns it doesn't get into trouble for slipping it to Dr Spire."

Nancy was deep in thought as she walked down the street, and did not see a petite, dark-haired young woman hurrying towards her.

"Nancy! What luck to run into you!"

"Helen Corning! Oh, I'm sorry," Nancy said with a grin. "I can't get used to your being Mrs Archer. How's everything?"

"Oh, just great, except for one thing. Nancy, I was going to call you this very afternoon. How about solving a mystery for me?"

Seeing her friend's look of interest, she chuckled. "I thought that would catch you. Could you come to my apartment tomorrow evening at six? I'll tell you all about it then. Besides, Jim would love to see you."

"I wouldn't miss it," Nancy replied, "but I think it's only fair to tell you I'm already working on a mystery."

Helen smiled. "Then this is just one more. You're so clever, Nancy, I'm sure you can solve both at once!"

Nancy laughed. "Give me a hint."

Helen explained that her Grandmother and Grandfather Corning had recently moved to Sylvan Lake. "They have a dreamy stone house on a hill. It is beautiful. But now Gram and Gramp are afraid to stay there because of something queer that keeps happening."

"What is it?" Nancy asked.

Helen glanced at her watch. "I'd love to tell you, but I must run. See you tomorrow. We'll drive out to the lake and have dinner with Gram and Gramp. Thanks a million, Nancy!"

As Helen Archer hurried away, Nancy stood on the pavement musing. "Um—another case." Then she turned towards home.

When Nancy reached it, Effie opened the front door. "I heard you coming," she said in a loud whisper. "The pigeon man's here." She gestured towards the living-room. "He's very good-looking."

"Thank you," said Nancy, and went to greet the caller, hoping he had not heard Effie.

A tall blond man in his twenties got up as she entered. He introduced himself as Donald Jordan, secretary of the local branch of the Pigeon Fanciers association. He showed her his credentials.

"I'm so glad you came," said Nancy. "Please sit down. I'll get the pigeon and the message."

Nancy hurried to the garage and saw with relief that the bird seemed stronger.

"Oh, I hope Mr Jordan won't take you away," she murmured to the bird. "I want you to get well enough to fly to your home loft. Then I'll follow you!"

Nancy carried the pigeon to the living-room. Mr Jordan examined the bird gently, noting especially the number on its leg band. Then Nancy took the message from her bag and handed it to him.

"This is the second pigeon seen in this area with an unregistered number," he said. "The other was found dead on the highway. I mentioned it to a detective friend of mine. He thought criminals might be using this means of communication, thinking it safer than telephone or telegraph or letter."

Nancy nodded and told him she had reported the incident to the police.

"Good. That saves us the trouble." The young man arose. "Well, thank you for notifying me, Miss Drew. Now I'll take the bird and—"

"Oh, please don't!" Nancy exclaimed.

Mr Jordan looked surprised. "Surely you don't want to be bothered with a sick pigeon?"

"I don't mind," said Nancy. "I'd like to try to nurse it back to health."

The young man shook his head. "I'm afraid there's not much chance, but if that's what you want, it's okay with me."

He made copies of the leg-band number and the strange message, then wished her luck and left. Nancy returned the pigeon to the garage. She immediately went to Hannah Gruen's room to tell her about the latest developments in the case.

"And about time," said the housekeeper. "I never hear any news up here."

"How are you feeling?" Nancy asked.

"Much better. If it wasn't for that fussy doctor, I'd be up and working like I should."

Nancy laughed. "You just take it easy while you have the chance!"

Late in the afternoon Mr Drew called to say that he could not be home until eight o'clock. To keep Hannah company, Nancy and Effie ate dinner on trays in her room and afterwards watched a television play.

At the end, Effie sniffed in disappointment. "Not enough love," she commented. "Now that handsome Mr Kyle should have—"

She stopped speaking as the front doorbell rang. "Dad must have forgotten his key," Nancy remarked. "I'll go."

She hurried down the stairs and started to open the door. Instinct told the young sleuth to be cautious. She flicked the wall switch to turn on the porch light, then opened the door a crack. The porch was dark! Nancy thought the bulb must have burned out.

"Dad?" Nancy called quickly.

There was no answer, but from somewhere in the shadows came the sound of heavy breathing.

·5·

Blue Fire

"Who's there?" Nancy called sharply into the darkness. She heard a stirring near the porch, but could see no one.

"Never mind who," came a rasping whisper from the shadows. "We warned your father to mind his own business. Now we're telling you: forget the doctor's story or you'll be sorry."

Just then headlights swept up the driveway. Instantly a dark figure dashed across the lawn and disappeared into the night.

Nancy recognized her father's car. Moments later Mr Drew parked beside the house and hurried up the porch steps.

"Is something wrong?" he asked. "Why are you out here?"

"A man rang the bell, Dad, but wouldn't let me see him. He gave us another warning."

The lawyer's face was grim. "Did you recognize his voice?" he asked.

"It sounded something like Adam Thorne's," Nancy replied, "but I can't be sure because he spoke in a whisper. The man was big, though, like Thorne."

Nancy explained why the light was not on, and turned to examine it. "The bulb's gone!" she exclaimed. "I suppose the man took it out so I couldn't see him. I'll put in a new one."

"I'd like to wring that fellow's neck," her father stormed. "I'll put the car away, then report this to Lieutenant Mulligan."

"Dad, before you put the car in the garage, would you drive me to the flower show? I'm just a little bit curious as to who won the prizes."

He grinned. "Of course I'll take you." He patted her shoulder. "While I phone Mulligan, go tell Hannah and Effie where we're going and *not* to answer the doorbell."

Twenty minutes later father and daughter arrived at the greenhouse on the Blenheim estate. The display was beautiful, but the cut flowers were beginning to wilt. Nancy's pulse quickened as she approached her own entry.

"Dad!" she cried out. "Look!"

Attached to her bouquet of larkspur was a dark-blue satin ribbon with the inscription FIRST PRIZE!

"Nancy, that's wonderful," her father said. "Congratulations! Maybe you ought to give up solving mysteries and raise flowers."

"Not a chance," she said.

"But it's far less dangerous," he countered. "Take this present mystery, for instance. It might be wise for you to drop it."

Nancy looked shocked. "Why, Dad! Think of the poor old woman who is a prisoner.'

"But, Nancy, my first concern is for your safety. You are more important to me than all the mysterious old ladies in the world!"

Nancy's face showed her disappointment. "Oh please, Dad, no."

With a crash Nancy's flowers were knocked to the ground

Mr Drew looked uncomfortable. "I know, I know. You're like me. You'll never be satisfied until you lick the problem. Go ahead."

"Thank you, Dad," Nancy said happily. "I will."

"Hold it, Miss Drew!" said a voice nearby.

Nancy looked up to see a news photographer pointing a camera at her. "There! Stand right next to your exhibit."

Before she could comply, Nancy heard another voice say, "Go get her!" At the same instant a big, vicious-looking dog sprang at her!

"Oh!" she screamed, dodging just in time. The Great Dane crashed into the vase of prize flowers, knocking the exhibit to the ground and shattering the vase. He yelped in fright, then ran off.

"Who owns that beast?" cried the photographer.

No one claimed to be the owner. The Drews guessed Thorne was behind the attack, but could see him nowhere in the crowd. He—or his henchmen—had taken advantage of the excitement to escape.

Nancy reported the incident to Mrs Winsor, who told her to take the blue ribbon home. When she and her father reached the house, Hannah and Effie were delighted to hear that Nancy had won first prize in the delphinium class. "Here's hoping," said Mrs Gruen, "that you'll come out ahead in your mystery, too."

"You're sweet," Nancy told the housekeeper, then kissed her good night without |telling of the dog episode. But she was alarmed over it.

Nancy went to her pretty yellow-and-white bedroom. There she changed into nightdress, dressing-gown and slippers, then seated herself at her desk. She was determined to figure out the strange message which the pigeon had been carrying.

She opened a gardening book and turned to bluebells, then delphinium and larkspur. She learned that bluebells were different from the others. Delphinium was a perennial flower and usually blue, though some were white or lavender. Larkspur, the annual flower of the genus, occurred in pale and dark blue, mauve and other shades. In common usage, however, the names delphinium and larkspur were often interchanged.

"Well, that's interesting," Nancy thought, "but it doesn't get me much further." She closed the book with a sigh and put it away. "Maybe if I just forget the whole thing until morning an answer will come to me."

She stretched out on her comfortable bed and tuned in the clock-radio to her favourite musical programme. But her mind kept returning to the problem.

"I have larkspur on the brain. Larkspur—larkspur," she mused, clasping her hands behind her head. "Funny name. I wonder how they came to be called that. Maybe because the blossoms have little points or spurs. But why the lark? Why not sparrowspur or ostrichspur?

"Spurs are for horses, and horses don't look like larks, and larks don't suggest anything that wear spurs. Larks sing and—Oh!" Nancy sat bolt upright. "I have it! I'll bet that's it!"

She raced to her father's study and knocked. Mr Drew called, "Come in." He looked up from the letter he was writing when Nancy exclaimed:

"Dad! I think I have a clue to the kidnappers' hideout. It's larkspur! *Singing horses* stands for lark—spurs!"

"Nancy, that could be it!"

"Maybe the kidnappers got the idea of using that flower in their code, because it grows at the headquarters of the gang!"

The lawyer nodded thoughtfully as Nancy went on, "There may be bluebells there too, but I'm not sure. *Blue bells* in the pigeon's message might mean something else since it is two words. I'm going to drive through the countryside until I find a place—a house, a street, or something else—that has larkspurs, bluebells, or both as its most conspicuous feature."

"It's certainly a lead worth working on," said her father. "Better than trying to follow the pigeon to its home loft."

In the morning Nancy studied a map of the River Heights area and decided to ride through the countryside east of the town on her search for the tell-tale flowers. She drove tirelessly, stopping only to ask people if they could direct her to places where either larkspurs or bluebells grew. Here and there she found larkspurs in gardens of private homes too small to be the place Dr Spire had described. After lunch she drove on, but had no luck. At four o'clock she gave up, disappointed.

"My score is exactly zero," she thought. "Well, tonight I hear about the Corning mystery."

Back home again, Nancy went to Hannah Gruen's room to see how the housekeeper was getting along. "I'm feeling much better," Hannah reported, and told Nancy that her father would not be home for supper.

Nancy showered, put on a pretty lime-green dress with a matching sweater, and left the house. Twenty minutes later she was ringing the bell of Helen's apartment flat. The door was opened by Helen's handsome husband, Jim Archer.

"Hi, Nancy!" he said, smiling. "We're ready."

"Jim will drive his car out to the lake," Helen said as she came into the living-room. "Leave yours here."

On the way, Helen asked about Nancy's two close girl friends, Bess Marvin and her cousin George Fayne. "How are they?"

"They've been holidaying in California," said Nancy, "but they're coming home tomorrow." She chuckled. "Won't they be surprised when I tell them I have two mysteries they can help me solve!"

Helen grinned. "It's my guess they won't be a bit surprised!"

Presently Jim turned on to the side road which led to the lake. When they reached it, the setting sun had turned the water to a golden colour. A few sail-boats, silhouetted against the red sky, were heading towards shore.

"What a lovely scene!" Nancy exclaimed.

The road circled the lake and at one point branched on to a drive which led up the wooded hillside. The Corning's modern house was nestled among the trees and rocks at the top, overlooking the water. The drive wound around it to a large flagstoned area, surrounded by shrubs. Jim parked the car there.

"The front door is at the back," Helen said with a laugh as she led the way to it and rang the bell.

The door was opened by a middle-aged man-servant with red hair. He wore neat dark trousers and a white jacket.

"Hello, Morgan," Helen said cheerfully. "How are you?"

"All right, thank you," he answered, but did not

smile. Nancy wondered if he, too, was worried about the strange happenings here.

Mrs Corning hurried into the hall to greet her guests. She was a pretty woman, with short fluffy white hair, and just as petite as Helen. She took them into the big living-room with a huge picture window.

Mr Corning rose from a chair. He was a tall man with a bold, aristocratic nose. Though he had to use a cane to support his frail-looking body, his dark eyes were alert and usually sparkled with humour. But now, Nancy noted, there was a strained expression on his face.

"What is frightening the Cornings?" Nancy wondered.

She had no hint until after dinner when the group returned to the living-room. As the girls seated themselves in deep pumpkin-coloured chairs, Mrs Corning went to the window. She began to draw the soft beige curtains, shutting out the dark wooded hillside below and the few lights of houses on the opposite shore.

"Oh, please leave the curtains open, Gram," said Helen. "Let's watch for the thing tonight. After all, that's what Nancy's here for."

"Thing?" Nancy repeated, leaning forward in her chair. "Please tell me about it."

"Of course," said Mr Corning. As his wife opened the curtains again, he began, "One night about two weeks ago, my wife and I were sitting here enjoying the view when we saw a large circle of blue fire at the bottom of the hill."

"Blue fire!" Nancy exclaimed.

Mr Corning nodded. "Yes, it's a circle about as big as a car wheel, and glows with an eerie blue fire. It's approximately seven feet off the ground."

"Sounds weird," Helen remarked.

"How long did it last?" Nancy asked.

"About five minutes—then vanished. The next night it came again—this time closer."

"We've seen the thing every night since," put in Mrs Corning. "It has come nearer each time. Somehow, I feel it is a threat."

"In the meantime," her husband went on, "there have been strange happenings in the house. I want to show you something." He arose unsteadily, then suddenly gasped. Seizing the chair back with one hand, he pointed with his cane out of the huge window.

"There's that spooky blue flame again!"

Nancy leaped to her feet. In the darkness of the woods, not far below the house, glowed a large blue fiery circle.

"Helen! Jim!" Nancy exclaimed. "Let's go see what it is!"

"Be careful!" Mrs Corning urged as the young people dashed from the room. The trio let themselves out of the main door.

"Helen and I will go to the right," Nancy whispered. "Jim, you take the left. When we're even with the light, let's close in on it."

As Jim slipped away in the darkness, the girls went quietly down through the woods. The blue circle continued to burn steadily.

"Queer," Nancy murmured. "What is it?"

Unfortunately, Helen slipped on a stone and turned her ankle. Involuntarily she gave a cry of pain. Both girls froze, their hearts pounding.

For a moment the circle of light did not move. Then, slowly, it began to turn towards them!

· 6 ·

Mysterious Morgan

HELEN seized Nancy's arm as the eerie blue circle of fire moved towards them through the woods. Nancy squeezed her friend's hand reassuringly, though she herself was not certain that the ring meant harm to them.

Closer and closer it came. Suddenly Helen could stand the suspense no longer and gave a shrill scream. *Instantly the circle vanished!*

Nancy darted to the place it had been, but now nothing was there. She tried to peer through the darkness, but the night seemed blacker than ever.

At the same time, she could hear Jim shouting for Helen and running towards them. "What's the matter?" he panted.

"That weird fire was coming at us," said Helen. "I lost my head and screamed. I'm sorry, Nancy," she added. "It spoiled your chance to find out what the thing was."

"Never mind. I'll see it again, I'm sure."

Back in the house, the Cornings met the three with a flood of anxious questions. They had heard Helen scream and were badly shaken. Quietly Nancy explained what had happened.

"I'll ring for Morgan," said Helen's grandmother.

"I think we could all do with a cup of tea to settle our nerves." She pushed a button on the low table beside her.

Five minutes later the manservant had not yet appeared. "I'll go for him, Gram," Jim offered, but returned to report that he could not find him. "I looked everywhere, including his room."

"Perhaps he went outside to investigate the blue fire," Nancy suggested. "I think we ought to search the woods for him."

"I went out and called," said Jim, "but got no answer."

The elder Cornings exchanged worried glances. "Never mind, Gram," said Helen. "I'll make the tea. You tell Nancy the rest of the story."

"It was two weeks ago," said Mrs Corning, "that we first saw the circle of fire. And it was exactly two weeks ago that Morgan changed."

"How do you mean?" Nancy asked.

"He used to be such a cheerful fellow," she replied, "always ready with a little joke. Nothing we asked was ever too much trouble. I can't tell you what a tower of strength he has been. Over the years he has become like a member of the family. But now—he's a stranger."

"He forgets things," said Mr Corning. "Sometimes we ring and he doesn't come. Afterwards he mumbles a flimsy excuse."

"Several times I heard noises at night on the ground floor," said Mrs Corning. "I came down and found Morgan wandering around, fully dressed, with a strange, frightened look on his face. We've asked him a number of times to tell us what's the matter, but he avoids answering."

"How long have you known him?" Nancy asked.

"Fifteen years," replied her host. "He came to us with excellent references. And now I don't know what we would do without him."

"Perhaps he needs medical help," Nancy suggested.

"Maybe he does," said Mrs Corning, "but I feel sure the reason for his trouble is the blue fire." She arose, went to a modern-looking desk, and returned with an envelope. From it she took a folded card.

"On the morning of the day the fire first appeared," said Mrs Corning, "a letter came in the post for Morgan. A little later when I went to the kitchen, he was sitting in a chair, very pale, with his hand on his heart. The open envelope was on the table but the card had dropped to the floor. As I picked it up, I couldn't help noticing it was an ordinary greeting card."

"Did you see a signature?" Nancy asked. Helen's grandmother shook her head.

Mrs Corning explained that they had called a doctor, who said Morgan had suffered a bad shock. But the manservant would answer no questions.

"That afternoon," Mrs Corning went on, "I called a taxi and went to the little shopping centre across the lake. I found a duplicate of the card there. I wanted to get a close look at it." She handed the card to Nancy.

On the front of the card was the picture of an attractive cottage with the door wide open. Above it were the words "OPEN THE WAY TO FRIENDSHIP". The inside was blank.

"Did you see any marks on the original?"

"None. It was exactly like this one—just an innocent card."

"Not so innocent, I'm afraid," said Nancy. "It had no signature and that makes me think the card was a message from someone Morgan knows and probably fears. Have you reported any of these happenings to the police?"

Mr Corning sighed. "We discussed doing so, but Morgan begged us not to. I thought he might have another attack if we did. No, Nancy, we'd like to get to the bottom of the matter quietly."

Helen returned with the tea trolley. As Mrs Corning poured, she suggested that the young people stay overnight. "To tell the truth, we'd feel better with you here."

They agreed and Nancy went to call her father. Before retiring, she asked, "Have any of the lake residents seen the blue fire?"

"There is only one other house near ours," Mr Corning replied, "but it's empty. Folks across the lake don't bother about what goes on here."

Jim spoke up. "Gram said Morgan often disappears for a while after the blue fire is seen. He probably spots it from his room, which is at the end of the house and faces the lake."

"I imagine he's back by now," said Mrs Corning. "I'll check after I show you to your rooms."

She led the three guests into the hall and up a spiral staircase. Nancy was given a room which had a full view of the lake.

"There are several nightdresses in the dresser," Mrs Corning told her. "Help yourself."

Nancy waited until her hostess had checked on Morgan. He had not returned! As the young sleuth got ready for bed, she wondered where the mysterious manservant had gone.

In the morning, when she followed Helen and Jim to the dining-room, Nancy found Mrs Corning setting the table while her husband watched, white-faced, from a chair.

Morgan was still missing!

"His bed hasn't been slept in," said Helen's grandmother, "and our car hasn't been used."

"He might be lying hurt in the woods," Nancy suggested. "We'd better search."

The three young people hurried towards the front door. But as Jim made to open it, Nancy exclaimed, "Wait!"

Sticking out from under the door was a piece of white paper. She picked up the paper and unfolded it. It contained a message written in pencil. Nancy read it aloud:

" 'Don't worry about me. Have to be away for a while. Don't call police. Will explain later.' " It was signed "Morgan".

"He must have slipped this under the door late last night," said Nancy.

The three returned to the dining-room and Nancy showed the note to Mrs Corning. "Yes," she said, "that is Morgan's handwriting."

"Gramp, I think you should call the police," said Helen.

Her grandfather shook his head. "For the present, we'll do as Morgan asks."

"Of course, we can get along without him for a day or two," said Mrs Corning, "but I'd feel safer if someone were here at night."

"I wish I could be here," said Helen, "but—"

"No, no," her grandmother said firmly. "Your place is with your husband."

"Perhaps Nancy could stay," Helen suggested. "Would you?" she asked her friend.

"I'd love to," said Nancy, "but you know I am also working on another case."

Mrs Corning smiled. "This could be your headquarters for both." Suddenly she frowned. "But I don't like to think of you working on this case alone. It might be dangerous."

"Maybe Bess and George could come," Helen said eagerly. "You three could have lots of fun here when you're not working on your mysteries."

"I'll see what Dad says," Nancy promised. "Anyhow, I'll come back tonight. I'd like another chance to catch whoever is responsible for that ring of blue fire."

After breakfast she walked down the hill to where she and Helen had seen the strange phenomenon the night before. Here and there she found singed twigs and leaves, but had no time to look for other clues. Jim was waiting with the car.

When Nancy entered her own house a little later, she found Effie whistling cheerfully in the kitchen. Her hair was topped by a pink bow.

"Oh, hello, Nancy! Your father's gone already, but he said to tell you he'd see you tonight. Your friend Bess called. She and George are back. They want you to phone them right away."

Just then the back doorbell rang. Nancy opened the door to see a small boy standing there.

"Hello, Johnny," she said.

"Hi, Nancy!" he said. "What's in that box in your back garden?"

Effie cut in quickly, "A pigeon. And don't you touch it!" The girl explained to Nancy that she had taken the pigeon's box from the garage and placed it in the yard. I put on a lid with holes in it. Now he can get air and a little sunlight."

"I peeped through a hole," said Johnny, "and I saw something move. Is it a bird? I like birds. My Mummy has a parakeet. Oh, Nancy, can I have some biscuits?"

Nancy laughed and gave him the last one in the tin. "That's all."

"It's okay. I'll go play with your bird."

"No, no," Nancy said quickly. "Leave the bird alone. I don't want it to fly away."

The telephone rang and Nancy went to answer it. The caller wanted the library. "I'm sorry," Nancy said, "you have the wrong—"

She broke off as Effie's shrill cry sounded from the kitchen.

"Help, Nancy! The bird is loose!"

With a gasp of alarm, Nancy hung up the phone and dashed for the kitchen. Effie was standing at the back door, wringing her hands. Outside, Johnny was squatting beside the box, holding the lid in his hand. The pigeon was looking over the edge.

"Don't move, Johnny!" Nancy called, and hurried out with Effie behind her.

"He wants to fly," the little boy said. "He flaps his wings like anything. See?"

The bewildered bird hopped to the edge of the box and sat there, balancing and stretching.

"Stay still, Johnny!" Nancy warned. "Don't frighten it!"

"He isn't scared of me," the boy answered confidently. "He likes me. See?"

Johnny's chubby little hands swooped towards the

bird. Alarmed, the pigeon flapped its wings, rose awkwardly into the air, and landed just out of reach on a kitchen window-sill.

"Oh dear!" said Nancy, hardly daring to breathe. "We must get it down."

Effie was already dragging a light lawn chair to the window. "I'll get him for you."

"Wait! That won't hold you."

Before Nancy could stop her, Effie leaped on to the chair seat and reached for the sill. Nancy grabbed for the chair. Too late! It tipped. With a wild cry Effie toppled off, her arms flailing.

The frightened bird flew away!

Unfriendly Keeper

"EFFIE! Are you hurt?" Nancy cried. But even as she helped the girl to her feet, Nancy's anxious glance went to the bird flying across the garden.

"I'm all right," Effie said breathlessly. "I'm sorry I scared him away. Oh, there he is!"

She pointed to the pigeon who had come to rest on the garage roof. Then, flying slowly and uncertainly, it flapped about in a circle and took off towards the front of the house.

Nancy grabbed Effie's hand. "Come on!" She pulled Effie towards her car, which was parked near the front door. "I'll drive. You watch for the bird. We must follow it!"

Flustered, Effie climbed in beside Nancy, taking off her apron and chattering apologies.

"Don't talk! Just watch," Nancy said crisply.

Effie, clutching her pink bow to keep it in place, gazed skyward. "There he goes!"

The pigeon was flying low along the street in front of the houses. Nancy started the engine and began to follow slowly.

"I don't think this will work," Effie said, "because we have to stay on the streets and the pigeon can fly in any direction."

"Maybe you're right," Nancy said grimly, "but we're going to try!"

"He's turning left," Effie announced. Quickly Nancy turned left into a side street and followed the bird until it veered again.

"Lucky he's flying low and slow," said Effie.

Now and then the bird fluttered to a rest on a roof or tree branch, but the girls managed to track it until they had reached open country beyond the suburbs of River Heights.

"My neck is stiff from watching," Effie said with a sigh. "Where's he going, anyway?"

"Home to its owner," Nancy replied. "Where is it now?"

"He went that way," said Effie, pointing across a field, "but I can't see him because of those trees."

"Oh, we mustn't lose it!" Nancy exclaimed. She stopped the car and scanned the sky.

Effie gulped. "I'm sorry. I can't see him. Oh, I could cry!"

"Well, don't," Nancy commanded. "That pigeon is one of my best clues. I must find it!"

Suddenly she spotted the large grey bird flying out of the clump of trees. "There he goes!" Nancy exclaimed.

Luckily the pigeon flew parallel to the road and Nancy drove along behind it.

"Please watch the bird, Effie," Nancy implored as her companion looked away.

"I'm not even blinking both eyes at once," Effie assured her. "I blink one eye at a time." After a mile, Effie suddenly pointed to a grove of elms that towered over the flat fields. "Look! He's going round and round over those trees. I think he's dizzy."

"No," Nancy said, and felt a quiver of excitement. "That's where it lives. I see buildings in the grove." A second later the pigeon disappeared amongst the trees.

Nancy halted the car beside a stone wall over which honeysuckle tumbled. A short distance ahead was a driveway.

"Listen, Effie," Nancy said firmly, "we are going in there and you are not to say a word about our keeping the pigeon or following it here."

Effie's eyes were wide. "Is there a gang of kidnappers in there?" she asked timidly.

"I don't know who's there," Nancy replied. "But we must be prepared for anything." Then, seeing that Effie was trembling, she said, "Would you rather wait here?"

"Oh, no! I don't want to stay alone! But maybe I— I could hide in the boot."

They got out of the car and Effie scrambled into the luggage compartment. She left the lid open an inch so there would be fresh air.

Nancy slipped behind the wheel again and turned off the little-used, sandy road on to a well-kept gravel driveway. It swept in a great curve towards a long rambling white house.

Nancy drove nearly a quarter of a mile. Then the path dipped under the trees, and Nancy saw that the house was a mansion. Whoever occupied it must be very wealthy. White columns supported the overhanging roof of a porte-cochère.

The young sleuth did not stop there, but headed towards the outbuildings, to the far right of it. She pulled up in front of a stable.

Quietly Nancy got out of the car. Her sweeping glance took in a nearby shed and a large coop beside it containing a number of pigeons. On the roof rested the pigeon Nancy had been following.

The yard was empty. Except for the cooing and flutterings of the birds, the place was silent. Was it deserted? Nancy wondered.

Suddenly she was startled by a noise that sounded like a pistol shot. She whirled. In the shadow of the stable doorway stood a dark, thin-faced man wearing a riding habit. He carried a long, knotted, leather whip which he cracked again.

With an unpleasant grin, he said, "Scared you, didn't I?"

Keeping her voice cool and even, Nancy said, "Good morning. Is the owner here?"

"Nope," he said, studying her carefully. "What do you want?"

"I'd like to buy some pigeons," Nancy said.

"They'll be expensive," he said. "Ours are specially trained to fly both day and night. How many birds you want?"

"Two," Nancy replied. "Do you take care of these all by yourself?" she asked casually, hoping to get a lead on how many men worked at the place.

"Sure," he said. As he walked towards the coop, he spotted the pigeon on top of it. "Oh—oh!" he exclaimed softly. "So you finally got here!" He hurried over and picked up the pigeon.

The keeper looked it over curiously, then opened the capsule on the bird's leg. With sinking heart, Nancy remembered that the message was no longer there. She had intended to replace it before releasing the pigeon, but the bird's sudden escape had made this impossible.

When the man saw that the capsule was empty, he bit his lip and frowned. After putting the pigeon into the coop, he turned and walked back to Nancy, his eyes narrowing.

"It's a lovely house and grounds," she remarked innocently. "Who lives here?"

"I'm kind of busy this morning," he said curtly. "What kind of birds you want?"

"Any healthy pair will do," Nancy replied.

While they had been talking, the man's eyes had roved over the convertible and now he gazed at Nancy as if he were trying to make up his mind about something. Had he recognized her? Had Adam Thorne warned his accomplices to be on the lookout for her?

Suddenly the man said, "Okay. I'll get you a pair. You pay inside the house."

"Oh, no," Nancy thought. "I won't risk that. I think I'd better be ready to leave fast!"

As the pigeon keeper walked towards the coop, Nancy got back into the car and started the engine. Instantly he turned and hurried back.

"Hold it!" he said sharply. "I think you'd better come with me and pick out your own birds."

Nancy's heart began to thump. "No, thank you," she said coolly. "You can do it."

"Get out!" the man snarled and swiftly seized Nancy's arm with one hand. He tossed away the whip and reached into the car to turn off the engine.

Suddenly a weird sound came from the rear of the car. *Effie!* It sounded as if she was having an attack of hysterical giggles!

Startled, the man let go of Nancy's arm. "What's that?"

Instantly Nancy released the brake and roared off in reverse. In a shower of gravel she turned, then sped past the house and down the driveway. Fearing pursuit, she kept going for about three miles until she reached the small settlement of West Gramby. Here the young detective turned into the parking area of an old-fashioned timber-built hotel. Quickly she got out and raised the boot lid.

"Okay, Effie, you can come out now."

"Oh, Nancy, I'm sorry if I spoiled everything," said the red-faced girl as she jumped down. "When I heard that man order you to get out of the car, boy, was I scared! I wanted to scream, but all I could do was make a crazy laugh."

Nancy smiled. "Never mind. Your giggles saved the day."

To calm the excited girl, Nancy suggested that they have lunch in the hotel. While waiting for their order, Nancy phoned a neighbour of the Drews and asked her to give Hannah Gruen some lunch, and tell her that the girls would be home in an hour. Then Nancy questioned the hotel manager about the estate she had seen.

"The owner's name is Adolf Tooker," the man said, "and that's really all anybody knows about him. He's lived there a year or so, but he keeps to himself."

"Then he doesn't bother his neighbours?"

The hotel manager scowled. "His plane does, though, flying all hours of the day and night."

"Plane?" Nancy repeated.

"Little tan one, with a flying horse—or something—on the fuselage."

So she had been right! The pigeon had been released from the plane. Nancy was quietly elated, for she felt sure she had found the gang's hideout. But suddenly she remembered: *there were no larkspur!* And she had not seen a gate.

"The kidnappers must have two hideouts," Nancy decided. "The pigeons and the plane are used for messages and transportation between them."

When she and Effie reached home, they went at once to Hannah's room and told her about the pigeon incident. "You're having plenty of excitement, Nancy." The housekeeper sighed. "And here I am cooped up and no use at all!"

Nancy hugged her. "You've helped me so often you deserve a rest! And now I must call Bess and George."

When Bess heard about the invitation to the Cornings', she gave a whoop of delight. "Guess what?" she said. "I just finished talking to Dave. He and Burt are going to that very lake as camp supervisors. It happened suddenly, when three old supervisors dropped out. You'll probably hear from Ned soon. And now tell me more about the Cornings' mystery."

Nancy related it briefly, then phoned George. "I'll be ready whenever you say, Nancy."

Just before dinner that evening Nancy made up a bouquet of flowers from her garden and took it to the neighbour who had given Hannah lunch. On the way back, she noticed a black saloon parked across from the Drew house. Two men were seated in it with their hats pulled low. When they noticed her looking at them, the driver pulled away quickly.

"I wonder who they are," she mused.

Nancy unlocked the front door but could not push it

open. She tried harder. It still stuck. What had happened during her absence?

"Effie!" she called loudly through the crack.

In a few seconds an answer came. "Okay, I'll open it."

There was the sound of something heavy being dragged over the floor. Effie, pale and trembling, opened the door. "I put the living-room couch and a big chair here to keep those men out," she explained.

"What men?" Nancy asked.

"The ones in the car across the street. They—they tried to force their way in here, but I slammed the door in their faces."

"Good for you," said Nancy, both alarmed and amused. "Who were they?"

"I dunno."

"Well, they've gone, Effie, so don't worry."

Nancy herself was greatly concerned and peered from the window several times. The black saloon drove past every few minutes. It was not the one in which Dr Spire had been kidnapped. Just before Mr Drew arrived at dinner-time, the car parked once more in front of a house a few doors away. Nancy mentioned it to her father and asked if the police should be notified.

"Not yet," the lawyer said. "That would only scare them off. I want to find out what they're up to."

"I have an idea," said Nancy, and told him what had happened the night before and during the day. "The keeper passed along the pigeon story, of course, so they know I've seen one of their hideouts. And they probably suspect I have the note that was in the capsule. I think they tried to force their way in here to intimidate me so that I wouldn't call the police—or to take revenge on me if I had."

Mr Drew frowned. "Nancy, you are in great danger. You must get away—and secretly."

"Shall I go to the Cornings'?"

"Good idea."

"But how can I leave secretly, Dad?"

"I have the solution to that problem," he replied. "I'll give you my surprise present now."

·8·

Over the Wall!

"A SURPRISE!" Nancy exclaimed. "How could that keep those men from following me?"

Her father smiled. "Can't you guess?"

Nancy's eyes suddenly sparkled. "Oh, I think I know. Dad, you didn't! It isn't!"

The lawyer laughed. "I did and it is. Your new convertible is at Packlin Motors. I was going to surprise you with it next week, but I'll have Mr French bring the car round as soon as it's dark outside."

"Oh, Dad, how wonderful!" said Nancy, hugging him. "You're the most generous father—" After a pause, she added. "Those men will be on the lookout for me in my old car and I'll be spinning off in a shiny new one!"

Then Nancy became serious. "I must leave here without their seeing me. You could have Mr French bring the new car to the street behind our house. I'll sneak out the back way."

"That's what I thought," said Mr Drew.

While he called Packlin Motors, Nancy hurried upstairs and told Hannah the news, then packed a suitcase for her visit at Sylvan Lake.

After dinner she called the Cornings to say she would be there later in the evening. Helen's grandmother was delighted.

At nine o'clock both the doorbell and the telephone rang at once. As Mr Drew headed for the door Nancy picked up the phone. Bess was calling to say that the cousins would meet her at the lake the next day. "Mother will drive us out. Sorry we can't leave now."

"That's okay."

When Nancy entered the living-room a muscular young man was talking to her father. She recognized him as Henry Durkin, security officer of the building where Mr Drew had his law office.

"Henry's going to help us, Nancy," her father explained as she walked into the room. "I called him while you were packing. Hannah can stay with her sister while you're away. Henry will drive her and Effie there after we've gone."

"Are you coming with me, Dad?" Nancy asked, surprised.

"I certainly am," he said firmly. "I'm taking no chances on your being alone if those men pick up your trail. After Henry takes Hannah and Effie, he will drive my car to the Cornings', pick me up, and take me to the airport. I have a conference in Chicago tomorrow and a reservation on the midnight plane."

Henry Durkin frowned. "Mr Drew, if I were you I'd call the police."

"That'll be your job as soon as Nancy and I leave the house," the lawyer said. "I don't want those men in the car disturbed until then. As long as they're parked on this street, we know where they are. Nancy," he added, "as soon as I reach the airport I'll call Lieutenant Mulligan and tell him about the Tooker estate. Now we must hurry."

While Henry Durkin brought Nancy's case downstairs, she rummaged in the back of her wall cupboard and found an old suitcase. She carried it to the hall below where her father was waiting.

"I have an idea, Dad. Suppose I take my old car out of the garage and park it at the kerb. If Mr Durkin carries this suitcase out and puts it in the luggage compartment, the men in the saloon will surely think I'm leaving in that car."

"Good," said Mr Drew. He switched on the porch light. "We'll make the front of the house as conspicuous as possible."

"And meanwhile," Nancy said with a smile, "we'll slip out the back door." When her car was in place she gave the empty bag to Henry. "Carry that as if it's full and heavy," she said with a chuckle.

As he went out of the door, Nancy stepped out on to the porch and called loudly and clearly, "Thanks a lot, Henry. Put it in the back."

Then she went inside and followed her father to the unlighted kitchen. He was carrying her case and his own. Together, they stepped outdoors and peered into the darkness. They wondered uneasily if there were any unseen watchers. Quietly they felt their way towards the rear of the garden.

Nancy was first to reach the high brick wall. With the help of the tough vines growing over it, she pulled herself to the top.

"Hand up the cases," she whispered.

Mr Drew did so and began to climb the wall. By now Nancy's eyes had become accustomed to the darkness and suddenly she saw a figure detach itself from the shadow of the garage and disappear down the driveway.

"Dad!" she whispered. "Someone was watching!"

"We must move fast then," he said, and dropped the cases to the ground in the adjoining back garden.

Nancy leaped down, landing lightly a moment before her father. Mr Drew grabbed the suitcases and they sped through the neighbour's garden, then down the driveway to the pavement.

At the kerb stood a beautiful convertible, its polished metal reflecting light from the street lamp several houses away. Despite their desperate hurry, Nancy felt a thrill of excitement.

"My new car!" she whispered.

As she reached it, a figure stepped from the shadows and her heart pounded. But a second later she relaxed.

"Here are the keys, Mr Drew," said a deep voice.

"Mr French!" exclaimed the lawyer as he tossed the two cases into the back seat. "Many thanks. Sorry we're in such a rush. Nancy's old car is in front of our house. The keys are inside. Will you pick it up? Nancy can come tomorrow and change licence number plates."

"How beautiful this is!" Nancy said.

She slipped into the driver's seat and turned on the ignition. A deep purr came from the engine. At the same time, the young sleuth glanced into the rear-view mirror and saw headlights sweep round the corner.

"I think they're coming!" she said.

The next instant her car was zipping forward. Nancy turned the corner and several more after that. Then she slid into a driveway and switched off the lights. A moment later the black saloon raced down the street and disappeared in the distance. Its licence plate was dangling so she could not read the number.

As Nancy gave a long sigh, Mr Drew patted her hand. "You certainly used your head that time."

"Thanks, Dad."

She enjoyed the drive to the lake, sensing the power of the new car. Finally she said, "I loved my old car, Dad. It did a good job for me, but this one is just marvellous."

"Glad you're pleased, Nancy. You certainly handle it like a professional."

At the lake the Cornings welcomed the Drews cordially. Over cool drinks, the elderly couple reported that Morgan had not returned, nor had the circle of blue fire been seen that evening.

"We're still worried," their hostess said. "Mr Drew, it's kind of you to lend Nancy to us."

He grinned appreciatively at the implied compliment.

Presently Henry Durkin arrived. Mr Drew quickly said good night to the Cornings, kissed Nancy, cautioned her to be very careful, and left for the airport.

Shortly afterwards, Mrs Corning went with Nancy to the room with twin beds that she had occupied the night before. "Would you like your friends to be in here with you, Nancy?"

"It would be nice."

"Then we'll put in a divan tomorrow morning."

As Nancy unpacked, her thoughts turned to the missing servant. Since the fiery circle had not appeared after he vanished, possibly it had been a signal to Morgan to leave. But why?

"Did he go willingly?" Nancy wondered.

She hoped the next day would bring news of him. But there was no letter in the morning post nor a phone call. Nancy was inclined to think he had not left of his own volition, but had been forced to go.

Mrs Corning looked through her letters. "I have one from Brent's Department Store," she said. "A dress I ordered has come in. I'd like to pick it up."

Nancy quickly volunteered to take her to River Heights. "I must turn in the dealer's number plates on my car and get my own," she said. "Also, I have an errand at the jeweller's."

Helen's grandmother accepted the ride. While she was in Brent's, Nancy went to see if Mr Stone had learned anything about the crest on the gold bracelet.

"I was going to call you," the jeweller said, taking her into his office. "I heard from Abelard de Gotha today." Mr Stone handed Nancy a typewritten letter. "Read this."

"Dear Mr Stone:
The armorial bearings described in your letter are those of the Eldridge family, the crest dating back to Henry IV of England, and the quartering on the shield marking the union of the Eldridge house with the Gerrets in 1604.

At the time of the Louisiana Purchase, the New York branch of the family, consisting of Isaiah Eldridge, his wife Prudence and two children, received a large grant of land in what is now Missouri. I presume their descendants still live in or near St Louis, although I have no records to prove that.
                              Sincerely yours,
                              Abelard de Gotha"

"Does that help you in any way?" Mr Stone asked.

"Indeed it does," Nancy replied. "I'll try to contact any Eldridges in St Louis."

Nancy thanked the jeweller and hurried back to the car. Mrs Corning joined her a few minutes later. After new number plates had been put on the car, Nancy headed for the lake. When they reached the Cornings' home, Nancy went upstairs to leave her bag. As she opened the bedroom door, there was a cry of:

"Hi!" Bess and George rushed across the room and hugged her.

"Oh, Nancy, I'm so glad to see you!" Bess exclaimed.

George, with an affectionate grin, added, "You'd think we'd been separated for two years instead of two weeks!"

Bess was blonde, pretty, and somewhat plump. Her cousin George, a brunette with a short haircut and classic features, gave every indication of being a fine athlete.

"Nancy, I'm just bursting to tell you something," said Bess.

"No!" George protested quickly. "You promised not to breathe a word."

Bess gave a great sigh. "I don't know which is harder: to keep *on* a diet or keep *in* a secret."

Nancy laughed. "How long before you'll tell me?"

"This afternoon," said George, "you'll see for yourself."

"If I don't wither from curiosity first," Nancy said, chuckling.

After lunch Mrs Corning insisted that the girls sit on the beach to exchange news and take a swim. Though Nancy would have preferred working on the St Louis lead, she put her plans aside to please her hostess.

Presently the three visitors appeared in swim suits and beach jackets. Nancy's turquoise suit set off her smooth suntan perfectly, while Bess looked attractive in a butter-yellow costume. George was a trim contrast in sea green.

"How pretty you all are!" their hostess remarked.

She led them down a back stairway, through the small store room next to Morgan's bedroom, and out to the gravel driveway.

"There's the way to the beach," she said, showing them a footpath which led into the woods.

As the three girls started down the path, George asked, "Where did you see the blue fire?"

Nancy pointed across the slope. "Near that end of the house."

"I hope I don't see it at all," muttered Bess.

Before long, they came out on a flat, narrow bit of shoreline a short distance from a jetty. A little girl of five was playing on the edge of it, while two women sunned themselves in beach chairs above the waterfront.

"Marie!" called one of the women. "Be careful!"

Nancy and her friends sat down on the jetty, enjoying the attractive scenery. A circling speedboat roared towards them. The girls realized that it was going to pass very close to the jetty.

Suddenly little Marie jumped up to wave. "Marie Eldridge!" cried the same woman. "Come here!"

Nancy was startled to hear the name Eldridge, but before she could question the child, Marie lost her balance and toppled into the water. The woman screamed and her companion cried out:

"The boat! It'll hit her!"

Nancy had already leaped to the end of the jetty. Without hesitation she dived in after the child, directly in the path of the oncoming boat!

Surprises

As Nancy hit the water the prow of the speedboat loomed overhead. Swiftly she put one arm round the floundering child, and placed the palm of her hand over Marie's face. At the same time Nancy plunged below.

Down, down, down! The little girl squirmed, but Nancy held her firmly. Looking up through the green water, she saw the black keel of the speedboat whiz past in a froth of bubbles.

Instantly Nancy shot to the surface. Barely thirty seconds had elapsed but it seemed like an eternity. Sunlight dazzled her eyes as the strong arms of Bess and George reached down and lifted the child to the jetty.

"Marie!" Nancy panted. "Is she—is she all right?"

"She'll be okay," said George as the child began to cry. "Marie has swallowed some of the lake, that's all."

By this time the two women had rushed over. "Mummy!" cried Marie. Mrs Eldridge scooped up her small daughter and hugged her.

"My baby!" the woman murmured. As she fondled the sobbing child she looked at Nancy. "How can I ever thank you?"

"Please don't," Nancy replied softly. "I'm so glad I was here."

"I want to do something for you," said the grateful woman. "I live in the white cottage at the north end of the lake."

Nancy smiled. "Perhaps you can, Mrs Eldridge. I would like to ask you something."

"Anything—anything," the woman said warmly. "Come and sit down."

She led the girls to the beach chairs and settled down comfortably with Marie on her lap. The little girl had stopped crying and cuddled up drowsily.

The girls introduced themselves, and Nancy said, "Tell me, are you from St Louis?"

The woman looked amazed. "Why, yes, I am. How did you know?"

"I've heard that an Eldridge family settled in Missouri many years ago," said Nancy. "They were originally from New York."

"That could have been my husband's people," the woman said, looking puzzled. "What's the matter?" she added quickly, for there was a strange half-smile on Nancy's face.

"I just can't believe it," Nancy said. "This must be my lucky day."

"What do you mean?" Mrs Eldridge asked.

"A short time ago," Nancy began, "under rather unusual circumstances, I came into possession of an old-fashioned gold bracelet with a coat of arms on it, which I traced. It belongs to the Eldridges."

"A gold bracelet!" the woman exclaimed, her cheeks flushing. "Was there an inscription on it?"

" 'To my darling Mary from Joe'," Nancy replied.

The woman grew pale. "Where is the bracelet now?"

"Safe in my home in River Heights," Nancy replied reassuringly.

"It must belong to my husband's Aunt Mary!" Mrs Eldridge exclaimed. "How did you get it?"

As Nancy told the story, the woman listened intently, then said, "I must call my husband at once." She explained that he was in Richmond, Virginia, searching for his aunt.

"She has been missing since early spring. Our aunt is a very wealthy woman, rather eccentric at times. Several months ago she disappeared from her home, leaving a letter. It said she was on the verge of a nervous breakdown and was going to a hospital for a long rest. Aunt Mary asked us not to try finding her."

"I'm sure she is being held not far from here," Nancy said. "I, too, am trying to find her."

"And Nancy will!" George declared. She and Bess told Mrs Eldridge of their friend's success as an amateur detective.

"Miss Drew has already done me one great service," Mrs Eldridge said with a smile. She shifted the drowsy child to her shoulder and rose. "I can never thank you enough," she said as she started to leave.

Suddenly Mrs Eldridge stopped and looked back. "I forgot to tell you: Aunt Mary has a necklace which matches the bracelet. She wore the set almost constantly from the moment Uncle Joe gave it to her sixty years ago."

"I'm glad you told me," said Nancy. "It may be a helpful clue."

As Mrs Eldridge walked away, Nancy said to her friends "This has been a day of surprises!"

George grinned. "You haven't seen anything yet."

She pointed out to the lake. "Take a look at that!"

A long canoe with three young men was heading towards shore. A shrill whistle split the air as one of them waved.

"Ned!" exclaimed Nancy.

"And Burt and Dave!" Bess added. "That was our secret!"

"The boys called us last night," said George, "and when we told them we were coming here, they decided to paddle over today. Ned wanted to surprise you, Nancy."

"He certainly did and it's a grand surprise," she said with a broad smile.

The canoe grated ashore and the three athletic-looking boys jumped out. All wore dark-blue shorts with white shirts bearing the name *Camp Hiawatha*.

"Here we are!" husky, blond Burt Eddleton exclaimed with a grin. "The world's greatest camp supervisors!" He was George's special friend.

Dave Evans was a rangy boy with fair hair and green eyes.

Ned Nickerson, who was tall and handsome, grinned. "Now with us at the lake you girls can have some excitement!"

George and Bess burst into laughter and even Nancy had to chuckle.

"Nancy's way ahead of you today," said George.

"She usually is," Ned remarked. "Tell us about it. More mystery?"

"Two of them," said George. "And a rescue!"

Walking up the hill to the Cornings' house, Nancy told the boys all that had happened, passing lightly over the speedboat episode.

Ned gave a low whistle. "You're on two dangerous cases, I'm afraid, Nancy."

"Don't forget you can count on us," Burt said as they entered the store room.

Through an open door straight ahead they saw Mrs Corning in the kitchen. She was happy to meet the boys and at once invited the three couples to the yacht club dance across the lake the next night. "My husband and I belong and would love to have you accompany us as our guests."

"I'm sure we can get time off from our camp duties," said Ned. "We'll accept. Thank you."

Presently the boys said goodbye. "We have to get back to our young charges," Dave remarked. "See you tomorrow."

The girls dressed quickly and helped their hostess prepare a dinner of steak, potatoes, green beans, and melon. Afterwards, they insisted upon tidying the kitchen without her assistance.

It was twilight by the time they finished. Nancy excused herself and slipped out of the front door. Carrying a torch, she headed for the spot in the woods where she and Helen had seen the blue fire. After examining the singed leaves, Nancy concentrated on the ground beneath them. There were some bits of scorched brown wrapping paper. Picking them up, she wondered if they might help to explain the fire display. Nancy then hurried to her room and put the pieces away in an envelope.

"Maybe Ned can analyse them," she said to herself. "I'll check with him tomorrow night."

Though the group watched intently, the blue fire did not appear that evening. Before going to bed, Nancy told the Cornings that she was afraid Morgan might have been kidnapped. "Perhaps you ought to inform the police."

Mr Corning shook his head. "Morgan asked us not to," he said. "I'll give him another thirty-six hours."

Next day there was still no sign of the missing man-servant and Nancy asked for permission to search his room.

"Go right ahead," said Mrs Corning.

It was an attractive room with a large window over-looking the lake. Quickly and efficiently Nancy searched, but could find no clue to the man's where-abouts. She observed that the servant could leave the house by going through the store room and out of the side door without anyone seeing him.

"Has he a key to the doors?" Nancy asked Mrs Corning.

"Oh, yes. He usually came and went by the side door so he wouldn't bother us."

"Did he have many friends?" Nancy inquired.

"None that we know of. He was a quiet man and liked to stay by himself."

Nancy looked thoughtful. "The friendship card Morgan received makes me feel that an old acquaint-ance is after him for some reason. There may be a clue to this person in his references. If you still have them, may I examine the letters?"

Mrs Corning was not sure where the papers were. "I'll look for them tomorrow."

After lunch Nancy, Bess, and George drove to the eastern outskirts of River Heights to search for the larkspur house. They were riding along a shady country road. Nancy stopped in front of a small house where a woman was trimming the hedges. Under a nearby tree sat an old lady, shelling peas.

"Excuse me," said Nancy, "we're trying to find a large house in this area that has lots of larkpsur or bluebells round it. Do you know of such a place?"

"Can't say I do," the woman replied.

"What'd she say?" the old lady asked loudly.

"Nothing, Mother. Just some house they're looking for. She's deaf," the woman added to Nancy.

"I heard *that*!" the mother said tartly. "And I heard 'house' and 'bluebells'. They're lookin' for the bluebell house. And I know just where it is!"

· 10 ·

An Unwelcome Gift

"You girls listen to me!" the old lady shouted. "The house you want is over in the next township, just outside of Milford. Go right down Elm Road. You can't miss it."

The woman standing by the hedge shook her head. "I never heard you mention that place before, Mother."

The old lady's black eyes snapped. "I know lots I don't tell," she said.

The girls thanked the two women and drove off, excited at the lead. But as they neared the small town of Milford, Bess looked worried. "I'm beginning to wish I'd stayed home," she said. "I really don't want to meet any kidnappers."

"Now don't be a snob," George teased her cousin.

"It's all right for you to make jokes," Bess replied, "but I can't help it if I'm not brave like you two."

Nancy smiled. "I can remember times on some of my cases when you were way ahead of us."

"I surprised myself," Bess admitted.

Nancy spotted the sign marking Elm Road and turned into the narrow, treeless street.

"There it is!" exclaimed George. In the middle of the street was a garden full of bluebells.

"You mean there it *isn't*," Nancy said gloomily as

she pulled up in front of the white cottage. A faded sign BLUEBELL HOUSE hung by the door. "No mansion, no fence, no gate!"

"But whoever lives here must be interested in blue-bells," said Bess. "Maybe they could help you."

"Good idea," Nancy said, and the three girls went up the path to the door.

Their knock was answered by a thin, young woman wearing an apron. "Hello, girls," she said cheerfully. "I guess you want to see the china. Come on in!"

She walked quickly into a room off the hall, beckoning them to follow. Nancy tried to explain, but stopped short at the door of the room. Shelves and tables were filled with flowered china.

"All hand-painted," the girl said. "The prices are marked."

"Oh, how beautiful!" Bess exclaimed.

While she and George looked round, Nancy explained to the girl why they had called.

"There's no place like that around Milford," she said, "but have you tried the Brookdale section west of River Heights? I've heard there used to be lots of estates out that way."

Nancy thanked her and Bess bought three hand-painted cups and saucers.

"There's one for each of us," she said when they reached the car. "A souvenir of a wild-goose chase."

"It may not have been so hopeless after all," said Nancy, and repeated what the girl had said.

George looked thoughtful. "You told us Dr Spire rode about an hour to get to the house. Can't we narrow the search by going only to places that are about an hour from the road where the old saloon was parked?"

"We could," Nancy said. "But the chances are that the kidnappers drove a little longer than necessary just to confuse the doctor."

George grinned. "Nancy, you never miss a trick!"

A further search continued for some time but without success. Finally Bess reminded Nancy of the dance that night. "We'd better go home," she advised.

Hours later Nancy was seated with Ned on a bench outside the gaily lit porch of the yacht club. Lively music and singing came pulsing out from the wide open doors and windows.

"On a hunch I brought something for the chemistry expert," she said, and handed him the envelope containing the bits of paper she had picked up in the woods.

"I'm no expert," he protested. Ned's eyes filled with mischief. "You don't expect me to look at this, do you, when I could be looking at you?"

Nancy blushed and laughed. She was wearing a simple rose-coloured dance dress and her hair was piled high with a gardenia tucked in it.

"Please be serious," she said. "I have a hunch that the burning circle is made of fireworks which are carried by someone. I remembered that you once helped make a fireworks display at college."

Ned spilled the bits of paper into his palm. He looked at them carefully.

"Your hunch is right, Nancy. These are fragments of quickmatch."

"What's that?" she asked.

"The fuse which is used to light fireworks." He explained that it was a string coated with a mixture of gunpowder and glue and enclosed in a brown paper tube. "Then that's attached to the lances."

"And what are they?" Nancy queried.

"Paper tubes filled with chemical mixtures which burn different colours. The circle you saw is probably a wooden frame with long nails sticking out of it about an inch apart.

"The lances are forced upright on to the points of the nails. Then the quickmatch is nailed across the tops of the lances. It's rough to do," he added, "because the lances are very hard, and many times the nail goes into your finger instead. Well, does that help you?"

"Yes. If I can find out where the fireworks were bought and by whom, I may have a good lead."

The rest of the evening was pure fun and ended with supper on several of the members' yachts moored to the club's jetty. While taking the girls home, the three boys invited them to a swimming gala at the camp the next afternoon and the invitation was accepted.

By one o'clock the girls were ready for bed. Bess and George dropped off to sleep at once, but Nancy lay awake. Suddenly she sat up. There had been a noise downstairs. Quickly she put on her dressing-gown and slippers, then grabbed a torch from her suitcase.

Slipping past her sleeping friends, Nancy went quietly down the back stairs. At the bottom she heard a scraping sound in the store room.

Softly she opened the door and flashed on her light. Caught in the beam was a white-faced, frightened figure on his hands and knees. He looked up. The missing man!

"Morgan!" Nancy exclaimed. "What are you doing? Where have you been?"

"I—I dropped the door key," he stammered.

Nancy spotted the key and picked it up.

"Thank you. I was moving things, feeling around for it. Sorry I disturbed you."

"Morgan, we've been very worried about you," Nancy said. "Won't you please tell me what's wrong?"

"Nothing's wrong!" the man said quickly. "I'll explain in the morning."

He opened the door to his bedroom, stepped inside, and locked the door behind him. Nancy wondered if she should awaken her hostess to report the servant's return, but decided against this.

In the morning, before breakfast, Mrs Corning told the girls Morgan had already talked to her and her husband. She said he had begged forgiveness, and had told a rambling story about going to help a friend.

"I'm afraid it's not true, but we don't want to discharge him." She sighed, then said, "Here, I almost forgot."

She handed Nancy the names of the three persons who had written letters of recommendation for the manservant.

"If you don't mind," said Nancy, "I'll phone these men after breakfast."

An hour later she came down from the first-floor phone and reported to the Cornings in the living-room.

"Well, what did they say?" asked the old gentleman.

"None of these people have ever heard of Morgan."

The couple sat thunderstruck.

"Then the letters were forged?" said Mrs Corning.

"I'm afraid so," Nancy told her.

"*Morgan!*" *Nancy exclaimed.* "*What are you doing?*"

"Impossible!" snorted Mr Corning. "I remember talking to one of those men on the telephone."

"You must have spoken to an impostor," said Nancy.

"But—but why would Morgan do this?" asked Mrs Corning.

"Maybe his past made it impossible for him to get recommendations any other way," said Nancy. "Whoever helped him must feel he has a hold over Morgan. Perhaps that is the 'friend' who has come back into his life."

Mrs Corning said presently, "Now that Morgan has returned, maybe it's all over."

"I doubt it," said Nancy. "He's still frightened."

Her host spoke up. "Morgan's always been honest and a hard worker. I say we give him another chance. Do you agree, Emily?"

His wife nodded. The girls said nothing.

After church and lunch Nancy looked through the advertising pages of the telephone directory for fireworks companies in the area, but found none. As she put the book away, there was a sharp knock on the front door. Nancy went to open it.

No one was there, but on the porch floor was a long, narrow parcel wrapped in brown paper. It was addressed to Morgan. Suspicious, Nancy went to tell the Cornings about it.

"Under the circumstances," she said, "would you like to open this before Morgan does?"

"No," her hostess said firmly. "I feel that what's Morgan's business is his business. Take the parcel to him, Nancy."

With misgivings, she carried the package to the

kitchen and handed it to the manservant. He stared at it and began to tremble. With shaking fingers Morgan removed the string and paper. He seemed lost in thought and unaware that Nancy was still in the room.

When Morgan opened the paper and saw the contents, his face turned white and he suddenly slumped to the floor.

In the package lay a few stalks of blue larkspur!

· 11 ·

A Hazardous Drop

QUICKLY Nancy knelt beside the unconscious servant. "Morgan!" she said urgently, and lightly slapped his cheek. He did not stir. She wet a clean towel at the sink and patted his face.

A few moments later he moaned and muttered, "Last warning—tomorrow night—" Then his eyes opened and with Nancy's help he managed to sit up.

She called the others and while Mrs Corning telephoned the doctor, the girls assisted the man to his room. Mr Corning seated himself beside the bed, but Morgan would speak to no one.

In a short time Dr Bennett, an old friend of the family, arrived. He said that Morgan had suffered a slight heart attack, and ordered him kept quiet.

"That means no questions," Nancy thought. She had been mulling over the significance of the larkspur in the package. She put them in a vase. When the doctor had gone, she led the rest of the group into the living-room and told the whole story.

"Larkspur again!" exclaimed George. "I don't get it!"

"That's one of the clues in your other case, Nancy," Bess said, puzzled.

"Probably the two are connected," the young

89

sleuth replied. She told the Cornings briefly about
Mary Eldridge.

Bess looked surprised. "Why, what could Morgan
have to do with the old lady's kidnappers?"

"But Morgan has always been the soul of honesty,"
protested Mrs Corning.

"Perhaps not *always*," Nancy said gently. "I believe
he may have a prison record—under another name, of
course. It would explain why he needed forged
recommendations. Now Adam Thorne wants repay-
ment."

"Adam Thorne!" exclaimed George. "Why him?"

"Because all the years Morgan worked for the
Cornings, no one bothered him, but after Adam
Thorne broke out of prison, the friendship card
arrived and the blue fire began."

Mr Corning stirred uneasily. "You spoke of repay-
ment. What did you mean?"

"I think Thorne and his gang want to rob this house.
Remember, the friendship card had no written message
on it, but the picture showed a cottage with the door
open."

"I see," said Bess. "That was the message—open the
door."

Mrs Corning was pale. "Do you know when it is to
be?"

"Tomorrow night, I think," replied Nancy. "I believe the larkspur was a signal to Morgan—his last
chance to co-operate. Probably the gang showed the
blue fire and abducted Morgan to intimidate
him."

Mr Corning's face flushed with anger. "Scoundrels!
We'll get the police at once!"

"Wait!" said Nancy. "This is only a theory. If we hold off until tomorrow night, we'll see if we're right. Maybe we can catch the thieves red-handed and solve both cases at once."

"But, in the meantime," George said worriedly, "Morgan may have told the gang where you are."

Nancy nodded. "Yes, I've thought of that."

When Mr Drew telephoned her a few minutes later he had disquieting news. The lawyer had reported to the police before flying to Chicago and asked them to keep in touch with him.

"Lieutenant Mulligan informed me they had not been able to trace the kidnap car. Also, when they arrived at the Tooker estate it was deserted. The gang had taken the pigeons."

"I understand, Dad. My visit forced them to run. They'll be more eager than ever to get me out of the picture."

An hour later Nancy, Ned and their friends were watching the swimming races at Camp Hiawatha. In the fun and excitement she found it hard to remember the threat of danger. Cheers and singing filled the air as the young campers put all their high-spirited enthusiasm into the contests.

When the swimming gala was over, she said, "It was great, Ned! Your little boys did so well!"

"Thanks," he said proudly. "Now we can go swimming. Burt, Dave and I have free time."

The boys showed their guests where to change into the costumes they had brought, then met them at the water's edge. Tons of ocean sand had been transported overland to make a beach for the camp. A float was moored a few rods from shore with a tower and spring-board for diving.

The three couples swam out to the float on which a dozen young people were frolicking. Ned introduced everyone.

"Oh, you're the detective," said one boy, playfully shielding his face with one arm.

Nancy laughed. "I promise not to delve into any of your secrets."

George called, "But watch out, my friend!"

Suddenly Ned asked, "How about a little diving?"

One by one the group went off the high board. Presently it became an impromptu gala.

"Nancy, show them that new one you just learned," Bess urged.

"I'll try." She smiled. "But I may flop."

As everyone watched, Nancy balanced upside down on the edge of the board for a breathtaking moment, then thrust herself off. Her body revolved in the air and straightened out so that her pointed toes cleaved the water like a knife. Down she plunged into the green waters of the lake, then bobbed to the surface to hear the cheers of the spectators.

"Wonderful! Perfect!"

Panting, Nancy climbed back on to the float. As she threw herself down in the sun to rest, Ned came over. "That was a beauty, Nancy."

"Just luck," she insisted.

Later, when Nancy swam ashore with her friends, she was met by Mr Dennis, the camp director. "Great diving exhibition, young lady! How would you like a job as a supervisor?"

"Thank you," Nancy said, smiling, "but I already have a job."

"Well, you and your friends stay to dinner," the man said cordially, "and the evening camp."

As he walked away, a bugle sounded. "We fellows must go now," said Dave, "but we'll take you home tonight after taps."

Nancy called Mrs Corning to tell her they would not be home for dinner, then the girls went to the guest dining-hall.

During the meal two small boys appeared at their table with their arms full of anoraks.

"Ned, Dave and Burt sent you their coats," piped the tallest.

"'Cause you didn't bring yours," said the other. They put the jackets on an empty chair and fled as the girls thanked them.

It grew chilly after dinner and the trio were glad to put on the anoraks and pull up the hoods.

George flapped her dangling sleeves. "What a great fit this is!"

"Now you can't tell us apart," said Bess.

When it was dark, a long line of singing boys filed up a hill behind the camp. The girls followed their bobbing torches. At the top, the three stopped to look round. The wooded hill sloped steeply to a rocky cliff. Fifteen feet below it was a huge bonfire.

The girls watched the campers wind slowly down the path, and saw that the first ones were already seated on another slope to the far side of the fire.

"Come on," said Nancy, "but watch your step."

She went first, with George beside her and Bess on the right. As they picked their way downwards

they   could   hear   the   giant   blaze   crackling.
Smoke   billowed   up   and   Bess   paused,   coughing.
Suddenly a powerful push from behind knocked Bess off
her feet.

Screaming, she began to roll down the hill towards
the cliff and the leaping flames!

The Crystal Garden

"Bess!" George exclaimed, horror-stricken. "She'll roll into the fire!"

Nancy scrambled down the hill, George beside her. With a flying leap she threw herself on Bess and stopped her from rolling. At the same time, George skidded down and caught one of her cousin's flailing arms. The girls lay gasping, only a few feet from the cliff and the bonfire below.

"Bess," Nancy whispered, "are you hurt?"

"N-no," Bess said shakily. "Oh, Nancy, somebody pushed me! If you and George hadn't . . ."

Nancy looked grim. "I think someone mistook you for me. And I don't want him to know he was wrong."

As she spoke, three supervisors hurried down the hill towards them, calling, "What happened? Anybody hurt?"

Nancy squeezed George's hand. "We'll pretend *I* am," she whispered, then closed her eyes.

"Yes," George called out. "Nancy Drew! Please hurry. I'm afraid it's bad."

"She's unconscious!" quavered Bess.

Moments later, a husky young man was carrying Nancy up the hill while one of his companions ran ahead for the camp doctor.

"And get Ned Nickerson," George called.

Forty minutes later Ned tenderly placed Nancy on the Cornings' living-room couch as Helen's grandmother closed the curtains.

"Okay," said Ned. "All clear." Only then did Nancy open her eyes and sit up.

"You're some actress, young lady," said Mr Corning.

Nancy smiled. "I didn't have to do anything. Ned and Bess and George were the real actors."

Bess giggled. "And the camp director and the doctor were good actors, too. Mr Dennis insisted that we use his station wagon to bring Nancy home."

"I just hope we fooled the one who pushed Bess," said Nancy.

"Morgan must have told the gang you were here," said George, "and one of them trailed us to the camp, waiting for the opportune moment to strike."

Ned frowned. "Someone probably is still watching this house. To make our act look really good, we ought to call the doctor for Nancy."

Mrs Corning hurried off to put in the call. Soon she returned, and she reported that Dr Bennett would be glad to co-operate.

Nancy chuckled. "We'll make the gang think I'm out of action. Then they'll pay no more attention to me and I can work freely."

George spoke up. "I have a suggestion. If someone *is* watching this house, he'll probably plan to speak to Morgan. How about Bess and me letting ourselves out the back door and watching?"

"I'll do it," Ned offered.

"No," Mr Corning said. "That would look too suspicious. I often take a little stroll outside before going to bed. In a few minutes one of you can follow me. While I'm out there no gangster will come to talk to Morgan through the window."

He waved aside objections and left the room.

His wife said worriedly, "Oh, I hope everything will be all right. But suppose they strike here tomorrow night?"

"I have a plan," Nancy replied, "if Ned, Burt and Dave will help us."

"Sure we will," said Ned. "It's not our night off, but I know three fellows who'll switch with us."

"The thieves probably will go for the safe," said Bess.

Mrs Corning shook her head. "I'm afraid they're after something very special. Come," she added, seeing the questioning expressions of her guests, "I'll show you."

As their hostess led the way down the hall, Nancy quietly outlined her plan to Ned. "I'll tell the others later."

Across the hall from the kitchen, Mrs Corning opened a door and flicked a wall switch. The room remained dark, but at the far side a tall glass cabinet lit up.

Bess gasped. "Oh ,how beautiful!" She and the others stared, amazed. Inside was a sparkling array of crystal flowers and butterfles set on shelves lined with black velvet.

"My husband gave me one on each of our wedding anniversaries," Mrs Corning explained as she led them to the case. "They are made in France. Each flower contains at least one valuable jewel."

Nancy noted a ruby glowing in the heart of a rose and a topaz set in a daffodil. The butterflies had diamonds for eyes.

"How could the thieves have heard about these?" George asked.

"My crystal garden was written up in a magazine some time ago," Mrs Corning replied.

Nancy examined the case carefully. "Do you have a key for this?"

Mrs Corning showed her a tiny gold one which she wore on a chain round her neck.

Just then the doctor arrived. He listened to the story of what had happened, then went to check on Morgan, who was much better.

When leaving, Dr Bennett called back through the open door for the benefit of any outside listener. "Miss Drew must remain in bed for at least forty-eight hours."

Ned followed the doctor and went to join Mr Corning. Inside the house Nancy said to her friends, "Dr Bennett played his part well." Then she told them her plans for the next day.

Half an hour later Mr Corning and Ned reported no prowler near Morgan's window. Ned said good night and returned to Camp Hiawatha.

Shortly before dawn, Nancy ate a light breakfast, then slipped into the garage and hid behind the front seat of her car. At eight o'clock the other girls came out with a picnic bag. George took the wheel and they drove off.

When she was sure they were not being followed, George pulled to the side of the road and Nancy took the driver's seat.

"Now for the larkspur house!" she said happily.

"But where is it?" Bess asked.

Nancy said that since the Tooker estate lay south-east of River Heights and the pigeon and aeroplane both flew over it, the other headquarters were probably to the north-west.

"I'll try that, anyway."

After a while the road narrowed and there were no houses to be seen. The countryside was generously sprinkled with patches of woodland and open fields.

The girls explored every side road. Most of these were merely forest trails which ended within a short distance. At other times the searchers found a cabin and inquired if there was a hospital in the neighbourhood. The answer was always No, and again Nancy would go on.

Stopping only to eat a picnic lunch, the girls travelled all day, exploring the network of winding lanes. All three were tired, their nerves tense with the strain of being constantly on the alert.

Finally Nancy glanced at the clock on the dashboard. "Ten minutes past five," she said. "We'd better go back."

Nancy turned the car and began retracing the route to the main road. Suddenly she pressed down on the brake and they stopped short.

"Sorry," Nancy said, "but we just passed a sign that I didn't see when we drove along here before."

She backed a dozen feet and halted opposite a narrow dirt road. Nailed to a tree was a crude, hand-lettered board: L. S. LANE.

"What about it?" Bess asked. "That probably leads

to the cabin of a forest worker whose name is L. S. Lane."

"And on the other hand," said Nancy, "it could mean Larkspur Lane, and be a guide for the crooks."

"It's worth investigating," George remarked.

Nancy turned into the narrow roadway, wide enough for only one car. But here and there the side bank had been cut to allow a vehicle to park while another passed it.

Proceeding cautiously over ruts and bumps, Nancy presently pulled into one of the wider places on the right. She stopped the car close to the trees.

"This might be the right place, so we had better go on foot," Nancy said.

She led the way amongst the trees, keeping parallel with the road. The girls trudged through the underbrush for nearly a quarter of a mile but saw nothing unusual. The only sounds were the crackle of twigs breaking underfoot.

Suddenly Nancy halted. "Look!" she exclaimed softly. "Larkspur!"

A dozen yards ahead the trees ended. Just beyond was a high wire-mesh fence. Inside it grew a long border of exquisite tall larkspur.

To the girls' left a large gate across the lane shut off the entrance to the grounds. Next to it stood a small brown lodge.

"This is it!" Nancy whispered gleefully, and her friends nodded.

Beyond the gate the ground sloped gently. A gravel roadway led to the top of the rise, where a large white colonial dwelling with a broad veranda was visible amongst some trees.

"It's a beautiful place," Bess said in a low voice. "I can't believe crooks live here."

"We'll soon find out," said Nancy.

Cautiously the three girls moved forward, taking advantage of every tree trunk and bush for concealment. There was no sign of habitation. If anyone was inside the gate-house, he was not to be seen at the moment. Then, for an instant, a flash of white appeared in the distance near the brow of the hill.

"Did you see that?" George whispered tensely. "I'm sure it was a nurse's uniform."

"Listen! Do you hear a plane?" Nancy asked.

The girls peered upwards. Several minutes passed before the aircraft became visible. Then it shot overhead, flying low.

"It's the same type of plane that wounded the bird!" Nancy said quickly. "And it's like the one the hotel manager said flew into the Tooker estate. . . . Yes, there is that flying horse on the fuselage. This *is* the place!"

"Sure enough," said George. "Down he goes. The landing field must be behind the house."

The plane dipped low, lost altitude rapidly, and vanished behind the roof of the mansion.

"Now what do we do?" Bess asked.

"There is only one thing left," Nancy answered. "Somehow we must get inside!"

· 13 ·

Baiting a Thief

GEORGE frowned. "You're not going to try getting into this place now, are you?"

"No," said Nancy. "I'd probably end up a prisoner." She thought of the old lady who was being held against her will.

"It's getting late," Bess put in. "We'd better go back to the Cornings'."

"Yes," Nancy agreed reluctantly. "We have our work cut out for us tonight."

"Why don't you just tell the police where the hospital is?" Bess asked nervously. "Let them rescue Mrs Eldridge."

Nancy shook her head. "We must get her to safety before the police raid starts. Otherwise, the gang might harm the poor woman to keep her from talking. We'll have to find out exactly where they're keeping her prisoner in the mansion."

"It's such a big house," Bess said gloomily, "Mrs Eldridge might be hard to find."

"It's also possible she's not here any more," George said. "The gang knows the police are after them and they may have moved her."

When they reached the car, Nancy hid in the back again and George drove. At the Cornings' Bess was asked to go in first and make sure Morgan was in his room.

"No use having him learn my secret," Nancy remarked. "Thorne might get it out of him before I'm ready to have it known." Learning the coast was clear, she scooted up to her room.

Mrs Corning had dinner ready, so a tray was prepared for Nancy. The others ate in the dining-room, then went upstairs.

"Now tell us your plan for capturing the thieves if they come," Mr Corning urged.

Nancy said, "Here it is. First, remember that the crystal-garden room has two doors—one to the hall, the other to the TV room. Each has a key that's now on the inside."

Her host nodded.

Nancy went on, "The boys will be outside. Dave will be watching in the shrubs bordering the flagstone area; Burt, at the top of the patch which leads to the jetty; and Ned, on the garage roof.

"As soon as the thief—or thieves—enters the house, Ned will signal with a walkie-talkie to Mr Dennis at the camp and he will call the police. Meanwhile, Burt and Dave will be ready to tackle anybody watching on the outside. We girls will lock any intruders in the crystal room."

"But suppose they see you?" Mrs Corning asked.

"They won't," said Nancy. "Bess and George will hide across the hall in the kitchen. I'll be in the TV room. As soon as the thieves enter, I'll lock the adjoining door. At the same time, the girls will slip across the hall and quietly lock that door."

Mr Corning asked what he and his wife should do.

"I suggest you go to your room as usual," Nancy replied. "That will cause less suspicion."

At nine o'clock the lights were put out on the ground floor, the couple retired, and the girls took their posts. Nancy held the door to the crystal room open a crack, put the key on the outside of the lock, and watched. It seemed that she stood for ages before the other door opened.

There was a *click* and the light went on in the glass cabinet. Nancy gripped the key, ready to shut the door. Suddenly she froze. Only one figure approached the cabinet.

Morgan! A thief!

He was carrying a large suitcase, which he put on the floor. Nancy watched, hardly daring to breathe, as he took a small tool from his pocket and picked at the cabinet lock.

A few minutes later he pulled the glass door open. Then he swung back the lid of the suitcase. Nancy saw that it was divided into compartments and heavily padded with velvet.

"A special carrying case," she thought.

As the man's trembling hands reached towards a fragile crystal flower, he suddenly drew back.

"No!" he whispered hoarsely. "I can't do it!" He buried his face in his hands with a sob.

Nancy hurried to his side. "Morgan!" she said softly. The man whirled and gave a gasp.

"Don't be afraid," she said quickly. "Let me help you." He groaned and sank into a chair beside the cabinet. "How can you know—all this?"

"I know part of it," she replied. "Where is the gang? You were to let them in, weren't you?"

The thief pulled the glass door open

The man stared at her, amazed.

"Yes, but Thorne changed his mind. He said I should steal the crystal flowers and deliver them in this special case he gave me. I used to be pretty good at lock picking," he added, flushing miserably.

"That's how Thorne got his hold over you, isn't it?" asked Nancy. "He knew you'd been in prison and he helped forge your references."

The servant nodded. "I wanted to go straight and I did. I wouldn't hurt the Cornings for anything. But Thorne—he wouldn't leave me alone. Kidnapped me. Held me on a big estate. Said the larkspur would be the signal for this theft. I'd have to deliver—or else."

"There's a Mrs Eldridge being held prisoner there, too," said Nancy. "Did you see her?"

"Eldridge?" Morgan repeated. "I think I heard the name, but—" Suddenly he broke off. "Listen! There they are!"

The sound of a low whistle came from outside. Nancy flew to the switch and snapped off the light in the crystal case.

"I'll close it," Morgan whispered. The door clicked shut. "What—what shall I do?" he stammered.

"Listen," Nancy said quickly. "We'll have to get them in here. I have a trap set, but you must go out and tell the men you need help—that you're too weak to carry all the loot."

"They'd never believe me. I'm no good at acting."

"There must be some way to get them in here," Nancy declared. "Suppose you just don't go out."

Morgan gave a bitter laugh. "They'll go away. And in a day or so I'll disappear and never come back. Thorne will see to that. He won't stand for any double-cross."

Nancy had an idea. "Come with me!" She led the way into the hall.

At once the kitchen door opened. "What's up? George whispered. "Where's the gang?"

Nancy drew Morgan into the dark kitchen and explained to the girls. "But I've thought of a way to lure the gang into the house," she said. "If they find out I wasn't injured and am still working on this case, they'll come after me."

Bess caught her breath. "You don't mean you'd let them know?"

"Morgan will tell them," said Nancy. "Bess, you stay here and George will take over the door of the TV room. I'll go out with Morgan. If they don't believe him, I'll let them see me and then run in here. That should do it."

"No!" said the servant. "I won't let you, Miss Drew. Adam Thorne is dangerous. He will stop at nothing. It's too big a risk for you."

"I'm not afraid," said Nancy.

Suddenly Morgan darted away and ran through the store room. Nancy dashed after him, calling:

"Morgan! Come back!"

"No!" he called. "I'm telling Thorne, I won't do it. I don't care what happens to me!"

Nancy raced outside and grasped the panting man. "Thorne," he called, "I won't do it!"

"Morgan!" Nancy cried frantically. "Come inside!"

An instant later powerful hands gripped Nancy's shoulders and swung her away from Morgan. She reeled and fell backwards in the darkness. Nancy struck the gravel driveway hard and blacked out.

· 14 ·

The Matching Necklace

As NANCY's eyes fluttered open, she saw Bess's anxious face bending over her.

"Oh, thank goodness!" Bess exclaimed. "She's coming to."

George and Mrs Corning stood at the other side of the bed. "You're in your room, dear," said Mrs Corning. "How do you feel?"

Nancy sat up, frowning. "My head aches, but otherwise I'm all right. What happened?"

"The boys found you on the driveway," said George. "The gang got away." She explained that the boys had seen three men scuffling and finally one had been carried off through the woods. By the time the boys had rescued Nancy, their search for the others was hopeless.

"They took Morgan, then?" Nancy asked. "I was afraid of that." She told how she had been pulled away from him.

"Lucky the thug didn't know it was you," said George, "or you'd have been kidnapped, too."

"The boys are waiting in the kitchen," Bess put in. "I'll go down and tell them you're awake."

"Let's all go," said Nancy. "I think I could do with

a glass of milk and something to eat, if you don't mind, Mrs Corning."

The woman's face broke into a smile and she said, "That's the best news I've heard yet. Now I know you're feeling better."

As Bess and George served cake and glasses of milk, Nancy and the boys exchanged stories.

Dave raised his glass of milk. "Here's to General Drew!"

The others echoed the toast enthusiastically.

"I guess I wasn't such a good general tonight," said Nancy. "I certainly lost the battle."

"The campaign's not over," Burt told her cheerfully.

Ned smiled and patted Nancy's shoulder. "Better luck tomorrow."

Mrs Corning cleared her throat. "Nancy, dear, I'm afraid we had better—"

"Oh please, Mrs Corning! I know what you're going to say—that I'd better give up the case. But please give me another day to find out exactly what's going on at Larkspur Lane."

Ned and the others backed up Nancy's plea.

Mrs Corning hesitated. "Well, all right, but we can't wait longer than tomorrow night."

"I'll do my best to solve the mystery by then," Nancy said quietly. To herself she added, "And no mistakes, Nancy Drew!"

Next morning the girls again started out early. As before, Nancy hid in the back of the car and George drove. The sky was overcast, but Nancy's spirits were light. Some miles from the lake she took the wheel, her eyes shining with excitement.

"I don't see how you can be so cheerful," Bess grumbled. "You were knocked out last night and now you're going into more danger."

Nancy smiled. "I never felt better."

Familiar with the way now, she was able to make good time to the spot where the sign "L. S. LANE" marked the battle line.

"We're in enemy territory now," she remarked. "From now on, caution must be *our* password."

Nancy drove past the half-concealed driveway and into the woods, where she parked the car behind a tangle of creeper and bitter-sweet.

"No one will notice it here," Nancy said. "Now let's start through the woods ahead and see how close we can come to the house without using the road."

Cautiously the girls worked their way round bramble and bush until the roof of the gate-house came into view. They crept closer and looks of dismay came over their faces.

Tilted back in a chair against the gate-post was a man whom Nancy assumed was the gate-keeper. At his feet lay a brindled Great Dane, his tongue lolling and his eyes alert

Nancy gasped. "That's the beast that tackled me at the flower show!" she whispered. "Let's hope he doesn't scent us."

George said, "There's certainly no chance of getting in here. Let's go on!"

Nancy led the way to the right, still well within the trees, always keeping the tall fence with its border of larkspur in view. After trudging through the woods for a quarter of a mile the girls found that the fence turned to the left. It continued in a straight line up the shallow slope along the flower-lined enclosure.

"Ugh, it's rough travelling," Bess shuddered. "I'm afraid of snakes."

"Want to wait here?" George asked.

"I certainly do not," Bess retorted. "I'd be scared to death by myself."

Smothering her fears, Bess followed Nancy and George through the tangled undergrowth. At one point they came to a place where a clump of trees partially concealed the house. Nancy called a halt for a rest and consultation. She and George sat down.

"This wouldn't be a good spot to climb the fence," George observed, leaning back on her elbows. "You'd rip your skirt on that barbed wire."

Nancy looked at her in surprise. "You'd do more than that! Don't you see?" she asked, pointing to the top of the enclosure.

"I see a fence and two strands of barbed wire stretched along the top," George replied.

"Notice how the wire is fastened to the supporting posts."

"It's attached to little porcelain knobs. What does that have to do with it?"

"Those knobs are insulators, which means the wire is charged with electricity. If you touch it, you will probably set off an alarm and get a bad shock besides. You could be killed."

George gave a low whistle.

"It's a regular fort," said Bess. "Yet how peaceful it all looks!"

Through the wire fence the girls could see other flower gardens, occasional clumps of trees, and a view of the rear of the gate-house. It was truly a lovely spot, except for the sinister strands of charged wire.

"Rested?" Nancy asked. "Let's go!"

Since they were now approaching the house, the girls moved even more warily. Bess stepped gingerly, afraid of putting her foot down on a snake.

"It would just be like those people to let a couple of thousand rattlesnakes and copperheads loose round here," Bess muttered. "Ugh," the worried girl cried suddenly, and jumped sideways, clutching at her cousin. Caught off balance, George stumbled and fell, giving a muffled yelp.

"What happened?" Nancy whispered excitedly, turning back to them.

"I stepped into a hole, and I—I think my ankle is sprained," George said, her face white.

Nancy's heart sank. If any of them should become helplessly injured, detection would certainly follow.

"Oh, it's all my fault," whispered Bess. "I'm sorry, George. I thought I stepped on something alive." Her eyes filled with tears.

George managed a grin. "Take it easy. I'm not dying."

Nancy knelt beside George, and with deft fingers felt the injured ankle, wishing that Dr Spire was with them now!

"I'm sure it's not broken," she said softly.

George rubbed her ankle gingerly. "Go on, you two. I'll wait for you here."

"Sure you're all right?" Nancy asked.

"Yes. Go on, please."

Nancy and Bess resumed their cautious advance to the top of the rise. There they had a full view of all the grounds.

Surrounding the house was a wide lawn with gravel walks and flower beds. In the rear was a huge meadow which Nancy surmised was used as a landing field for the aeroplane. The craft was not in sight.

Just below the brow of the hill, and connected with the house by a long arbour, was a group of outbuildings —a carriage house evidently converted into a garage, a good-sized barn, and a chicken yard.

"Listen," Nancy said, raising a finger. "I heard cooing."

"Pigeons!" Bess exclaimed.

The girls moved ahead until they were behind the carriage house, where they saw a small wooden building which had no window on their side. Here they rested in the shade until aroused by soft cooing and the sound of a man's voice.

"You're getting better!" the listeners heard through the wooden walls. "I guess you'll be able to work again if we keep you warm with this electric light. That'll cure you!"

There was more cooing. Then the unseen man said, "You ought to be ashamed taking a couple of days getting to the boss's place and arriving there lame at that! And why did you go to Drews', you half-witted barnyard goose?" A door closed and all was silent.

"Did you hear what that man said?" Bess asked with a catch in her voice. "He mentioned your name!"

"Yes. That was the man I met at Tooker's estate. I recognized his voice," Nancy said as she walked ahead.

Once past the outbuildings, the girls saw a moss-covered sundial surrounded by a grassy court. In it stood a number of wheel-chairs, each occupied by an old lady.

A large woman in a nurse's uniform had her back to the girls. She seemed to be administering to one of the elderly women.

"It looks like a real nursing home," Bess whispered. "Perhaps our suspicions are all wrong."

Nancy put a finger to her lips. The nurse turned and walked towards the fence.

"That's the woman who stole my handbag!" Nancy exclaimed softly.

"The one who took the bracelet?"

"Yes. She's in league with Thorne and Tooker, I feel sure."

"One of those old ladies may be Mrs Eldridge," Bess said, "but how can we find out?"

"I don't know yet, but I'll think of something," Nancy replied. "Meanwhile, we'd better go back and help George to the car. If she were discovered, she'd have no way to escape."

The girls hurried back to their companion and the three made their way down the hill. George limped along as quickly as she could, but progress was slow. When they had nearly reached the gate-house, the girls paused and George sat down on a stump to rest.

Suddenly Nancy seized Bess's arm and pointed amongst the trees. On the other side of the wire barrier was an old woman, dozing in a wheel-chair.

"Stay here," Nancy whispered. "I'm going closer."

Bess clung to her friend's arm. "No! Suppose they catch you!"

"I must talk to that old lady," said Nancy. "She may be able to help us."

Cautiously, Nancy crept towards the fence. When she was a few feet away, still screened by bushes, she stifled a gasp. The elderly lady wore a necklace which looked like the gold bracelet Dr Spire had given Nancy as a clue.

"The missing Mrs Eldridge!" Nancy murmured excitedly.

· 15 ·

Daring Plans

"Do I dare go closer?" Nancy wondered, watching the woman behind the fence.

Just then the old lady awakened and for a moment sat up straight in her wheel-chair.

"Oh dear!" she said. "I thought—I guess I dreamed I was—"

Her wrinkled chin twitched and she leaned back with closed eyes. Tears crept from under her lids.

Nancy was about to speak when she spotted a white figure hurrying down the hill. The nurse!

"So there you are!" she said harshly, drawing near the old woman. "I thought so! Trying to hide again!"

A sob escaped the elderly patient.

"Come now, stop that crying!" the nurse commanded. "If you act like a baby, you will have to be treated like one."

The old lady lifted a fragile, blue-veined hand in protest, but let it drop limply.

"Very well, Mistress Contrary, you may sit there for half an hour," the nurse snapped. "Lucky for you I'm tender-hearted, or I'd take some of your privileges away. See that you're here when I come back." She strode up the hill.

As the patient closed her eyes wearily, Nancy edged closer. "Mrs Eldridge! Mrs Eldridge!"

The old lady's eyes snapped open and she looked wildly about her.

"Here I am on the other side of the fence, behind the trees," Nancy said. "Listen closely, I will bring you help."

"How do you know my name? Who are you?" Mrs Eldridge whispered.

Nancy moved closer. Quickly she told the woman who she was, then explained how she had identified her.

Mrs Eldridge clasped her thin hands. "Bless you, child," she said, "but you can do nothing."

"Yes, we can," said Nancy, speaking with confidence. "But you must be brave and ready to follow instructions."

Bess and George had moved up to Nancy, who quickly introduced them.

"We'll all help you, Mrs Eldridge," Bess said.

"You can trust Nancy." George spoke cheerfully, despite the pain in her ankle.

The old woman smiled. "What brave young girls!" Her chin lifted and a glint came into her eyes. "All right. I'll do my part."

Nancy glanced uneasily up the hill. "We'd better stay out of sight while we're talking."

The girls stepped back and crouched down behind the bushes. "Tell us where your room is," Bess urged. "We'll get you out, then call the police and they can rush the place."

"No, no!" exclaimed Mrs Eldridge. "We've all been warned that if strangers try to enter the grounds, we'll be locked in the cellar."

"The police would find you," George said.

"Yes, but some of the women here are heart cases. Many of them could not stand the shock. Hush! Dr Bell is coming!"

"Bell!" thought Nancy, recalling the bluebell code message.

Quickly the girls slipped back amongst the trees and watched. Striding down the slope was a tall, distinguished-looking man in a black suit. He had smooth grey hair and a pointed beard.

He spoke in honeyed tones to the old woman. "Well, well, what has upset our dear patient?" he asked, bending over and gallantly kissing her hand. "I'm afraid you fret too much. However, I must tell Miss Tyson to be less strict with our favourite guest. Shall I call Luther and have him wheel you through the gardens?"

"No, just leave me alone," Mrs Eldridge sighed.

"Yes, that is what you need—rest and quiet," Dr Bell agreed. "But," he went on, "we must talk business. Shall we get that little matter of signing the transfer papers over now?"

"Your proposition is nothing short of robbery, and I will not consent," Mrs Eldridge replied, sitting bolt upright.

"Dear me, how harsh you are," Dr Bell said soothingly. "When you came here, you had every confidence in me. You entered this place of your own accord. You didn't give your relatives any idea where you were going. Didn't you agree to that as part of your treatment?"

"Fool that I was, yes!" snapped Mrs Eldridge. "But you haven't kept your part of the bargain to me or to any of the other ladies. You promised a special secret treatment—so secret you don't want anybody to know about it. That's why you have this isolated place."

"The special treatment to restore youthful vigour isn't ready yet," Dr Bell replied. "But it will be very expensive. I must have the extra money now."

"Oh!" Nancy thought. "He's undoubtedly a fraud!"

"I demand that you let me go," Mrs Eldridge cried out.

"We can't do that," Dr Bell said. "It would discredit our hospital to have a person leave in a poor state of health. Besides, I have your signed declaration that you are a patient here of your own accord, and that you agree to remain as long as I think necessary. Naturally, I forbid you to go."

Mrs Eldridge glanced quickly towards the woods where the girls were concealed. In a loud, clear voice, she said, "You wish me to sign over to you many thousands of dollars, in addition to the three thousand I have already paid you".

"And why not?" Dr Bell retorted irritably. "There are other patients whom I have charged more."

"Well, I suppose that once the papers are signed, I won't live very long," the old lady said meaningfully.

"You will feel like a girl again," Dr Bell replied.

"I'd rather live without youthful vigour and be out of here!" Mrs Eldridge said, closing her eyes. "I won't sign a thing. If you should kill me, you won't get a cent. That's all. I wish you would go. I am very tired."

Nancy saw the doctor's face turn red. His beard seemed to bristle, and his eyes blazed with rage.

"You'll sing a different tune if you don't do as I say," he fumed. "I've wasted enough time on you. I will give you until nine o'clock tonight to come to your senses!"

"Oh, you are a brute," Mrs Eldridge cried. "If only some good angel would come to my little room in that hot south corner on the third floor and rescue me!"

"Say, what are you talking about?" Dr Bell asked, looking about him suspiciously. "You don't think any angels are listening to your careful directions, do you?"

The girls could not help grinning.

Dr Bell turned and shouted, "Luther!" A man in a white uniform came out of the gate-house. "Take Mrs Eldridge to the porch!" the doctor snapped. "Any word about the new patient?"

"A message arrived by Bird X that she will be here at nine," the attendant said with a wink as he wheeled Mrs Eldridge away.

Swiftly, the girls made their way towards the car. Nancy took the wheel and headed for the main road. As they drove along, the sun broke through the overcast sky.

"We're going to Glenville," she said. "It's about five miles from here. George can see a doctor there."

"What about Mrs Eldridge?" Bess asked.

"No plan yet," Nancy said tersely, "but I'm thinking."

Her companions asked no more questions. When they reached the small town, Bess went with George, while Nancy telephoned Ned from a telephone kiosk. She told him what had happened and alerted him to his part in the plan she had devised.

"You can count on me," he said.

An hour later the girls met in a coffee bar for a late lunch. "My ankle isn't sprained," George reported. "The doctor put on a bandage and it feels better."

"Good," said Nancy. "Are you ready for danger?" she asked soberly.

"Of course we are," George answered steadily.

"Anything to get those poor old ladies free and home to their families," Bess added.

"Then right after we eat, I'm going shopping, while you two hire a black saloon. You may have to drive to another town for it, so let's meet here about five. Then I'll tell you the plan."

At the appointed time Nancy came hurrying down the street, her arms filled with packages. Bess and George were waiting in Nancy's convertible behind which stood a black saloon parked at the kerb.

"What did you buy?" George asked in amazement.

Nancy grinned. "Black shoes, a black hat with a heavy veil, grey gloves, and a long black coat much too big for me!"

George's eyes grew wide. "Nancy! You're going to dress up like an old lady!"

"That's right. I'll be that new patient who is supposed to arrive at nine o'clock. Only I'll be there early."

Bess stared at the parcels Nancy was holding. "What's in that fifth bag?"

"A nurse's uniform and a pair of horn-rimmed glasses for you," said Nancy.

Bess gasped. "Me?"

"Yes. You'll have to drive the car into the hospital grounds," Nancy replied.

"Oh, my goodness," was all Bess could say.

Immediately George offered to go instead, but Nancy said No. "You never can tell what will happen." she said. "With that bad ankle, you wouldn't be able to run if it should be necessary."

Nancy put the packages in the convertible's boot and suggested that they eat tea. They found a small restaurant on a side street and ordered sandwiches and coffee.

"What's my part in the plan?" George asked.

"I want you to stay with the convertible—in the clearing where we hid it before," Nancy said. "Bess may need your help when she brings Mrs Eldridge out."

George nodded. "I see. I'll play it cool."

"But what about you, Nancy?" asked Bess. "You're not going to stay in that awful place?"

"Yes. We must get Mrs Eldridge out before nine o'clock. After that, I'll give the signal for the rescue of the others. A pigeon will carry it to the deserted Tooker estate where Ned is stationed."

Nancy glanced at her watch. "There's no more time to talk now. We must get started."

With George driving the convertible and Nancy the saloon, they returned to the clearing near Larkspur Lane. There Bess changed into the nurse's uniform and Nancy put her costume over her own clothes.

Bess, wearing horn-rimmed glasses, looked stern in her white uniform and cap. Nancy seemed small and frail in the long black coat and heavily veiled hat.

"I'd never know you," George exclaimed.

Ten minutes later in the gathering dusk, the saloon reached the gate-house.

"Now remember to give the password," Nancy whispered.

Trembling, Bess halted the car in front of the gates as the gate-keeper appeared and chained his Great Dane securely. The huge dog strained at his leash and barked furiously. His master advanced towards the girls.

Suppose the password has been changed?" Nancy thought fearfully.

"What's the good word?" demanded the watchman hoarsely, stepping closer.

"Singing horses!" Bess whispered, quaking.

Sleuthing

"Singing horses," repeated the guard. "Right you are."

Striding up to the gates, he opened them wide. Bess guided the car between the posts and the portals clanged shut behind them.

The password had permitted them to enter!

Both girls heaved sighs of relief as they sped up the gravel driveway. Halfway to the mansion, Nancy spoke.

"Stop. No one can see us from the house yet, and the lodge is concealed by those shrubs."

Bess brought the car to a halt and Nancy said, "Back the car off the drive into that clump of trees, Bess. Good! Lucky there's enough room. Get in as far as you can. Keep on backing—farther. That's fine! Now, you wait here. I'll return as soon as I can!"

"Don't be too long," said Bess, trying not to sound frightened.

Nancy squeezed her friend's hand and slipped out of the car. As she went up the hill, she could hear the dog down at the gate-house growling.

"I hope he's still chained," she thought.

Near the mansion, Nancy assumed a stooped posture and uncertain walk.

"I must be on my guard," she told herself.

Light streamed out on to the lawn from the windows of the house. Staying in the shadows, Nancy reached the walls of the mansion and made her way round to the back where she found an open door.

Peering through, she saw a wide, dimly-lit hallway with stairs ascending to her left, and guessed that this was a back door to the main corridor.

"Now for a trip inside," she murmured. "I hope my new shoes don't squeak."

Quietly she stepped into the hall. Half-a-dozen wheel-chairs stood about. Two of them had sleeping occupants, but there was no other sign of life.

Nancy moved on tiptoe towards the broad stairway, and had just reached the steps when she heard the tread of feet on the wooden floor. In a flash she darted to an empty wheel-chair, and muffled herself in the light woollen blanket left by its last occupant.

"I'll try to look as if I'm asleep," she thought.

At that moment a young woman in a striped uniform entered the hall. Nancy watched her apprehensively, fearing that the hat and veil would excite some comment. The nurse's helper, however, marched by humming to herself, giving none of the chairs a second glance.

As soon as she disappeared through a door, Nancy leaped up and dashed towards the stairs. A white head poked up from the nearest chair, and a cracked voice cried:

"Hi there, my dear. The doctor seems to have more than cured you. Why, you are young again!"

Nancy did not pause, but with hammering heart ran up the steps to the first floor. She glanced quickly round, then started the climb to the next storey.

At the top of the stairs, she peered cautiously down the corridor. Empty! Relieved, Nancy tried to get her bearings.

"The south corner room," Mrs Eldridge had said. "That would be to my right."

Quickly Nancy tiptoed down the hall and stopped before the last door. She bent to look through the key-hole, but could see nothing. Then she turned the knob.

The door was locked!

As Nancy racked her brains to think of a way to open it, she heard footsteps on the stairs. She darted across the hall and tried the handle of the opposite door. It turned, and she stumbled into total darkness. It was not a room, but a small broom cupboard.

It was a tight squeeze. Nancy did not dare move, for in the brief moment that the door cupboard was open, she had seen that the floor was filled with pails. Against the wall were mops, brooms, and other cleaning equipment. Her slightest movement would send them clattering to the floor.

With her ear to the door, Nancy waited. The footsteps approached, coming her way. They stopped outside her hiding-place!

For an instant she dared not breathe. Then there was the rattle of a key in a lock, and the clink of china on a tray. Nancy guessed that a bedtime snack was being brought to Mrs Eldridge.

Cautiously she opened the door and saw a white skirt vanish into Mrs Eldridge's room. Then came Miss Tyson's harsh voice.

"Wake up, Mrs Eldridge! Here is your medicine and some food. If you don't do as the doctor says, it will be the last snack you'll taste for a long time!"

The patient groaned faintly, and the nurse went on speaking.

"I have some nice hot consommé and toast and rice pudding. Doesn't that make your mouth water? Taste it, and remember that tomorrow there will be only stale bread and warm water for breakfast, lunch, and dinner if you don't obey our dear good Dr Bell, who is so kind to you."

An idea suddenly occurred to Nancy. "If that nurse is going to lecture Mrs Eldridge, I'll have some time to act," she decided.

Swiftly Nancy tore a strip from her veil and slipped out of the cupboard to the opposite door. It stood slightly ajar.

With the piece of net, Nancy plugged the slot in the door frame into which the bolt of the spring lock fitted. Then she darted back to her hiding-place.

"I hope my scheme works," she thought.

As Nancy stepped back and pulled the door shut, she bumped against a broom. The handle fell forward. Quickly Nancy caught it and another broom which toppled.

For a moment she clutched the wooden handles in the dark, her heart pounding. Then, very cautiously, Nancy propped them against the wall again.

"Oo! That's all I need!" she murmured. "One noise and I'll be trapped!"

Miss Tyson remained to threaten Mrs Eldridge a few minutes more, then left the room. She closed the door, and apparently thinking it was locked, hurried away.

Nancy listened for her to go downstairs, then ran to the door across the hall. Her trick had worked! The bolt had failed to lock! Nancy pushed the door open and stepped into the room.

"Mrs Eldridge," she said softly.

The old lady was propped up in bed, with two pillows behind her back, contemplating her bed-time snack. With a sigh she pushed aside the tray on her lap.

"Mrs Eldridge," Nancy whispered again, coming closer to the elderly woman.

The patient looked up and gave a sharp scream. Nancy flew to her side. "Don't be afraid! It's Nancy Drew, the girl who spoke to you through the fence," she whispered, quickly lifting the veil.

"I'm sorry! I—I'm nervous," the old woman gasped. "They have tried their best to frighten me so often. How in the world did you get in?"

"Don't worry about that. The thing to do now is for you to get out of here. I hope ho one heard you scream." But as she spoke, she heard someone running down the hall.

"I heard Mrs Eldridge scream," came Miss Tyson's voice.

"What of it?" said a second speaker.

"I suppose I'll have to chase into her room again," the nurse said irritably.

"I wouldn't bother," came another voice.

"But I can't let anything happen to her," said the nurse.

"She hasn't signed yet?"

"No."

Nancy looked round the room. There was not even a clothes cupboard to hide in!

Mrs Eldridge groaned. "Oh child! What will you do?"

As the doorknob turned, Nancy dived under the bed. It was very dusty there and she lay motionless, almost afraid to breathe.

Nancy saw a pair of white leather-shod feet stride into the room and pause at the foot of the bed, a few inches from her nose.

"You screamed!" Miss Tyson said angrily. "Why, Mrs Eldridge?"

"Oh, did I?" the patient asked in a weak voice. "I am sorry."

"Whether you are sorry or not makes no difference!" Miss Tyson snapped. "There are other patients in the house whom you upset by carrying on in that way. Why did you scream?"

"I am really very sorry," Mrs Eldridge said, trying to find some excuse for her outcry. "It won't happen again."

"I asked you why," the nurse said sharply.

There was no reply.

"Answer my question!" exclaimed the nurse, stamping her foot and raising a cloud of dust. Nancy pressed the hat veil to her face, trying not to sneeze.

"The—the consommé is very hot," Mrs Eldridge said. "It burned my tongue."

"A likely story." The nurse sniffed. "The broth is not as hot as all that after being carried up from the kitchen. No, that is not the truth, Mrs Eldridge, and I intend to find out your real reason."

"Oh, Miss Tyson," begged the patient, "don't scold me."

"I had to make a special trip up here on your account."

"That's too bad. I'm sorry."

"Well, why did you scream? What have you been doing?" rasped the nurse.

"Nothing," replied the old lady. "I haven't been out of bed."

"You've been acting strangely ever since this afternoon. You're up to something! Then the nurse added in a bullying tone, "You know what I'm going to do?"

"What?" asked Mrs Eldridge.

"Search this room!"

·17·

Attic Hideout

AT THE nurse's words, Nancy froze in horror. From her hiding place under the bed she strained to hear the old woman's reply.

"Well, go ahead and search," quavered Mrs Eldridge. "What do I care?"

"You spunky old dear!" Nancy thought.

The nurse snorted. "Hmm, I guess it would be a waste of time! Things are beginning to get on my nerves! You, especially!"

"I'm sorry," Mrs Eldridge said meekly.

"I think you screamed just to make trouble," snapped the nurse, "because you know another patient is due here, and you want to give the place a bad reputation! Well, spare yourself the trouble. The new patient's just telephoned that she will not arrive today."

Nancy nearly groaned. "If someone questions the gate-keeper, I'm sunk!" she thought. "I must get Mrs Eldridge out of here quickly!'

"I'll give you five minutes to eat. Then it'll be nine o clock. Zero hour for you, old girl. With an ugly laugh, the nurse stamped out of the room.

Nancy waited until the sound of her footsteps had died away before she crept from her hiding place. Hastily she brushed the dust from her black clothing.

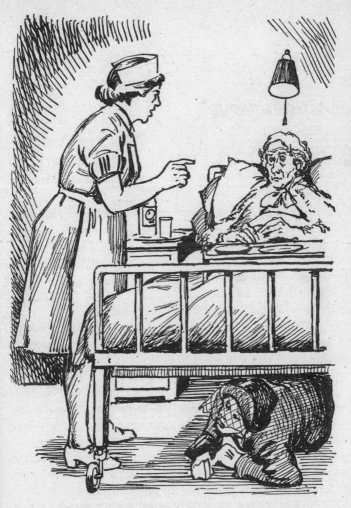

*From her hiding-place, Nancy strained to hear
Mrs Eldridge's reply*

"You were wonderful, Mrs Eldridge!" she whispered. "Now we must work fast and quietly. Can you walk?"

"Yes. They keep us confined to wheel-chairs to weaken us, but I'm still pretty spry. I walk up and down this room for a little exercise. Once I tried to climb out of a ground-floor window, but the creepers pulled loose and I fell and dislocated my shoulder."

"Is that how it happened?" Nancy marvelled at the elderly woman's courage.

While Mrs Eldridge talked, Nancy had taken off her long coat, hat, and gloves. Now she helped the woman to put on her own shoes and Nancy's costume. As she did so, the excited old lady looked at the supper tray.

"Food is cooked with drugs to keep us drowsy all the time," she said. "I eat as little of it as possible."

"How dreadful!" Nancy murmured as she helped her to the door.

"Don't take the main stairs," Mrs Eldridge whispered. "There is a service flight at the rear end of the hall."

"Yes. I explored this place in the dark until they took to locking me in at night. By the way, how could you open my door?"

"I'll tell you later," said Nancy. "Come now."

The service stairway was a steep flight of enclosed steps which Mrs Eldridge had to go down sideways, one at a time.

With maddening slowness, they reached the first floor and saw lights reflected under the door leading to the hall. The stairs squeaked and Nancy's nerves grew tenser. Near the ground floor the staircase divided and Mrs Eldridge said they should take the left branch.

"The other leads into the kitchen. This one takes you to the cellar landing and the entrance into the garden," she whispered.

A few minutes later they stepped into the open air. As fast as Mrs Eldridge could go, the two hastened to the car. Nancy's heart leaped with joy when she saw its hulking shadow amongst the trees.

"Bess!" she whispered. "Any trouble?"

"No, but I thought you'd never come! Bess choked back tears of relief as she and Nancy helped Mrs Eldridge into the back of the car.

"You'll have to sit on the floor, and keep your head down," Nancy warned Mrs Eldridge. "Go now, Bess. Good luck!

"Oh, Nancy, aren't you coming?" Bess whispered.

"No, I have work to do here."

"Well, for goodness sake, be careful!"

The car moved out of the shadows to the driveway. Nancy followed and watched the red rear-lights proceed towards the closed gate.

"Oh, I hope there'll be no trouble," she thought The watchman came out with a torch and shone it into Bess's window as she stopped. The dog began to bark frantically.

For what seemed an age, the gate-keeper held the light in Bess's face and Nancy heard him talking, but could not make out the words. *What was the trouble?*

At last he shrugged, opened the gate, and the car shot through. As the rear-lights disappeared down the lane, Nancy gave sigh of relief.

"Now to send Ned the alarm!"

As she turned back towards the house, Nancy saw that it was ablaze with lights. Figures darted back and forth across the illuminated windows. Reaching the mansion, Nancy concealed herself in the shrubbery alongside a wall. A window above her was suddenly flung open, and Bell's voice rang out.

"Emily, your carelessness is inexcusable!" he thundered. "I am not afraid of the old crone's escaping, but she will give us a pretty hour's work searching the grounds."

"Listen, Simon," Miss Tyson replied. "I can't be everywhere at once."

"You can keep your eyes open," he snapped. "Mrs Eldridge smuggled her bracelet to that doctor right under your nose!"

"Forget it," the woman retorted. "You've taken in enough money from these old women. Why don't you quit this business? Then we could all leave for South America as you promised."

"Not with several thousand dollars still to be had," Bell snarled. "See that every shrub and bush in this place is combed for Mrs Eldridge, and when you find her, bring her to me."

"All right."

"We will wring the money out of her tonight!"

Nancy peered upwards. She could see Bell's pointed beard thrust from the window. Suppose he saw her? But after a few moments he withdrew his head.

"So they are searching the grounds," Nancy mused. "In that case, Mrs Eldridge's room would be the safest place for me."

The Great Dane growled menacingly at the gatehouse. Nancy shivered. Suppose they let him loose!

She edged softly to the rear door by which she and the elderly woman had left, and crept up the steep, dark stairs. When she was halfway to the second floor, the door below her was thrown open and a voice asked:

"Has anyone looked in here?"

As light streamed into the stairway, Nancy ran on tiptoe to the top.

"I'll check the third floor," the same woman said.

As she started upwards, Nancy whirled and quietly sprinted up the narrow stairs, two steps in one leap. At the top was a low door. The young detective opened it, stepped into blackness, and closed the door softly behind her. From the musty smell she surmised that it was an attic. For a few moments she listened. Silence. Then came a scurrying noise and a squeak. *Mice!*

Nancy felt along the wall until her fingers found a switch. She flicked it on and a single bulb glowed in the middle of a great raftered room. Here and there stood trunks, barrels, and old furniture. Against one wall rested dozens of dismantled bedsteads.

In the middle a ladder led up to rafters and there Nancy could see a partial floor with boxes and piles of newspapers.

Suddenly she noticed a small, round window at one end of the attic. With a gasp Nancy quickly flicked off the light, hoping no one had seen it from the grounds!

She felt her way to the window and looked down. Several torches were moving near the outbuildings.

"That's where I'll have to go," she said to herself, "in order to send the alarm to Ned. I must reach the pigeon loft unseen."

Just then she heard a low sigh behind her in the dark attic. It seemed to come from above. "Who could be hiding here? Or maybe it's a prisoner. Morgan!" she thought. "So this is where they're keeping him."

Nancy felt her way back to the ladder and cautiously climbed part way up.

"Morgan—" she whispered.

There was a gasp. "Yes—who is it?"

"Nancy Drew. Are you well enough to move?"

"No," was the faint reply. "I'm very weak."

Nancy's heart sank. "Never mind," she said encouragingly. "I'm going to get you out of here somehow. Just—"

At that moment footsteps clumped on the attic stairs. Nancy scampered up the ladder and felt amongst the boxes and papers. Just as she crouched down, the light went on.

From a cramped position she saw that Morgan, very pale, lay on a mattress, well-concealed amid the boxes. Scattered at her feet were bits of torn newspaper.

Peering between boxes, she saw two men at the door. One had a thin, pinched face, the other was stout with pale, flabby features.

The big man was puffing. "There's nobody here, Tarr. All those stairs for nothing!"

"Chief said he saw a light."

"Chief's wrong."

The other man sighed. "We'd better search, anyway."

Very cautiously, Nancy tried to relieve her cramped muscles. But just as they walked beneath the platform, her foot slipped, pushing a small piece of paper off the platform. As it fluttered down, the two men looked up.

"Morgan?" Tarr called sharply. "You alone?"

The sick man groaned slightly.

"Forget it," said Jackson. "There's nobody with him. Probably a mouse disturbed the paper. Place is full of 'em."

"We ought to search," the thin man said weakly.

The heavy one grinned craftily. "Let's not, and say we did."

The other gave a weak laugh and they left, flicking out the light.

"I'll be back soon, Morgan," Nancy promised. As quickly as possible she made her way out of the attic down to the second floor.

"I'll wait in Mrs Eldridge's room," Nancy decided. "When I hear the searchers come inside, I'll sneak out to the pigeon loft."

Softly she turned the knob and stepped into the upper hall.

A startled scream rang out.

"Oh—oh—help!" A crash of crockery froze Nancy in her tracks. The nurse's helper was in the hallway, staring at Nancy open-mouthed, a tray of broken dishes at her feet.

Nancy darted past her and ran down the main stairs, while behind her she heard the girl shouting the alarm.

A chorus of excited voices came from the second floor, but Nancy reached the veranda without being seen. She ran along its entire length and dived into the shrubbery, panting. Then, hoping that she would not be seen, Nancy darted across the open lawn to a clump of bushes.

A moment later her heart leaped with alarm. Somewhere nearby she heard the dog sniffing. The next instant the animal broke into frantic barking.

Heavy footsteps raced up and a blinding light focused on Nancy's face.

"Here she is!" a deep voice shouted. "I got her, chief!"

· 18 ·

The Underground Cell

MORE running steps came closer and stopped outside the bushes.

"Come out of there!" ordered a harsh voice.

Nancy's heart sank. The speaker was Adam Thorne! Knowing resistance was futile, she crept from the bushes and stood up in the glare of a powerful torch beam. In the darkness just beyond, Nancy could hear the dog snarling and her captors breathing heavily.

"It isn't the old lady!" came Miss Tyson's voice. "It's Nancy Drew!"

Adam Thorne growled. "*What?* I thought we'd knocked her out of action."

Miss Tyson said in a worried voice, "That's what Tarr and Jackson reported. Tarr himself pushed her—"

"Quiet!" snapped Thorne. "She's tricked us. Take her to the house. We'll lock her up."

Quick as lightning, Nancy plunged out of the light and desperately raced down the hill. Taken by surprise, her captors hesitated, then pounded after her, the dog barking furiously.

Blinded by the sudden change from light to darkness, Nancy stumbled and fell. An instant later the Great Dane leaped on her.

"Grab that leash!" shouted Thorne. The dog was

yanked back, then someone jerked Nancy to her feet.

"We'll take her to the house!" panted Thorne.

With the ex-lawyer in the lead, flanked by the nurse and the attendant, and guarded in the rear by the gate-keeper and his dog, Nancy was marched to the mansion. Bell was waiting in the main hall.

"Who is this?" he demanded. "Where's Mrs Eldridge?"

"We haven't found the old fox yet," Thorne answered. "This is the Drew girl I warned you about."

Bell's eyes narrowed. "What do you mean by trespassing on private property?"

"I meant no harm," Nancy replied truthfully.

Thorne snorted scornfully. "She's been spying. It's your fault, Bell. I told you not to bring Dr Spire here. If the old woman's shoulder was dislocated, you should have let it stay that way. Too bad you aren't a real doctor," he added unpleasantly. "You could have set it yourself."

"Never mind that," Miss Tyson put in sharply. "How did she get in here?"

"Luther, bring the gate-keeper quickly!" Bell ordered. "Just how did you get in, Miss Drew?"

"I came in at the entrance," Nancy replied. "The larkspur is beautiful—"

"I'm not interested in flowers. I think—" Bell checked himself.

He turned to Adam Thorne and spoke in an undertone, but Nancy, straining her ears, heard him say "password to Larkspur Lane" before their voices became hushed.

After a few minutes the attendant appeared with the

gateman. "Jones, have you ever seen this young woman?" Bell demanded, glaring at the man standing before him.

"I? No, sir," the guard declared, not recognizing Nancy dressed in her own clothes.

"Did anybody come in by the gate tonight?" Bell asked sharply.

Nancy saw fear flicker in the man's eyes as he met Bell's hard stare. Through no fault of his own, the gateman had let intruders into the grounds!

Jones swallowed. "Uh—no, chief," he said. "Nobody came in or out."

A wave of relief swept over Nancy. No alarm would go out for Mrs Eldridge. The gang would continue to think she was hiding in the grounds.

"All right," Bell said. "Get back to the gate." Then, turning to Thorne, he said, "Let's continue this in my office."

Miss Tyson grinned maliciously as she prodded Nancy along and into a large, luxurious room. A thick green carpet covered the floor and in the centre stood a large mahogany desk. The walls, panelled in a rich-looking wood, were hung with costly oil paintings.

"Shut the door, Luther," Bell ordered.

Bell seated himself behind the desk, motioning Nancy to stand opposite him. There was tense silence for a moment. Then Bell reached for a desk telephone.

"I am going to call the police, Miss Drew, and turn you over to them on a charge of trespassing, breaking, and entering with intent to steal."

"I wish you would," Nancy replied, "if it is possible over that dummy telephone."

"Didn't I tell you she was sharp-eyed?" Thorne

scolded. "You can't fool her. Follow my advice and put her away. This is a waste of time."

"What do you mean? Do you wish to have me summon the police?" Bell blustered. "Why do you call this a dummy telephone?"

"Because, in answer to your first question, I should be happy to be escorted from here under police protection," Nancy retorted. "I know the telephone is a dummy because there are no—"

She checked herself abruptly. No use proving her powers of observation!

"See here, Nancy Drew," Bell said, pointing a finger at her. "Stop all this talk and tell me how you entered these grounds—and why. I know all about you. Sylvan Lake is a long distance from here, and you did not walk."

"There are various ways of travelling."

"Bell, I'm telling you it's just foolishness to try to match wits with this girl," Thorne put in. "I know a way to make her talk—and what's more, I'm sure her illustrious father will pay plenty to get his precious daughter back."

"An excellent idea, Thorne," Bell said with an evil smile. "What would you suggest we do first?"

"Put her in the cistern," said Thorne. "I guess a couple of days without food or drink, down in the dark and cold with the rats and spiders, will make Miss Drew answer any questions we ask."

Miss Tyson laughed harshly, looking straight at Nancy to see if she winced at the prospect. "That will take some of the snap out of her," she said.

A shiver went down Nancy's spine, but she did not change expression.

Bell's cold eyes studied her carefully. "You've caused us a lot of trouble," he said softly. "Because of you we had to give up our other headquarters. My partner Mr Tooker will not overlook that very readily." Bell toyed with a sharp-pointed letter opener on his desk.

Miss Tyson spoke up. "The pigeon keeper guessed she had found that bird, kept it, and then followed it to Tooker's. Now I'm sure he was right. Only from the message that pigeon carried could she have learned the password. And I still say she couldn't have entered without it."

Luther cleared his throat. "But Jones said—"

"He was lying," Miss Tyson broke in. "Where's the car you came in?" she asked Nancy.

Nancy thought it best to keep stalling. The farther away Bess, George, and Mrs Eldridge got, the safer they would be.

Nancy smiled. "Why don't you search the grounds for the car?"

"That's enough!" snapped Bell. "Take her away."

Nancy knew she was in a hopeless predicament, and reasoned that more was to be gained by strategy than by a desperate attempt to break loose. As she was marched out of the room, she heard Bell say, "The disappearance of the Eldridge woman and the Drew girl showing up have me so upset I can't think. I'm going upstairs and tell Adolf. Let him handle this. It's dynamite."

"Do as you please," Thorne said coldly.

Nancy, her arms pinned behind her back, was shoved out on to the porch and towards the buildings beyond the house. Just outside the pigeon loft, Thorne stooped and jerked at an iron ring in the ground. It was

attached to a round steel lid about three feet in dia-
meter. Beneath it gaped a black hole.

"Well, down you go, Nancy Drew!" Thorne
laughed.

Nancy looked round desperately. There was no
escape. As the nurse pushed her, the trapped girl was
forced to start down a swaying, flimsy wooden ladder
into the dark, damp hole. Down, down, ten or twelve
feet Nancy went, until she could feel the slimy bottom
under her feet.

"This is worse than I bargained for," she thought
ruefully.

The ladder was jerked up and Thorne called, "Don't
worry. You may have it back."

There was a series of splitting noises, and pieces of
the ladder came raining down around Nancy's head.
As she threw up her arms to protect herself, she heard
Thorne laugh sardonically.

Then the lid clanged shut!

Caught!

DESPAIR filled Nancy's heart and she shivered. The dampness of the old cistern covered her like a clammy hand.

She took a deep breath. "Come on now," Nancy scolded herself. "Brace up and try to find a way out!"

Stretching her arms wide, Nancy could feel nothing, so she knew her prison was wider than its three-foot lid. When her eyes became accustomed to the darkness, she noticed tiny gleams of light coming from above. Perhaps the lid did not fit tightly.

"Or maybe it's a phosphorescent glow from some decaying thing," Nancy thought with distaste. "Whatever it is, I must find out."

Balancing herself with outstretched arms, she walked cautiously across the slippery floor. It was uneven and Nancy stepped ankle-deep in cold water. A moment later her fingers brushed the moist stone wall. She stared upwards and saw light coming through chinks in the wall directly above her.

"I must try to reach those openings, but how?" Then Nancy remembered the pieces of ladder Thorne had mockingly thrown to her.

"Maybe I can use them after all," she thought. Repressing a shudder, Nancy slid her fingers over the slimy floor for the fragments. "Now's no time to be squeamish."

Finding a piece of wood, Nancy fingered it anxiously for a nail. Feeling one, she pulled it loose from the rotten wood and noted that it was long and strong.

"Maybe this will work, and maybe it won't," she said half-aloud.

To her horror, she was answered by a throaty chuckle. Nancy gasped. As the sound was repeated she dropped the nail, unnerved. Then, fighting for control, the desperate girl located the noise—it was coming from above. Was someone watching through the chinks?

"*Kel—ek—koo—oo—oo!*" As the new noise blended with the chuckles, Nancy suddenly grinned in relief.

"Pigeons! The light must be coming from the loft!"

Frantically she sought the lost nail. Locating it, Nancy began to dig vigorously at the loose mortar. Soon she had hollowed out space enough to give herself one toehold. A little farther above, Nancy dug again, and repeated the process until she could reach no higher on the wall.

Then she climbed up and chipped out another hold. The mortar was hard and her fingers, clutching the nail, grew cramped. The higher she went, the more difficult the task became.

Finally the imprisoned girl was forced to cling to the damp wall, her toes and the fingers of one hand digging into the niches she had scooped out. With her free hand she scraped a higher grip for herself.

At last Nancy's fingers found the openings through which the light filtered. A big stone rocked under her hand!

Mingled excitement and alarm shot through her Here was the way out! "But suppose I can't move the stone or I fall!" she thought. About eight feet below was the stone floor of the cistern.

Nevertheless, Nancy forced herself to try pushing the stone aside. She failed, but suddenly it came loose and fell inwards over her head. As the stone plummeted down, it grazed her shoulder, but Nancy managed to grab the top edge of the hole and hold tight.

With a sigh of relief she pulled herself through the enlarged opening and up to freedom! On the earthen floor of the pigeon loft, the young sleuth fell back exhausted and closed her eyes. A few moments later she opened them to the sound of fluttering wings and sleepy cooing. The loft was lit by a large bright bulb under a small cage containing a pigeon.

"This is the sick bird," Nancy conjectured, "and it is being kept warm."

Capsules for messages lay on a shelf. "Good," Nancy thought. She took a pencil and small pad from her blouse pocket and wrote three identical messages: "SP at once". Nancy inserted them in the capsules, then caught a pigeon and attached the capsule to its anklet. Quickly she caught another bird, then a third.

"I'd better turn out the light for a few minutes so I won't be seen releasing these pigeons," she decided, and unscrewed the bulb.

Nancy now felt her way to the door, opened it, and released the birds, "Fly straight to Ned," she muttered. "He's waiting at the Tooker estate."

Hoping no one had seen the light go off, Nancy replaced the bulb again and fled from the coop to the carriage-house garage.

Here she considered her next move. Nancy knew there must be lights on the landing field, because the gang used their plane at night. "But how do they turn them on? Perhaps at a switchbox in here?"

She opened the door wide enough to squeeze through and saw two large saloons. One was the old car used to kidnap Dr Spire. Walking past it, Nancy glanced inside and stopped short. She had glimpsed a white blur! Was it a face she saw?

Nancy turned quietly and stepped nearer. As she stared, a figure in one corner of the back seat moved. Someone was seated there, bound and gagged. Quickly Nancy opened the car door. Removing the gag, she asked, "Morgan, how did you get here?"

"They brought me down," he said hoarsely. "Thorne's going to finish me off to keep me from talking. But they'll do it where no one will find me." He breathed heavily. "The gang's ready to escape. Tooker has given the signal to clear out."

"How soon?" asked Nancy as she quickly worked at his bonds.

"I don't know," he whispered. "Soon."

"What about the patients?"

"They'll herd 'em into the cellar." Anger gave the weakened man strength to continue. "The gang isn't worried about them. They figure the shock'll kill some of the old ladies and the rest'll be too confused and terrified to be of much help to the police."

"Those men are brutes!" Nancy exclaimed. "They mustn't get away!"

Quickly she climbed from the car and took the nail from her pocket. Nancy inserted it into a tyre valve, holding it open until all the air had hissed out. She did the same to the rest of the tyres on both cars, then hurried back to Morgan.

"Do you know how they turn on the landing-field lights?" she asked.

"Big oak," he said weakly, "at the edge of the field. Switch box nailed to the tree."

"I must turn them on," she said. "I'll be back!"

Nancy dashed from the garage and ran down the hill towards the level field at the bottom. The moon was coming up and the sloping lawn was bathed in pale light."

"If only they don't see me!"

From somewhere behind Nancy came the deep-throated bark of the Great Dane. Was he loose on the grounds? she wondered.

At one end of the landing field, Nancy could see the plane and at the other a clump of trees. She angled left and raced down towards them.

Reaching the shadow of the trees, she stopped and tried to spot the oak. Again, she heard the dog's bark—this time closer.

Nancy looked back.

The huge beast was silhouetted on the brow of the hill, straining against a leash held by the gate-keeper. He began pulling the man down the slope.

"Does he scent me?" Nancy tried not to think about it, and pressed deeper into the clump of trees.

There was the oak! And gleaming in the moonlight a metal box nailed to the trunk! Nancy darted to it, opened the door, and pulled the single switch inside.

Out on the field, spots of light were coming up through the short grass. "Clever," she thought. "They're sunk in the earth, and aren't noticeable in daylight. Now for the plane!"

The far side of the landing area was bordered by woodland. Nancy ran from her shelter to the woods, then hastened along the edge of the field, keeping within the tree line. At the far end, she crouched low, dashed across the clearing, and crept under the low wing of the small plane.

Nancy knew that the fuel drains were on the underside of the wings. She felt along the surface until her fingers encountered a T-shaped metal valve.

"This must be it," she decided, and pressed upwards. A stream of fuel flowed to the ground! Nancy found that by turning the valve slightly she could lock it open. Then she hurried to the other wing and did the same thing.

"Now," Nancy said to herself, "that should ground the gang! I'll get back to Morgan and hide him before the men go to the cars."

As she started to move, however, Nancy heard the Great Dane growling. Coming down the field were the dog and the gate-keeper, with four men running behind them. Nancy recognized Thorne, Bell, and Luther, but the fourth was a tall stranger. As they drew nearer, she saw he had a gaunt, cruel face, and guessed he was Adolf Tooker.

"I'm telling you I didn't turn on the lights," came Luther's voice.

"Well, somebody did," Thorne growled. "Jones, can't you shut that dog up?"

"There's a prowler down here," replied the gateman. "That's what's the matter with him."

As the party reached the plane, they stopped less than thirty feet from Nancy. The dog strained towards her hiding-place, whining.

Nancy took a deep breath. "I'm really in a tight spot!" she thought. If she moved from the shadow of the plane's wing, the men would see her. If she didn't, the dog would attack her!

Suddenly shouts came from the hillside and Nancy saw the bobbing rays of torches. "Wait for me!" called Miss Tyson. "Something's gone wrong!" her shrill voice warned.

The tall man said sharply, "Jones, take that dog and find out what the trouble is! We'll search down here for the prowler."

As the gate-keeper pulled the dog away, louder shouts came from the hillside and the four men looked up towards the moving lights.

"It's now or never!" Nancy thought. Crouching low, she ran out on the moonlit field.

The SP

NOT daring to look back, Nancy raced for the shelter of the woods, wondering if she could make it before being detected.

Suddenly she heard a hoarse shout. "Look, chief! There goes a girl!"

The young sleuth's heart sank.

"Catch her!" Thorne yelled.

"No, you fool," barked Bell. "We haven't time! Into the plane, everybody! Go ahead, Adolf!"

"Wait!" came the tall man's hard voice. "I smell petrol."

Thorne gave an angry exclamation and Bell said, "I do, too. Where's it coming from?"

"There's probably a leak in one of the fuel tanks," said Luther. Quickly he ducked under the wing. "One drain valve is open!" he shouted.

"Open?" thundered Bell. "Who did that?"

At once Thorne climbed into the plane. In a moment he gave an angry yell. "We have no fuel!" he cried and jumped out. "The gauges read empty!"

Miss Tyson raced up to them with three men and a girl at her heels, followed by the gate-keeper and his barking dog.

"Everything's gone wrong!" she exclaimed.

At that moment a plane swooped soundlessly out of

the sky. Before it taxied to a full stop, several armed police officers jumped out and surrounded the criminals. A powerful searchlight was turned on the confused gang.

A voice over a loudspeaker ordered, "Stand where you are! No one move!"

"Ned!" Nancy cried out.

She raced from the woods and reached the plane as he leaped from it, followed by Dave, her father, and the pilot.

"Dad!" Nancy exclaimed as Carson Drew caught her up in his arms.

"Are you hurt?" he asked quickly.

"No, Dad, but I'm so glad to see you! Ned, you're just wonderful!"

"Oh, Nancy, you take such chances," he said. "But I was sure happy I could come to the rescue."

In a moment a second noiseless plane skimmed down on to the field. Out jumped Burt, Lieutenant Mulligan, and two members of his detective squad. They joined the others in the circle of light, while the officers began snapping handcuffs on the prisoners.

"Miss Drew," Lieutenant Mulligan said, "Ned Nickerson informed me of your plan and I called the police."

"I'm glad the mystery is solved, Lieutenant," said Nancy, then turned to Thorne. "Where are the old ladies?" she asked anxiously.

The gang members had been staring at Nancy in disbelief. "You!" Thorne spluttered. "How did you get out of the cistern?"

"First answer my question," said Nancy.

"They're in the cellar," Bell replied shortly.

Miss Tyson spoke up. "They are not in the cellar."

As Bell looked at her, puzzled, she added, "I didn't have time to put them there! As soon as I saw the air was out of our car tyres, I knew something had gone wrong with the plans. I wanted to get away—fast!"

"What did you do with Morgan?" Nancy asked quickly.

"Nothing. He's still in the car."

Nancy explained Morgan's condition to the police, who promised that the sick man would be taken to a hospital.

Thorne glared at Nancy. "How did you get out of the cistern?"

"Climbed out," Nancy said directly. "I used the ladder you gave me."

Miss Tyson gasped. "That's impossible."

Briefly, Nancy told how she had escaped and sent for help.

" 'SP at once'," Ned said with a grin. "Sailplane at once!"

"Also, send police," Nancy added.

"These aren't gliders?" Tooker asked.

"No," Ned answered. "They're motorized sailplanes. They were perfect for this job because we flew them here using the motor, then cut it out and landed soundlessly."

He grinned at Dave. "All we had to do was find two sailplanes. We finally rented these from an airport in the next county. The police provided the pilots."

"Dad," said Nancy, "how did you hear about the plan?"

"Ned briefed me. He called our house on the chance that I'd returned from Chicago." Looking at Adam Thorne, Mr Drew added, "I'm proud of my daughter,

Thorne. She planned to take you and your accomplices by surprise, so you couldn't harm the old ladies before you bolted."

Lieutenant Mulligan cleared his throat. "Miss Drew, you're a fine detective."

Nancy smiled and thanked him.

Adolf Tooker turned to Bell and said angrily, "This is the girl you said would be no trouble?"

"I warned Bell about her," Thorne spoke up, "but he wouldn't listen!"

"It's not my fault," said Bell, his voice rising nervously. "It's Thorne's. Ever since he read about the Cornings' jewelled crystal collection he wanted to steal it. Then he dragged us into the scheme and bungled it! My men were doing all his work!

"Whenever I wanted Tarr and Jackson, they were trailing Nancy Drew in the saloon or spying on that Sylvan Lake place. They even set the dog on her. Twice they snatched Morgan, and Jackson showed the blue fire night after night to scare him. It finally worked. Then suddenly Morgan wouldn't go along with us, so we had to teach him a lesson.

"As for Tarr," Bell went on bitterly, "he spent days making the firework wheel and rigging up an asbestos-lined box for it."

Tarr gave a sickly grin. "All I had to do was shut the door of the box and the blue fire was gone—like magic!"

Jackson's face was pale. "We only did what Thorne ordered."

"Be quiet, all of you!" barked Thorne. "Don't you know there are police listening?"

"It doesn't matter," Adolf Tooker said wearily. "They'll find all the evidence they need here."

"Is this your whole gang?" Mulligan asked sharply.

Tooker looked round the group which included the gate-man with the dog, the pigeon-keeper, and the nurse's aide whom Nancy had startled in the hall.

"Yes."

Miss Tyson's assistant was shaking with fright. "I was only doing what Dr Bell ordered. He told me the patients were too nervous to have visitors."

"He's no doctor," Nancy told her. "And I find it hard to believe Miss Tyson is a real nurse."

The hard-faced woman shot her a venomous look.

"The police will find out about them all," Lieutenant Mulligan said grimly.

At that moment two helicopters appeared, lights flashing. They landed on the field and the rotors were silenced.

"Last stage of Nancy's plan," Ned said. "Reinforcements!"

"Okay," called a police officer to the arriving men. "Load this gang in the copters and take 'em away!"

An hour later Nancy had the biggest thrill of the evening. As she walked into the Cornings' living-room with her father and the boys, she saw Mrs Eldridge seated in a big chair with little Marie asleep on her lap. At one side stood the child's mother, on the other a tall stranger.

"Nancy," the old woman said happily, "this is my nephew John. Nancy Drew is the girl who—" Tears filled her eyes and she could not go on.

"Yes," he said, "Nancy Drew has done a wonderful job. Thank you, Nancy."

"The hospital called," said Mrs Corning. "Morgan will be all right! We're so grateful to you for clearing up the mystery about him."

"Will you take him back?" Bess asked.

"Of course. He is honest and faithful. We know his true story. There can't be any more trouble."

Nancy thanked her friends for helping her. She gave Bess and George each a hug and quickly excused herself to change her clothes. When she came downstairs, Mrs Corning had a tray of tempting food waiting.

"Oh good!" said Nancy. "Tea was a long time ago. I'm famished!"

While everyone ate, Mrs Eldridge told what she had learned while a prisoner at Larkspur Lane. Tooker, whose real name was Van Hofwitz, was an international confidence man.

"The hospital was his idea," she said. "He made Bell a partner and he was to pass as a doctor. Thorne had put money into the venture while in prison. As soon as he escaped, he joined the others."

Mrs Eldridge went on to say that Von Hofwitz ingratiated himself into various social circles. He would introduce the fake doctor to wealthy ladies who complained of old age.

"I see now how silly I was," Mrs Eldridge said. "I was taken in by their suave manners and my own vanity."

She revealed that the unscrupulous pair would persuade the women to go secretly to the hospital. There, using drugs and threats, Bell prevailed upon the patients to sign away large parts of their wealth to him.

Mr Drew spoke up. "Thorne is a very sharp lawyer and no doubt the contracts he drew up for you women to sign seemed harmless enough, but could not be changed, even if your relatives tried to break them."

"But your courage, Mrs Eldridge," said Nancy, "helped to put an end to the whole scheme. There are two questions I hope you can answer," she added. "Why did the gang use *blue bells* in the code?"

"Because Bell was so conceited he wanted his own name in it. Blue, of course, was the colour of the flowers growing so profusely round the estate."

"And why was the pigeon released from the plane?"

"Tooker was flying from the mansion to an appointment with an old woman in Pennsylvania that day. He let the bird go on the way so that it would reach his estate more quickly."

"Thank you, Mrs Eldridge, for the answers to my questions," Nancy said. "And now I'll go upstairs and get your bracelet for you."

"No, dear," said the old lady. "I want you to keep it as a memento."

"How wonderful!" Nancy hugged her.

Mr Corning spoke up. "And I am going to order crystal earrings in the form of tiny larkspurs for you and the other girls."

"Oh, how exciting!" Bess exclaimed. "Thank you very much."

George grinned and added her thanks.

Nancy protested that she wanted no reward. "I'm just happy everything turned out right."

Ned grinned. "If I were to give Nancy the reward she'd like best, I'd hand her another mystery to solve. I'll find you a mystery by tomorrow morning," he promised jokingly.

"And I'll be ready for it," Nancy said with a twinkle in her eyes. "But make it very, very complicated and original." *The Bungalow Mystery* proved to be both!